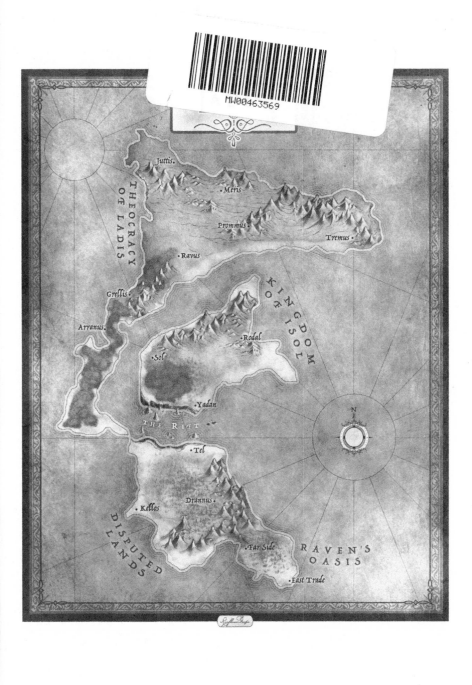

SPEARS OF LADIS

First Edition. December 4th, 2018

Written by RG Long

RG LONG

SPEARS
LADIS
of

LEGENDS OF GILIA

BOOK 9

1: The Will to Fight

Ealrin stumbled as he tried to regain his footing. The rocks and gravel beneath his feet mocked him as he attempted to climb higher up. His ears were full of the clash of steel and the screams of men. If he fell now, he would not recover. Exhaustion was taking its toll on him.

He barely held onto his sword, which was inexplicably warm in his hands. The rest of the world around him was cold and dark.

With one last effort, he felt his foot slide and the weight of the past months come down on him. He was falling. He was going to slip back down into the battle and never come back up again.

And some of that was alright with him.

At the last moment, he felt a strong arm grab him and pull him up onto the rocky cliff face. He didn't look up to see who it was. He knew.

"Just a bit more," Holve said.

His voice was rough and calloused. Ealrin had once felt reassured to hear him speak. It had always been a welcome sign that he was where he needed to be. Now it only reminded him of his doubts and current struggles.

"Up here," Holve said and directed Ealrin to their group. They had gathered on top of this hill for a defensive position. He could see the same worn look on their faces that he felt deep within him. They were broken. Taking in each face, Ealrin nodded at them, still panting from his climb. They returned his gaze.

Well, Ealrin thought bitterly, most of them did anyway.

All around them the battle raged. The blue of Isol clashed against the green of Ladis. Dotted throughout the shifting tides of battle, the brilliant shining purple lights.

The demons were ravaging the soldiers. No matter where Isol and Ladis fought, the great four-legged demons tore through them.

It was only in these places that the green and blue did not battle each other but instead turned to face the more pressing attack.

Ealrin let out a deep sigh that seemed to push all the air from around him further away. In the middle of the fighting, a circle of destruction and magic exploded as three forces collided. Yada's terrible blue light struck out at the purple of Prince Dram. Ealrin saw the flashing red of the demon-possessed one as well. All three danced in a horrific explosion of power and magic.

"Can't we stop them?" Ealrin said out loud, feeling hopeless as the great beasts tore through the armies, seemingly uncaring about who they devoured with their power.

Holve stepped forward, spear in hand. Its tip was glowing with a pearly white sheen. Ealrin knew what it had cost him to face one of these demons the last time. He guessed that was what reeled through Holve's mind, even though his exterior remained calm and collected.

Then Ealrin saw something flash in the corner of his eye. He knew what that was. It felt familiar and powerful.

"No!" he yelled, trying to step towards the light, but he found that he couldn't move.

Her magic was strong. He knew that all too well. But she was too tired, too hungry, and too spent to go up against these terrors.

Not now.

"You can't do it, Blume!" he shouted.

She was just as tired as he was. Perhaps more so. They had both been through the same ordeal only to arrive at this battle. They had both suffered and run and fought only to find themselves in the midst of a struggle they had no control over.

How could she possibly have the energy to go against such terrible enemies? They should have fled when they could. They should have gotten off of Ladis when the opportunity presented itself. This was not their war. It wasn't connected to any part of them.

Except for Holve.

He looked sideways at the older man and glared at him for just a moment. He was the reason they were here. A wave of energy hit and caused him to snap his head back to Blume.

Ealrin could feel the power emanating from the girl he so admired.

And was so fearful of losing.

"I have before," she replied, stepping in front of their group and facing the battle. He couldn't see her face, but he could hear the determination in her voice. She was preparing to fight. She was going to defend her friends.

"You're too weak," Ealrin pleaded with her.

Blume spun on the spot and faced him.

The bracelet with a piece of rimstone she had been given glowed in her hand. She held it tightly as she glared at Ealrin. An aura of green energy filled the air around her. Even her eyes took on a gleam of the magic.

"I," she said with as much ferocity as he had ever heard her speak. "Am not weak."

With those words, she turned and ran towards the towering figure of Yada and the demon, fists and eyes glowing, a scream erupting from deep within her, magic spilling out into the battle.

2: Capital Fires

Jerius stumbled to one side as he made his way down the hall. He and the high priest had been called from their study when the castle began to quake. It was no small thing; Prommus was supposed to be the most fortified city on the continent. If it was under siege and suffering already, that did not bode well for the Temple.

Or the people who lived there of course.

Jerius did his best to right himself as another tremor shook the temple hall. Guards were running in different directions, putting statues back into place, addressing the needs of prophets who were shouting orders, and for the most part ignoring Jerius completely.

That didn't bother him.

Not at the moment.

He had more pressing things to consider than sieges and the respect of women.

Clutching the worn book to his chest, he began trotting down the hallway again, determined that he should reach the end of the temple quickly. His message was not one to be delivered late.

There was a small part of him that was resenting being a messenger once again, but when he grasped the codex in his hands a little more tightly, he began to think that he may be able to endure it for a little while longer. It may not be as long as he thought before he was no longer anyone's errand runner.

The great doors that separated the Temple from the Castle of Prommus stood before him. The guards who were assigned to these doors must be otherwise occupied at the moment. Not a soul was around.

Except for Luca.

She looked over at Jerius and stumbled towards him as another blast shook the castle.

"My Priest," she said, Jerius noted, through slightly gritted teeth. "The nation of Isol has come to Prommus. All of the defenders have been brought inside the city's gates. We are awaiting a ceasefire so the King can speak to the attackers."

"Yes Yes, I am aware that Isol is..."

"My Priest," she said again, slightly more forcefully. "They've employed some type of heretical...cannon against us. They are firing magic at the castle walls. With every blast that hits an entire section falls to the ground. We will not last the night."

This caused Jerius to come up short. He stuttered as his mind tried to keep up with the information he was presented with. The High Priest had told him to go and speak with the king, delivering the message. But if the king was to be talking with Isol soon, then he would not be in the throne room.

"Then we will go down to the city walls," Jerius commanded, walking through the giant portals that lead from the temple to the castle. That was the way out.

"My... My priest?" Luca asked. Her tone was undoubtedly one of confusion, but Jerius didn't mind.

He had a message for the king.

One that would change everything.

***

The city of Prommus was ablaze. Blasts of blue energy were flying over the city, hitting the mountain behind the capital and the castle. Parts of the mountain were exploding with dangerous force. Chaos was everywhere. As Luca and Jerius made their way down the road that led to the gate, a frenzied populace filled the streets.

Some were soldiers who had abandoned their posts and were fleeing in whatever direction seemed to please them. Others were families who were running from burning home to burning stores to piles of smoking rubble.

Jerius cared nothing for them. They were small obstacles to the earth-shattering realization he had come to.

"My Priest!" Luca shouted from behind him. If she hadn't been so loud, he might not have heard her. The intensity of the explosions was growing as they came closer and closer to the walls of Prommus. Each blast shook the ground beneath their feet. But Jerius was so determined that with each stumble, he simply righted himself and continued on his quest.

"This is not wise!" Luca shouted. Jerius looked back to see her squinting her eyes forward and raising her hands to block her face. Bits of rock and city wall were raining down on them intermittently. None of them were large enough to cause significant damage, but they were irksome.

"An incorrect assumption!" Jerius answered, turning and caring little if she heard him softly speak his next words or not. "This is monumental."

The castle's defenders were in plain sight now. Soldiers of Ladis were running in every direction, following the orders bellowed to them by their captains and their sergeants. Jerius scanned them quickly, knowing where both the king and the generals would be: a safe distance from the fighting, but able to see the siege taking place.

A tower, set back far enough from the wall but still very much in the front of the city, was heavily guarded by troops. Jerius knew just by looking at it that the king must be up there. That or someone who knew where the king was would be there.

Another blast rocked the city walls as Jerius approached the guards of the tower. He could tell they recognized him, or at least his priest's garments.

"You cannot pass!" the taller one said, looking down at Jerius. The other put out his spear to block his path.

"And you will not deny a priest of Ladis his audience with the king!" Jerius retorted, throwing the spear back and walking underneath it. "I have a message from the high priest!"

The men did not try to stop him, but Jerius could see their hesitation. They would soon see just how valuable the church was and how insignificant they were. Luca followed behind him as he began to climb the stairs that wrapped around the outside of the tower. Every so often a landing and a door appeared. Inside officers and soldiers discussed plans and strategies.

Jerius gave them no heed as he looked for the king in each room. He came upon the fourth such landing and was impeded by another set of guards. These were king's guards, dressed in full plate and carrying halberds. They turned their helmets to face Jerius and did not speak a word.

For a moment, he felt as if he might quail beneath their stare, but he shook himself. He was a priest of Ladis. He could not be intimidated by fancy armor or sharp weapons. He was powerful. He would show them all just how dominant he was.

Even the High Priest.

He passed between the guards, who did not attempt to stop him like the others and made his way through the stone archway that served as the door for the room. Advisors and generals surrounded the king. They sat looking at a map of the castle, with several painted stones resting on the parchment. Jerius suspected these represented the opposing soldiers as well as their troops.

The numbers looked even, but Jerius wondered if the generals were being optimistic.

He chuckled to himself. He would offer up something that these generals could not. He had heard the rumors of how Grellis and Ravus had fallen so quickly to the forces of Isol.

The king would be anxious and he, a Priest of Ladis, would be the one to relieve his fears.

"What are you doing here, priest?" snarled the king. Gravis' blonde hair was a stark contrast to his red face. Sweat was pouring down his brow, which only made Jerius smile as he bowed.

"My king," he said with triumph in his voice. "I have found a way to quiet the heretic's magic and cannons once and for all!"

3: Useless

The scraping noise of the rusted and chipped ax along the gravel road was all that could be heard along the horizon. No bird gave its call or sang a song to mourn. Creatures did not stir from their dens. Nothing moved. Not even the wind blew. The stillness in the air was as unnatural as the sight of the boy who walked down the road, dragging his bloody ax in his wake.

His feet dragged along the road, the shoes he had once worked so hard to keep together so he could diligently work his father's farm now barely clung to his tattered ankles. His shirt hung off one shoulder, and his pants were shredded above his calves. David was a wreck of a boy.

He could hardly remember the last time he had slept. There was no memory of food in his mouth or his stomach. The pain that he felt there was numbed only by the horrible images that flashed over and over again in his mind. A mother shielding her newborn, a father protecting his son, two young children cowering in a corner. All of these and countless others he had cut down mercilessly. Each one screamed and pleaded for mercy.

Mercy was not a memory he could recall either.

On top of each image of murder and misery was of his mother's screams and the demon who held her life on a string. The face was burned into his mind's eye. There was no escaping it, no running away.

There was only obedience.

He must obey the Goddess of Blood.

"Woah, son," said a voice to his left. "You look like hell."

David didn't turn to face them. He didn't need another vision in his mind. He tightened his grip on his weapon and prayed it would happen quickly.

It had to be over quickly.

"That's putting it kindly, Grax," said another, younger voice. "He looks like he's just come from a war."

"Think he's a refugee from Ravus? I've seen some others like him before, though that was a few weeks ago and further south."

"Naw, can't be..."

David saw the two move in front of him. His lips quivered as he stared down at the road.

"What's your name, son?" the man named Grax asked. "Where you from?"

David tightened his grip on his blade and looked at the ground. There wasn't anything he could do. Nothing within his power to stop what was coming. It had happened all too often now. Still, perhaps there was one last hope.

"Run."

He had barely breathed the word. It had required so much of his strength to utter the syllable.

"Eh? Say what?" the other man asked.

It was too late now, David knew. He had known it as soon as they had foolishly stopped him.

"The Goddess of Blood requires a sacrifice..." the voice in David's head called.

He breathed out long and hard. Tensing his muscles, he prepared for the onslaught.

Power filled his being as he lifted the ax with one hand and swung it with dizzying speed at the first older man. His head would have gone flying, had the blade not been so dull. Instead, the old traveler's body flew off the road, a grievous trail following in his wake as he spluttered in surprise.

"What in the name of the gods!?" screamed the young man.

David lifted his eyes to see him, for the first time, and take in the face of the man he would slaughter. The face that met him was no older than he was. In his mind, he had imagined a man, but this was a boy turned hard by the road. Perhaps it was his father who lay groaning several paces away?

Of course, David didn't care. He only desired to kill. To save his mother. To appease the goddess of blood.

He swung out with his ax again, but this time, instead of meeting flesh, his blade met steel. The boy had drawn a sword. David frowned at this. Whenever they fought back, it always turned out worse.

Skidding against the gravel, the boy took up a fighting stance. David barely paid it attention. His hand tightened over the handle of his ax once more, preparing for the strike.

With three swipes of his blade, he had taken the sword from the boy's hand. With another swipe of his elbow, he had thrown the boy a span into the air. With a final slam of his hand, he sent the boy colliding into the ground.

It had all happened in an instant. David saw the cold sweat on the boy's face. He felt the fear emanating from his body.

"What the hell are you!?" the boy screamed from the ground, his forehead bleeding and one eye closed. He held up a hand, perhaps in a vain attempt to stop David's killing blow.

Nothing would prevent him from saving his mother's life.

Nothing at all.

"Useless," David answered.

The crunch that followed the swing of his ax echoed along the path. The stillness returned to the area, just as eerie as before. David looked down at his weapon. It had broken in two in this last fight. He dropped it.

Graxxin whispered into his ear, or at least it's what it felt like to David. He had never seen her in person. He didn't need to. She was his master. He was her servant.

"Bleed him," she ordered, her voice reverberating in his skull. "He still has enough life in him to appease my wrath."

"Yes," David replied, hating himself and the task. "For the Blood Goddess, I will serve."

4: Wounded

Snart was licking his wounds with his forked tongue. Several of his Veiled Ones warriors were doing the same. Some had lost limbs in the vicious attack, while others had fared only slightly less worse.

Now that the bloodlust had gone out of his system, Snart was trying to figure out what obsession had overcome him in the moments before attacking the human camp. They had sought to sneak up on the humans and attack them little by little. Yet he, like all the rest of his warriors, had been overcome by an insatiable desire to kill and eat.

Not that he was complaining. They had been able to kill many men and fill their bellies on their flesh. But the victory seemed hollow. He had lost so many of his Veiled Ones. Their numbers were greatly diminished.

The humans hadn't put up as much of a fight. The Veiled Ones had caught them off guard and were able to feast long before any resistance could be put up by the men of Isol and their terrible speakers.

No, the issue had been the great beasts who came after that. Swinging weapons of fire and steel, their purple flames had decimated the ranks of Veiled Ones who were so focused on eating that they didn't see the great danger they were in.

Snart had only just woken up out of his bloodlust when a great, four-legged beast landed next to him and his guards. With one swing of its mighty blade, the entire group had been laid to waste.

All but for Snart.

This encouraged him in a way. It was a sign that he and he alone was supposed to lead the Veiled Ones. But now that they were so diminished, who would he lead? And how would he fulfill what he had promised his faithful followers?

If he couldn't deliver, they may turn on him.

The thought filled his mind as he licked the wound on his left arm. He was grateful for the blood. It had been what had taken him out of his hunger. A man with a spear had sliced his flesh, causing him to howl in rage and wake from the desire to kill.

He had stared up into the eyes of the terrible beast. For a moment, only a moment, he had been too terrified to move. The four-legged creature was as tall as a house. In one hand it could've quickly picked up Snart and crushed him to dust. In a blink, Snart had turned himself invisible with the gift of his people and darted underneath the creature before it could swing it t him again.

The blood of his companions was still wet on him as he fled.

Those who had survived escaped to a nearby network of caves and tunnels. Whether or not the humans or monstrous beasts knew about these caves did not matter to Snart. All he wanted to do was hide and think of their next move.

Movement out of the side of his eye told him that he was not the only one contemplating the next steps of their congregation. As quick as a flash Snart picked up his spear and hurled it at the Veiled One who had been attempting to sneak up on him. The blue lizard let out a streak of pain, dropping both of its spears as it tried fruitlessly to pull the projectile out of its chest.

With one last ragged breath, it fell to the ground in a heap.

Using his good hand, Snart picked himself up off the ground and looked around at the glowing rimstone and eyes that found him in the dark.

"Snart, "he said as loud as he could. "Boss boss!"

The call was not returned with enthusiasm.

"Boss, bosssss." came the lackluster reply.

Snart knew this was not the call of loyal followers. That was the answer of lizards who would instead follow any of their number other than him. And if he valued his life, he needed to show them that he was worth supporting.

He slinked over to the lizard who had come to attack him and pulled his spear from its chest. The dead body flinched at this disruption. Snart dared not take his eyes off the lizards who were seated all around the dark cavern. Who would be the next that would try to take a bit of his flesh with him?

Snart flexed his good hand and knew that he had to show them something worth following. The rimstones woven into his vest began to glow with a blue, shaking light. Several lizards hissed at the sight of this light in the dark cave. Some began to move away from the sight of it. Others put claws on their own spears, unsure of what Snart was going to do.

Good. He needed them to be afraid of him.

He moved around the cave, jabbing with his spear and clutching his fist even tighter. As he did so, the intensity of his glow grew brighter and brighter. He felt a pang of hunger in his gut, but he ignored it. It was helping his cause.

"Snart!" he yelled out as loud as he could. "Boss, bosssss!"

With the last word, he jabbed his fist at a lizard who was taking a few steps closer to him. From his fist, a blast of light flew like a spear at the lizard. It hit the blue lizard square in the stomach. The cave went dark just as the lizard divided into two.

Screeches and hisses from the congregation as a whole filled the cavern. Snart himself took a step back, at a loss at his power. Then again, he was meant to be the Veiled One's ruler.

Wasn't this his right?

He made a fist again, and his vest erupted in blue light. This time, no Veiled Ones came forward to challenge him. He looked at them out of the corner of their eyes. Their spears and weapons lay at their sides. He knew he had it now.

Their fear.

"We have eaten man flash!" Snart shouted. "We will grow stronger!"

He looked around the tunnel and his followers. They were too few. But there had to be more Veiled Ones somewhere. They had come from the mountains in the south. Were there any of their kind in these mountains of the north?

"We will seek out these caves," he said pointing with his spear over the heads of the lizards. "We will find more Veiled Ones. Those who have tunneled deep in the cold, cold."

It was a plan. Not the best, but potentially one that would save Snart's life. Those who had escaped the battle had at least tasted the fresh meat that could be eaten with more victories. If they could find more Veiled Ones, they could mount another assault upon demand.

Snart balled up his claw again.

And with this power that he would grow within him, Snart would need these new Veiled Ones to follow him.

He was strong. He was a leader. He was Snart of the Veiled Ones.

Stepping forward, he motioned with his free claw that they should follow him deep into the caves. He did not know how far down they went, or what they would find there. It didn't matter.

Whatever beast or monster they located, it would serve him and him alone.

He was Snart.

He was boss boss.

5: Back Again

The night air chilled him enough to stir a small shudder from him. It wasn't supposed to be this cold in the fall, but perhaps that was just how the landscape around the north of Ladis worked. Restless bugs chirped at the night sky, which had only just begun to show its moons through dark clouds.

He crouched with a group of people hidden just outside the massive city walls, looking towards a familiar sight.

"I thought we just escaped from here, ya know?" Tratta said as their party looked up at the bleak city walls of Meris.

Their party had positioned themselves behind a clumping of large boulders, hoping that they would be shielded enough by the rocks as to not be seen by any guard who spent too long observing the plains outside the city. They made for an odd bunch.

"Kind of like going back to the pan after jumpin' out of the fire, huh?" Maccus mused.

Ealrin had to agree that there was a certain amount of irony that they were considering sneaking back into the city they had only recently made their way out of. Then again, as with most of their adventures, plans changed when new information came to light.

The fact that the princes of Juttis and Meris both seemed to be caught in an alliance of sorts with the demons who they had fought on several occasions made things difficult. That was why they needed Holve. He would be able to tell them what was going on and why it was happening the way that it was. He would be able to let them know what happens when a man gives himself to the demons from the Dark Comet.

If only he had told them sooner.

Ealrin caught himself thinking that last thought more and more as they ran from Juttis and the impending demon invasion that seemed to be just behind them. Streaks of purple had burst from the comet just as they had fled the city. They all were concentrated on Juttis, though some flew out ahead of them. If the demons really were cascading down from above, they needed all the help, and information, they could get.

And so they had decided they needed Holve more than risking letting him get himself out of jail.

If he was still alive.

That particular notion didn't stay with Ealrin for long. The old man had evaded death more times than Ealrin could count. And if any of the stories he had heard about him on Ladis were true, it seemed Ealrin had a long list of other times to catch up on.

"Well if you're so familiar with this place, surely you can get us in and out without any issues," MIss Rivius said pointedly. Ealrin glanced back at her and Master Ferrin, the bodyguard she had insisted come along with them.

They made for an odd group.

Maccus and Tratta had escaped from Meris with them, after pretending to kidnap them. That still didn't make sense to Ealrin, but he trusted Holve's word. Plus, they had helped them escape with Gregory, a rather grim man who had worked for Holve in a time before this. Then there was Olma, the girl they had found amidst the wreckage of another city lost to Isol.

Adding them to their original group from Ruyn of himself, Blume and Jurrin, seemed like an odd combination.

Especially Miss Rivius.

Ealrin was curious why she had come. It could have easily been said of her that the insurgent group she had harbored had no relation to her whatsoever. That she had been taken in and was repentant of her apparent crimes.

But she had refused any such reasonings. Instead, she had made up her mind to attend to their group and come with them. For maternal reasons, she had said, looking at Blume, Jurrin, and Olma, then at Gregory, the oldest of their group, disdainfully, as if he should be ashamed of himself for allowing such young ones to travel through such dangerous lands.

Gregory had shrugged his assent, and Tratta voiced her objections.

"I'm more than capable of being maternal, ya know!" she had complained.

Miss Rivius wouldn't have it.

Ealrin thought the whole thing was ridiculous and not worth arguing about. If Miss Rivius wanted to come trekking back down to another hostile city and put herself in danger, that was on her. He wasn't the leader.

Not really.

"What do you think, Ealrin?" Gregory asked, catching him off guard.

Ealrin looked over toward the gruff man and realized he had been thinking of a plan, whether anyone asked him about it or not. He let out a sigh.

"Well," he started, realizing that everyone was turning to face him. "I seem to remember a certain one of our members making a rather large hole in a dungeon."

***

It didn't take them long to make their way to the edge of the city where Blume had decimated the dungeon. They could see the castle's tall peaks peering out over the wall and the guards who walked alongside it. It didn't seem any more heavily guarded than the rest of the wall.

Ealrin was at the very least pleased with the fact that there wasn't a more substantial guard presence. They had caused quite a stir.

"What's that over there?" Blume asked, pointing towards a spot beyond the wall. Ealrin tried to find the point she indicated and realized that the city of Meris was glowing. Not a sickly purple glow of the demons, but it was orange.

And then the smell hit him.

"What's on fire, I wonder?" he asked no one in particular.

"I do not like it," Gregory said grimly. Ealrin turned to look at the older man and nodded.

"It could just be something close to the castle. Burning waste or..."

"That's not like Meris," Maccus interjected. "They don't go burnin' things unnecessarily. You've seen how much wood for fuel they have. It's too late to have torches goin', and it looks like it's getting brighter."

At just that moment, the guards on top of the walls began to assemble. It looked very much to Ealrin that something was going on down in the city that was concerning to them. Most of the soldiers ran out of sight, while only two appeared to guard a very long stretch of wall.

"I don't think we'll get a better chance than that, ya know?" Tratta said, looking up at the wall and rubbing her hands together.

"We don't know what's going on in there," Ealrin cautioned. He felt odd about the whole situation. "It could be any number of worse scenarios."

"Worse than sneaking back into a city that already tried to lock you up?" Tratta asked.

At that very moment, a shout rose up from inside the castle walls. It wasn't just the shouting of one or two, but Ealrin was quite sure it was the shouting of a chorus of people. Whether it was the guards who had descended the castle walls or the residents, Meris was apparently in an uproar.

"Looks like we already have our diversion," Miss Rivius said. "What now?"

6: Break Out

Gregory had taken the time to acquire a rope before leaving Juttis, and this one piece of equipment proved to be their doorway into the city. Whatever commotion was going on inside the walls had distracted enough of the guards to allow them to climb up along a buttress of the defenses without being spotted.

At least, Ealrin hoped no one was watching them, as he put hand over hand and climbed the rope as quickly as he could. Blume and Olma followed Maccus and Gregory. Then Jurrin climbed right before Ealrin. Tratta, Rivius, and Ferrin would be the last up the wall.

He scraped his knee along the rough stones as he tried his best to climb the cursed rope. If Blume could do it, in her weakened state and after being so drained in Juttis, then surely he could. Their travels had included so many acts of skill and strength that he thought he would be able to climb a silly rope.

The challenge was harder than he had anticipated.

"Just one hand over another, Mister Ealrin!" Jurrin called over his shoulder. Ealrin looked up at the halfling and was frustrated at how high he had managed to climb in such a short time. He was almost to the top of the wall, while Ealrin struggled in the middle.

He let out a grunt of frustration, before using his feet to try to find some hold in the stones. Ealrin found a footing and, using the rope to pull as he put his feet outward, he discovered that the task became easier.

Slightly easier, in any case.

He was panting heavily when he finally reached the top of the wall. Gregory helped him over before turning to assist Miss Rivius and Ferrin, who both climbed up quickly after he did.

"Just a quick challenge before the real fight begins, I suppose," Miss Rivius said.

"Yes, Ma'am!" Ferrin echoed as they hopped over the stone wall and stood with the rest of the group. Miss Rivius didn't even look winded.

Ealrin found this more frustrating than he cared to admit. Perhaps the journey had taxed him more than he wanted to acknowledge. Maybe the lack of food, shelter, and a good night's sleep anywhere was beginning to do damage to his body.

No, he decided. He wasn't that soft. He would pull through.

Looking over at Blume and Olma, who were both staring over the castle wall to the city below, he decided he wouldn't let the aching in his feet and arms bother him. Not at the moment, anyway.

"What's going on down there?" he asked the two girls. It took a breath or two, but he then realized there had been silence between them. They hadn't been speaking to one another, which seemed odd to him. They were so close in age that maybe, he thought, they might become friends and be a comfort to one another.

Well, how comforting can you really be when being chased from warzone to warzone?

"Everything looks a little off," Blume replied. "The fires seem to be coming from over there."

She pointed out a spot that looked to Ealrin like the market towards the entrance to the city. If there really was a fire, it was far from the castle and the dungeons. But then why did the guards leave?

"I don't think we'll have a better chance," Gregory said, pointing down at the courtyard the castle faced. Ealrin knew that on just the other side of that square, there was a hole that Blume had blasted from the dungeon to allow their escape last time. "It looks as deserted as I've ever seen it in the castle grounds."

Ealrin took a deep breath. It was time already. His arms ached, and his feet were tired, but he had already decided not to let those things bother him.

"Alright," he said, turning to face the group. "I don't think we should all go. Blume should come. And Gregory and Maccus for sure."

"I'm coming too, you know?" Tratta said, stepping forward. "Maccus is lost without me there."

"Ha!" Maccus said, not contradicting her, but pushing her from behind all the same.

"So that leaves Olma, Jurrin, Rivius, and Ferrin to guard the entrance," Gregory said. "I think that'll suffice."

"Two children?" Ferrin said with a smile on his face. Ealrin could see the doubt that lurked behind his eyes.

"One child, Mister Ferrin, sir," Jurrin piped up. "And I wouldn't discredit Miss Olma either. I've seen her take on her fair share of guards and lizards!"

Olma gave Jurrin a winsome smile, and the little halfling bowed down at her.

Gregory shrugged and made his way down the wall.

"There are some stairs this way. We ought to get going quietly before the guards come back from whatever it is they're doing."

And so, as quickly and quietly as they could, the group followed him down the wall and to the first set of stairs they came to. Ealrin felt like they were being watched the whole time, but no matter how often he looked over his shoulder or down at the grounds below, he couldn't spot any soldiers or guards.

The longer they walked without coming across any other person along the wall, the more it unnerved him. They were heading for the rear of the castle. Surely it should be better guarded than this?

Just as the thought crossed his mind, an arrow skidded off the rock wall beside him.

"Down!" Gregory shouted.

All around them arrows began to fly and hit the stones they ducked behind. Ealrin felt one zip right past his head and bounce off the opposite stone wall.

"The stairs are just a few steps away!" Gregory called.

"And we'll be pincushions if we try to climb down them!" Miss Rivius called.

"Just give us a sec!" Tratta replied.

Ealrin looked over his shoulder to see her and Maccus taking their bows off of their shoulders and fitting arrows to them.

"I can't see where they're shootin' from!" Maccus said, peeking over the wall quickly. He ducked down as another hail of arrows rained down against the wall.

"There!" Olma pointed. Ealrin looked and saw that a light was in one of the towers of the castle ahead. Several guards moved back and forth in the tower, pulling back their bow strings and letting their arrows fly.

"We'll keep them hidin'," Maccus said, letting his arrow fly. It hit near the window and sent some of the guards beyond the open portal. Tratta let hers fly just as soon as one peeked around the corner.

A yell and a delayed crunch let Ealrin know she had hit her mark.

"We're pretty good shots, ya know?" Tratta said, picking up an arrow they had fired and putting it on her bow. "Plus they're giving us tons of bolts to give right back!"

Gregory nodded.

"Just try to keep them off of us while we cross the lawn. It'll be no good dying on the castle grounds."

And with those grim words, Gregory turned and scurried to the stairs, staying low to avoid being hit with an arrow. Ealrin and the rest followed him in a similar manner.

The stairs were narrow and, unlike the rest of the wall, had no barrier in between the inner grounds of the castle and themselves.

Ealrin figured that was normal. The city wouldn't need to be defended from itself.

Gregory held up a hand and looked back at Maccus and Tratta. The two were both lifting their bows and looking down towards him. He put his hand down, and they begin firing arrows as quickly as they could towards the tower above. Gregory stood up and ran down the stairs. Ealrin saw Jurrin, Blume, and Olma follow him before he took off.

A sudden panic hit Ealrin.

What if they were shot and killed here in Meris? What if they met their demise in such an unforgiving city? What if, because of his need to rescue Holve, they lost another member of their party? They had lost many since this adventure had begun. How many could have been prevented? How many might have been saved if he had been a better thinker?

He shook himself as his feet hit the path below.

There was no time to rethink this plan now. They were here.

It was either rescue Holve or die in the attempt. That was all there was.

Ealrin's feet pounded against the stones that made a path from the wall to the castle grounds. They only had a few more paces before they could round the corner of the castle and they would be able to see the large hole Blume had made for them to escape last time. Just as they were about to come upon it, a group of guards came bursting out from a side door. Ealrin spun to face them and drew his sword. There were no less than five, though it was hard to tell in the half-light of the moon.

"Go!" Ealrin shouted to the ones in front. He couldn't stand the idea of them being hurt because of his foolish idea to rescue Holve. He would make sure they made it. "I'll hold them off!"

"Not by yourself, lad," Ferrin said, taking a large ax from his back and hefting it onto his shoulder.

Ealrin nodded and stood ready as the first guard came rushing towards him. The man let out a yell and swung his sword. Ealrin was ready. He threw own blade out and defended the blow. Ferrin put his shoulder into the man's ribs just as soon as the guard's sword was up in the air.

A second guard was ready to take his fallen comrade's place. Ealrin swung up and made sure he never got a blow in. The guard fell with a horrible gash across his chest and face. Ferrin felled another guard with his large ax, the poor man's head separated from his body.

The last two took weary steps towards them. The loss of three companions in such a short time certainly must have cooled their fire. One seemed to take a step backward. Ealrin lunged at him, his sword coming down in a smooth arc. Then, just as he was about to make contact with the guard's sword, an arrow slashed his left arm.

He cried out in pain as the bolt tore through his flesh. It passed through his shirt and coat. Ferrin was right beside him, using his blade to knock aside the sword that was coming for Ealrin. Another swing felled the guard who had tried to cut off Ealrin's other arm.

The last guard turned to run, but an arrow caught him in the neck, and he dropped.

Maccus and Tratta were standing on the wall now Through the pain, Ealrin could see them with bows drawn, and arrows pulled back. They were waiting. The threat from the tower must be over.

Ealrin looked down at his arm and saw his blood staining his coat. No time to make adjustments. He nodded at the two and turned to head for the hole Blume had made and the one, he hoped, his friends had gotten down into without further trouble.

So far, this rescue plan was not going well.

7: Tunnels

Blume scrambled over the dirt and debris and began the descent down into the dungeon. She didn't remember making the tunnel quite this large, but that didn't matter at this point.

They were trying to save Holve.

Rocks and dirt were loosely shifting under her feet as she followed Gregory down the tunnel. They had only recently gotten out of this place. It was surreal to be going back down into it. But that was the plan. Get Gorplin and Holve out.

They had done a similar service for her before. It was the least she could do for them.

Ealrin and Ferrin had stopped to give them time. They needed to rush as quickly as they could to make good use of it. Blume felt her feet give way as she stepped on a loose stone and she fell hard on her bottom. A small burst of blue light escaped her ring as she hit the ground. A sound like "opmh" escaped her mouth as she landed.

An arm was pulling at her in an instant.

"Come on Miss Blume. We can't be tripping along the way!" Jurrin said as he struggled to help her up.

Blume shook herself as she tried to put her other hand down to get herself up and walking again. Another hand held her as she made her way up. She looked back, thinking to see Olma there, but it was Miss Rivius.

Olma had continued down with Gregory.

"Such a mess of a place," Miss Rivius said. "And bringing children no less."

"I'm fine," Blume said defiantly as she stood and began walking again. The footing was no more stable than it had been, but she continued on all the same. She didn't need another person telling her she was little.

She was nearly a grown woman now. Seventeen or sixteen, depending on the days. She had lost track somewhere along the way.

"Can you make a little more light?" Gregory asked from below. "I want to see something."

It took Blume a minute to realize he was speaking to her. His grim voice had not directly addressed her since they had begun this adventure.

She nodded and focused on her ring, muttering under her breath.

A gentle blue light began to fill the tunnel as her ring glowed more brightly. Roots and rocks on the tunnel's ceiling came into focus as she made its glow increase. But so did something else.

"Tunnels," Gregory said, looking at them with his eyebrows furrowed.

Indeed, there were small tunnels leading off the sides every few paces. Blume was almost sure those had not been there the last time they had been inside this hallway of earth. Then again, she really wasn't paying attention the last time. She was running.

"Oh I hope there aren't any more of those giant bugs," Jurrin said. "Remember the bugs, Miss Blume?"

"I do," she said, remembering another time when they were underground. She shuddered at the terrible thought.

"Let's keep moving," Gregory ordered. "I see some faint torchlight down below. Go ahead and put that light out."

Blume nodded and concentrated again, waiting for the light to dim down.

But it didn't.

The light glowed just as brightly as it had when she had ignited it. If anything, it was shining brighter. Gregory took a few more steps forward and then turned around to turn up an eyebrow at Blume.

"I..." she began, confused as the ring's lack of submission. "It's supposed to go out."

"Cover it up then," Gregory said, turning and again making his way down the tunnel towards the place where Blume and the Prince of Merris fought.

Curious and frustrated, Blume put her hand over the ring, dimming its light slightly and awkwardly made her way behind him. Why wouldn't the rimstone respond to her command? It always had before. Well, it had sometimes reacted when she was angry or upset. Magic had come out of her without her express permission, but it had never disobeyed her directly.

Pondering this, Blume stumbled down the path until the torchlight from below became bright enough to see by. Gregory held up a hand, asking them to stop. He took a few more steps forward before poking his head into the hall. It was have evidently clear because he waved them on down.

Olma, Jurrin, Rivus, and Blume all followed his lead, making their way down to where earth gave way to formed and shaped stones. The dungeon looked as dreary as it had the first time. Small torches lit the chamber but allowed large dark patches of the hall to remain.

"We'll need to split up," Gregory said. "As soon as Ealrin and Ferrin get back we'll search both ways."

Blume looked to see that the dungeon hall went for a long way in two directions. Cells lined each hall. Not a single guard could be seen patrolling the corridor. That was either because of the lack of guards due to whatever was going on in the city, or the Prince's confidence that his locks held fast. Even with the hole in his dungeon, he must have thought highly of the cell doors.

"No need to wait," came a voice from behind them. Blume spun around to see Ealrin and Ferrin clumsily making their way down the tunnel. Ealrin was wrapping a cloth around his arm. She took her hand off of her ring so that she could illuminate the area and saw red dripping from him.

"You're hurt!" she exclaimed, before Gregory clamped down on her ring, shutting out the light.

"Keep that dark," he commanded. "Let's not draw any more attention to ourselves."

"I'm fine," Ealrin said.

Blume didn't believe him. He looked pale in the blue light of her ring. Was it from loss of blood or the adrenaline of the fight? Either way, she knew she could attend to him when they had a moment. She had healed him before. She would do it again.

Gregory split them up. Ferrin, Rivius, and Jurrin were to go one way, while the rest were to follow him. Search the cells, find Holve, Gorplin, and Donald, then get out as quickly as they could.

"Easy enough," Blume said once the plan was laid out. Gregory gave her a look that she couldn't discern, then shook his head. He made his way down one path the tunnel offered them, while the others went in the opposite direction.

Blume glanced into each cell. Some were empty. Others held feeble prisoners who just barely turned their heads to glance at the strangers walking by. Some moaned out calls for help, while other just lay still.

She tried to ignore the smell that came from those cells and what that might mean.

"I don't see them," Ealrin said once they reached the end of their row. A solid wall greeted them, with no doorway or stair leading in any direction. There were no more cells to check.

A low whistle came from the other end of the hall, and Blume turned. By the torchlight at the furthest point in the other direction, Ferrin was waving at them.

Hopefully, that meant they had found Holve and the others.

By the time they reached them, Blume could tell something was wrong. Jurrin was kneeling down and talking in a low voice, and Miss Rivius had her arms folded and was shaking her head.

"Are you sure, Mister Gorplin?" Jurrin was saying.

Olma knelt beside Jurrin and put a hand out to the dwarf.

"Oh Gorplin!" she said, reaching into the cell. "I'm so glad you're alright."

"Aye, lass," he replied. "They can't break me so easily."

Blume felt a mixture of joy and annoyance. She was glad the dwarf was ok as well. Their little band wouldn't be the same without his constant presence, however ornery he got. But Olma hadn't been that friendly towards her since they had escaped Merris the first time. She felt... lonely.

"Where's Holve?" Ealrin asked.

Blume moved over so that Ealrin could wedge himself past her and get a better view of Gorplin.

"Bah. They took him up for questioning," Gorplin answered. Blume could hear in his voice he was trying to sound strong, but that his body was quite weak. "Maybe three hours ago."

"I've never enjoyed those sessions," came a voice from deeper inside the barred room.

Blume tried to get a glance at who said it, but she couldn't see in the darkness.

"Light," Gregory said.

That was an easy thing to make. She took her hand off her ring, and the blue glow penetrated the darkness. Blume gasped when she looked inside. She was taken by surprise at how beat up Gorplin looked. His face was covered in scratches, and one of his eyes was swollen shut.

But the reason she had lost her breath was that his cellmate was a Skrilx. It was hard to tell if he was naturally that dark brown color, or if the dirt and grime of a very long imprisonment had taken its toll.

"Galp," he said, nodding his snout at them. "I take it you are the friends Gorplin has said travels with a distant relation of mine? I'd be most interested in meeting the fellow. But, as you can see, we're rather locked up tight."

Blume blinked, absolutely stunned. That was more words than she had heard Urt say in a year. She had long since operated under the assumption that the entire Skrilx race was of the strong, quiet variety.

But, to be fair, this was only the second one she had ever met. Whereas Urt, the stoic sailing sidekick of their previous captain, was a strong creature who towered over them all and barely spoke, Galp was lean and thin. Blume felt terrible looking at him with her jaw open. She tried to shake herself and adjust her face to a look more suitable for the moment.

"Where did they take him?" Gregory ask, cutting in across the chatter of the poor looking creature.

Gorplin looked back at Galp who shook his head.

"The Temple," he said sadly. "Usually they question us just out in the main chamber and chain us up for the other prisoners to see. The priest himself came and got him just a bit ago. Not many come back from his interrogations, I'm sad to say."

8: Fortunes Vary

Ealrin shook his head at the inevitability of the situation going from bad to worse.

"What do you mean the temple is on the other side of the city?" he said, gesturing wildly with his hands. "We barely got into the dungeon in one piece, and we're going to have to carry out Gorplin and Galp if they're going to make it!'

"Bah!" Gorplin protested as he stumbled from the jail cell. "Try to carry me, and I'll make you regret it!"

Blume had managed to make short work of the lock in the door, which now was swinging freely open. Olma and Jurrin were inside helping Galp to his feet. He claimed that he hadn't been free of shackles in more than a year, which helped explain his pitiful state. Gorplin may not need to be carried, but the Skrilx certainly would need assistance.

"We have to get Holve," Gregory insisted.

Ealrin puffed his frustration out into a breath. He knew they needed to get Holve. He was integral to not only their success on Ladis but their eventual escape too. The man knew the ports, the captains, and the right cities to go to. He was also a marked man, to be fair.

"Well," Ealrin said, knowing what was right and also seeing the task that was ahead of them. "What do we do?"

"The city is still in an uproar," Gregory said. "There's a chance we can get to the temple in the middle of the chaos."

"And what if the chaos is happening around the temple?" Ealrin shot back.

"Aye," Gorplin said. "The priest did look all kinds of flustered when he came and demanded Holve. Dirty beast."

"Fine," Ealrin said, feeling flustered and heated. He didn't want to take chances that would endanger the group. "But it'll just be me,

Ferrin and Gregory. Everyone else can stay back and get Galp and Gorplin to safety."

This caused immediate arguments from several of their group. Jurrin didn't want to miss out, Miss Rivius refused to be separated from her bodyguard, and Blume insisted they would need her along the way. Olma stayed mostly quiet.

"We can't all go!" Ealrin shouted back.

"Hey! What's going on down there?" came a distant shout.

Everyone froze. Ealrin looked at Gregory, who was staring up a long corridor that had a set of stairs leading from it. One torch lit the stairs the rose out of sight into the rock above. He turned slowly back to Ealrin.

"You're right," he said darkly. "We can't all go. Some of us will need to stay back and help these two. The dwarf is too weak to fight right now, though I don't doubt he's a considerable opponent."

Gorplin muttered at this. Ealrin wasn't sure if it was agreement or dwarvish curses. They went on.

"Is anyone willing to stay behind?" Gregory asked.

Olma raised her hand sheepishly.

"We'll stay with her," Miss Rivius said. "Ferrin and I will help get these two out of here and be with little Olma."

Ealrin noticed the girl she was referring to gave her a look at the word "little" but didn't protest. He nodded and looked at the others. Blume's eyes were wide with daring. He knew that look. They also didn't have time to debate.

"Then you three get Galp out of here," he said. "Meet up with Tratta and Maccus and try to see what's going on in the city. We'll meet back up with you on the outskirts of the southern border. Gregory, Blume and I will go find Holve."

***

There was no good way to describe the situation. Blume and Gregory were the ones who could go with him. Maccus and Tratta were, hopefully, able to protect the others as they got Gorplin and Galp to safety. In the meantime, Ealrin was going to do his best to make sure Blume stayed safe, and Gregory got them to where they needed to go.

And while all this was happening, they had a hallway of guards to deal with.

The path to the prison was familiar to Ealrin. They had traversed this way recently in reverse, so he knew the route well enough to know that there was a turn up ahead that would lead them to the castle's grounds. Unfortunately, that turn also seemed to be inhabited with every guard the prince of Meris had.

Voices and the clanking of metal armor reverberated down the hallway as the three of them stood in the shadows. They tried to take in everything they could while also not poking their heads out to be seen by any guard who was suspicious about the path to the dungeon. If any went that way currently, they would find several of their companions unconscious or otherwise out of the way.

Gregory had a very stealthlike manner about him, which was helpful.

Up to this point.

"I could make a path..." Blume offered.

"And risk having every other guard in the castle on us as well," Gregory said, stating what Ealrin was thinking. He knew Blume was good, but even she wasn't that talented. Plus, her magic had been a bit finicky as of late. They couldn't risk it.

Blume looked put out, but Ealrin shook his head at her.

"It's not worth it," he said.

"And every moment we stand waiting around, Holve gets tortured more," Blume protested in a harsh whisper. "Shouldn't we get going!?"

Ealrin smiled at her, just a bit. He never thought she particularly liked the old man. He was rather short with her most of the time. Then again, he was one of the two who had rescued her at the beginning.

"I know," Ealrin said. "But we don't want to cause..."

His sentence was cut off by a loud crash that echoed down their hallway.

"What in the world?" Gregory said, poking his head out.

Several shouts and clanging of metal followed the crash and what sounded like most of the guards moving away from the spots they had been occupying.

"Can't ask for better," Ealrin muttered. "Let's go."

Gregory moved out first, followed by Blume. Ealrin took the rear, making sure that Blume was covered if they needed to make a quick getaway. In any possible circumstance, she would be the one who could enable them to escape if needed.

The stone hallway gave way to an arched door, where the soldiers had been standing. Gregory peeked around the corner, taking a moment to see whatever was beyond it. Ealrin took a breath, steeling himself for a fight. He held the sword he had borrowed from a stash of Ladis weapons in Juttis. It still didn't feel right in his grasp. He missed his old sword, but now was not the time to lament his losses.

Gregory nodded and waved them forward before taking a step out himself. Ealrin crossed the archway at the same time as Blume did, not wanting her to engage unaccompanied. Instead of a castle courtyard filled with soldiers, they saw that it was utterly deserted.

The last time they had made their way through this courtyard, it had been filled with nobles and lords who were celebrating the birthday of the Prince. Expensive food and drink were abundant, and the decorations were elaborate.

Now the courtyard was barren, save for a large crater in the middle of it that was not there the last time they had walked through.

Even a few things seemed to be out of place. A stray shield lay against a turned over barrel. A spear stuck into the ground had a bit of cloth hanging on it. A cat even walked alongside the other end of the courtyard, observing the newcomers with indifference.

And not a soldier could be seen.

"Weren't they just..." Ealrin started to say.

Gregory pointed, rather than spoke.

Ealrin followed the direction of his finger and saw the castle gates wide open. Not a single guard was left to defend it.

"Why would they just leave like that?" Blume asked.

Ealrin didn't know, and he saw Gregory shake his head.

"I'm not sure," he said in his gritty voice. "But whatever the reason, it can't be good."

"Do we head on towards the Temple?" Ealrin asked.

"This may be our best opportunity," Gregory answered.

Blume stepped in front of them both.

"Then what are we waiting for? Let's go get Holve!"

Ealrin found it hard to share her enthusiasm, but he agreed with the idea. They needed to take advantage of whatever good fortune they had wondered upon. If something was occupying the soldiers of Meris at the moment, they didn't have time to think about why or what.

They needed to head straight for the temple.

"Let's go," Ealrin said. "Take us to the Temple, Gregory."

9: Bitter Tastes

Once they had left the confines of the deserted castle grounds, Blume found herself in the oddly familiar territory of large houses and well-groomed lawns of Meris. It was so unlike the place they had initially entered. She had a moment of remembrance running through these same houses and bushes with Olma, but she pushed that aside.

No matter how hard she tried, the only girl who was relatively close to her age kept pushing her away. She had hoped to find a friend. It seemed that all she could do was scare the girl from the jungle.

Blume found herself resenting Olma for it. They had such similar stories. They had even been plucked up from certain death by the same group of people. Why couldn't they bond over their experiences? Few people could ever understand them. Their parents were killed. Then they were accepted into a group of strange and wonderful adventurers. She wanted a friend.

So far, it only felt like she had received an enemy.

Gregory was jogging through the streets of Meris, keeping to the far side of them. Ealrin was right behind her as they ran. As the sky darkened, a more magnificent orange glow came from the city's entrance. The shouting seemed to get louder as well.

"Exactly where is the temple?" Blume asked as she attempted to keep up with Gregory's long strides.

"Up ahead," he answered, pointing out the large structure that stood above the houses that surrounded it. "That's the temple's tower."

Small rocks crunched under their feet as they continued their run. The streets were devoid of life. No guard, occupant, or temple priest was anywhere to be seen. Bluem supposed that was for the best. If they ran into any one of those groups of people, it might alert the authorities to what they were doing. Plus, they very much needed

38

the group who would meet them outside the walls of Meris to make it there unscathed.

Hopefully, they could find some supplies they could take with them on their trip back down south. Blume knew their stores were running low.

Gregory stopped abruptly and put up a hand for them to follow suit. Blume skidded to a halt and nearly fell forward. Ealrin grabbed onto her shoulder and steadied her, and he stopped as well. The air was still, and all Blume could hear around them was the distant shouting and the quiet night. Her ring glowed with a slight blue tint as she felt apprehensive about no longer moving forward, so she covered it with a hand.

Then the sound met her ears.

Footsteps.

Lots of footsteps.

"This way," Gregory said, running for a house's lawn and hiding behind one of the massive columns that held up the houses' portico. Blume and Ealrin followed his example. Just as her hair flipped around the pillar, Blume caught a glimpse of temple guards marching down the street, weapons in their hands and torches lighting the night sky.

At their head was a temple guard who was tall and intimidating in his appearance. He was shouting at his fellows.

"They can't kill our priest and get away with it!" he yelled at the crowd. "The prince may have sided with the demons, but we know better! We'll show him with the man he was so eager to imprison. We'll take him to the prince himself and have them see who the true gods are! That'll put a stop to the people's rebellion!"

With that, he pulled on a chain he was holding, and a man stumbled forward, pulled by the guard.

Blume let out a tiny gasp as comprehension dawned on her.

It was Holve.

He looked awful, even from this distance and in such pale light, Blume could see cuts and bruises all over his face. They must have mistreated him terribly.

"Gregory," Ealrin whispered. Blume turned around. Ealrin had seen who they pulled on several chains as well.

The grim-faced man looked out at the crowd of guards and then back at the two of them. Blume knew he must be weighing their odds. Three to a dozen or more. Blume knew they had faced worse and come out on top. But what would he think?

Before giving him time to consider whether or not they could take them, she leaped around her column and let out a yell of fury, followed by words of Speaking.

Tendrils of power flew from her ring and assaulted the guards as they pulled hard on Holve's chains. Some of them began to rush Blume and the porch she was standing on. Gregory came around his column with a bow and an arrow notched and ready. Beside her, Blume heard the arrow sail through the wind as the bowstring snapped. The first guard fell dead with a scream, the projectile straight through his eye.

Ealrin jumped in between her and the second guard and let his blade sing, taking down the second guard even as he advanced on them.

Now the remaining guards were in a sort of panic. It seemed to Blume that some wanted to flee, while others held Holve's chains and shook their weapons at her and her companions.

A smirk crossed her face. She felt powerful. She felt alive.

How delightful would it be to end the miserable lives of these guards who held her friend captive? With a flick of her wrist, the weapons of each guard flew from their hands and went soaring high into the air. The chains that held Holve tightened and glowed with a bright blue light. She felt the air tighten within her grasp as the weapons soared back down towards their owners, tips and metal blades aimed to kill.

"Blume!" a voice called to her. It seemed far and distant. The air around her grew lighter. A blackness that she had not realized has consumed her vision receded. Strangled cries of anguish filled her ears, and her feet touched the ground hard. Had she been floating? She blinked.

The chains around Holve fell in a smoking heap. The collar that had been around his neck and the cuffs around his wrists broke into pieces as he gasped for air.

Blume breathed deeply of the cold night air and realized that moments had gone by without her realization.

The guards around Holve all laid dead on the ground. Holve himself was on his knees, gasping for air. Gregory was with him, helping him to his feet and hurrying him towards the house as fast as he could.

Blume was aware that someone was holding onto her arm. She didn't like it.

"Ah!" a voice said. She looked to her side to see Ealrin shaking his hand frantically. "Did you do that?"

She looked down at where she had felt a hand and saw that her shirt was smoking there. Had she burned his hand? Had she meant to do that?

"I don't know," she answered. And she really didn't. The ring on her finger glowed brightly as Gregory and Holve stumbled up to the house. Blume took a moment to take in Holve. He looked terrible. The bad light from the street hadn't done his injuries justice. Still, he seemed every bit as stubborn as he usually did.

"Where's Galp?" he asked, looking at the three of them.

Blume raised her eyebrow at him.

"Thank you, would do just fine," she replied, standing to her feet and crossing her arms. She gave him a hard look. They just risked life and limb to save him, and this is how he showed his gratitude?

By asking about a Skrilx they hardly knew?

Blume could feel her mouth go dry as she opened and closed it several times. She didn't like the taste it was leaving, and she felt a great mix of anger and frustration coming up from her, like a wave of power. Blue sparks radiated from her hair as Ealrin put a cautious hand on her shoulder.

"Calm down," he whispered.

Blume didn't want to calm down. She wanted to blow things to pieces with her magic.

Holve shook his head.

"If we can save Galp," Holve started, looking around at their surroundings. "We can end this conflict and deal a strike against the foul things that spawn from the dark comet."

Blume looked at Holve and blinked.

"You mean he knows how to..."

"Defeat the demons of darkness for good?" Holve interjected, putting a hand on a column and freeing himself from Gregory's helping hands. "He does."

10: The Plans of Gods

Jerius walked quickly down the path. He was breathing heavily as he hadn't yet taken a break since the suns had risen early that morning. Since he had spoken with the king and explained the plan to him, he had been going from general to general, relaying the details of the great quest to rid their continent of the Isolian threat.

Some of the generals were willing to take whatever measures it required to get the magical heretics off of their lands. Others looked at Jerius with skepticism. He couldn't blame them. There wasn't much trust he had for them to see this through either.

Clutching the tome he had carried from the high priest's private study in his arm, Jerius climbed the last set of steps he would need to before heading back. He took the steps quickly, making sure that he touched each one. Even in his rush, he wasn't going to fall down these steps.

A priest had his position to think of, even in the chaos of a siege.

Jerius made his way up the stairs until he reached the top of the tower. Before he registered the people who were standing within the tower, he saw the carnage that was going on out in the fields of Prommus. The army of Isol was back further than he could remember seeing. They had positioned themselves just outside the range of Prommus' best artillery. This had to have been their intention.

Those blasted cannons of theirs, however, could shoot further than anything Prommus had in its arsenal. Another shot came careening towards them, and several of the officers in the tower looked to see if it would impact the wall.

It did.

A thunderous explosion reverberated throughout the city as another portion of the wall came crashing down. A few more direct hits like that and Prommus would have no barrier left to defend itself.

43

Jerius nodded resiliently. He had the answer in his hands. Now he only needed to convince one last general.

"Pardon my interruption," he said, bowing to the room at large. " Who is the commanding officer for this section of the wall?"

He knew the name of the general very well. He didn't, however, want to leave the impression that he was starstruck. Oranius was a name known by many in the Theocracy. He was a hero in the Disputed Lands. Leading troops to victory after victory had made him grow from a soldier to a general in a short amount of time. No one had the strategic prowess he seemed to possess. Even the king spoke highly of him.

Jerius knew the name, but not what the general looked like.

A large, very scarred man stepped forward. Jerius could see why this man would be respected, but something was off. He didn't wear the same uniform as the other generals he had spoken to that day. This man was a captain. Jerius almost opened his mouth, assuming that the famed general had lost his life and this captain had taken rank, but it wasn't so.

The scared man made a motion to a younger looking man. Younger than Jerius. He wore the gray stripes on his arm that denoted him as a general. Jerius couldn't believe it. Every other man he had met today had been twice his age at least.

How had this youth become a commanding officer? Was he the one who had commanded troops in the Disputed Lands and led battalions to victory against the speakers?

"I am General Oranius," he said in what he probably thought was a commanding voice. Jerius had to hold back a smirk. The boy's voice nearly cracked as he said the words. The longer Jerius looked at the boy in front of him, the younger he looked. The priest held himself up as high as he could and puffed out his chest.

This general, he would be able to convince without worry.

"I bear a message from the king: the wall is to be abandoned. Haad back to the inner defenses and remove all your soldiers from atop the walls. The priests of Ladis will be delivering Prommus from ruin."

A soldier laughed, but no one joined in with him. Jerius surveyed the room and could tell that most of them probably felt the same way that lone soldier did. Each of them, to a man, looked at the general in the tower. Another cannon blast shot past them and blasted against the mountains behind them. The tower shook slightly, but no one blinked.

"This message comes from the king, does it?" General Oranius said. "I'll need to see the paper orders, prophet."

"Priest Jerius of Arranus," Jerius said, inclining his head. He was a high ranking member of the Temple of Ladis. He did not have to bow to a general. It was only a good gesture to do so. And he was feeling himself run out of goodwill.

"Priest Jerius," the General said, correcting himself. "I will need to see His Majesty's seal before I perform any duty other than the one he commanded me to: defend the wall."

Jerius nodded and took from his arm, a paper signed by the king himself. Regis had been reluctant at first, but he had given in. There was no way they would win this fight against Isol in this manner. The heretics had already taken down two cities. Prommus would just be another notch on their belt.

Unless they did something.

General Oranius was scanning the letter with a furrowed brow.

"I do not see the King's seal here," he said, handing the paper back. "I will not remove my men unless the order comes from the king. This is the central wall and the gatehouse of Prommus. I will not abandon my post or my liege at the command of a Priest."

With that, he gave the paper to the broad, scarred man and turned back to the tower's balcony where the battle was still unfolding. There wasn't much of a struggle from the Isolian side of things. Only a few companies of soldiers had gone out to meet the invading army head-on. They had met much the same fate as the crumbling wall had but in a much bloodier and terrible manner. After those companies were shattered, no more were sent.

Prommus appeared to wait it out.

And slowly lose its defenses in the process.

Jerius brought his attention back to the general. Pointing with his robes hand, he indicated the troops that were retreating off the walls and moving inside to the inner walls of Prommus.

"The rest of the army is already following the orders of the king," Jerius said, looking back to the general. "I suggest you do the same."

Oranius took two very deliberate steps toward Jerius and the soldiers who stood in the room with him tensed. Jerius did his best to remain calm. He was a priest, after all.

"I do not take well to being ordered around by a temple lackey," he said in a low growl.

"Then listen to its High Priest," came a voice from behind them.

Jerius smirked, not needing to turn to know who spoke. Oranius stepped back and bowed his head, though Jerius could tell it was not out of respect, but an obligation.

The high priest outranked all by the king himself.

And Jerius knew there were plans for that as well.

"High Priest Regis," Oranius said. "You must understand that my orders come from the king."

"As do our own," Regis replied. He looked regal in his ornate robes and High Priest hat. His stare held as much hatred for Oranius as the general held for him. The two stared at each other for just a moment, and Jerius wondered if the general would be as obstinate as he had heard he would be.

Oranius seemed like he was going to open his mouth when the noise of more people ascending the stairs came from behind them.

This time, Jerius was curious who would be accompanying them in this room that was beginning to feel very cramped.

"We are ready to serve, High Priest," came the feminine voice of a temple guard. Jerius kept his smile inward at the sight of thirty or more temple guards coming up the stairs. Luca was apart of the group as well. She made no indication that she saw Jerius, and he didn't look her in the eyes.

She was his servant, and she was in her rightful place. That was all that mattered.

Looking back to Oranius, Jerius could see the man seething at the sight of the guards and the priest and the High Priest all standing before him.

He knew he was cornered.

"And what does the king command of me?" Oranius asked with his teeth clenched.

High Priest Regis took a step forward.

"To rid this land of the heretics and magic speakers who would threaten to undo the efforts and ideologies of the Theocracy," Regis answered. "To ensure that they never again affront our great nation and that we succeed in what the almighty Decolos intended to do a thousand years ago."

"That is my purpose here," Oranius began to say. Regis held up a hand to quiet him. To Jerius, it looked like Oranius was deciding if he and his men could really take on the thirty temple guards and get away with it. He looked livid.

"But you have so far been unsuccessful," Regis continued. "The great Decolos foresaw a time when the armies of the Theocracy would fail and that we would need to call on a power higher than men can reach."

"Our deity certainly has knowledge beyond that of mortal men," Oranius said.

Jerius knew the young man was offended. He was being told that he and his army could do little to repel the Isolian invaders. On the one hand, he had to see that it was true. The Isolian cannons were ringing out shot after shot at the city of Prommus. They couldn't take many more direct hits without allowing the army to come unhindered into their capital.

On the other hand, Jerius knew it bothered the general to be told that he could do nothing more. Especially one as decorated as he was.

"Indeed," Regis replied. "Now, this tower is where we will begin our necessary steps to rid ourselves of the Isolians. You are free to leave, or stay if you wish to witness the victory of the Theocracy!"

The scared man made a scoffing noise but quieted with a look from Oranius. He bowed and moved aside, letting Regis step towards the balcony.

"Jerius," he said, not looking behind him. "Prepare the ritual."

Pulling the ancient tome from his robe, Jerius laid it upon the stone table that was in the middle of the room. He turned to the page he and the high priest had studied for countless hours the week before this moment. Putting a finger down on the correct page, he read aloud.

"Blood for the driving out of the heretic and purging the land of the Speaker. Blood for the one who is in exile. Blood for the return of the scourge of the rimstone. Blood for the fire of the sky and the destruction of the time yet to come."

"What is this?" Oranius said as he took a step forward, looking at the book that Jerius was pointing at.

Jerius paid him no heed.

"Blood of the strong to call the strong," he finished. "Blood to call the ones from the dark above into the light beyond."

"Now!" Regis commanded.

As one, they obeyed.

Jerius pulled a knife from within his sleeve and shoved it into the unprotected armpit of Oranius, drawing out a gasp of pain and surprise from the decorated general. His soldier moved forward with cries of rage, but the temple guards were spilling into the room, swords in hand and fire in their eyes.

Jerius watched as the expression on Oranius' face turned from anger to pain to blank as blood poured down his hand and onto the floor of the tower.

And out on the plains, a flash of purple light lit up the night sky.

11: Crumbling

Another blast from the cannons on the plains in front of Prommus sounded out as cheers rose from the Isolian camp. The city was falling to them and their magical power.

Octus stood with arms crossed, a look of passivity on his face.

"Why do you hate it so much?" Yada asked him. She had been brought to the front where she could see the devastation better and was reclining on the couch. Octus didn't reply at first. Though he knew he would be punished if he didn't respond soon, Octus reveled in the idea of making her wait to hear from him,

It was a small bit of rebellion that he could afford at the moment.

"I do not enjoy death and war as much as your soldiers do," he said, while not looking at her. Another blast shot down a large tower from within the walls of the city. Cheers rang out from the soldiers as they watched it fall. Octus knew that Speakers would walk into the city and reconstruct that same tower in hours. It was wondrous to behold. And terrible.

Those same speakers would clear the streets of the dead bodies of the defenders. They would carelessly lift them into piles and then burn the dead as other soldiers collected their possessions.

Having seen this play out twice not, Octus was sick of the sights.

He wanted very badly to do his worst to Her Holiness and then search for his niece.

He would do anything to know she was safe.

"But you were a soldier in the wars against my people once," Lady said. "You fought bravely, I'm told. You were a hero to them."

"I'm no hero," Octus replied. "Does Her Holiness require anything?"

He heard a dry chuckle from Yada. He knew what that meant. She was on to him.

"I'll not dismiss you until I'm quite satisfied you've seen enough of your capital burned to the ground," she answered back.

Octus breathed but did his best to keep the sigh from making noise. He knew that he could be punished for such things. He had been in the past when Yada was in a foul mood. Fortunately for him, she had been in high spirits ever since marching to Prommus. The campaign had seen some trials, but when it involved taking the cities of the Theocracy, Isol and Ydda flourished.

Another blast of magical energy shot out from the ranks of Isol and shook the castle walls. Octus looked down from the chaos. He knew it would not be long before the capital of his country, the one he had fought for and bled for, fell to these horrible wizards and heretics.

"Eyes up," Yada said with jubilation in her voice. "This will be our final stroke."

Octus looked over at the women he hated so much. She had her hand in the air as if to signal something. The blue crystals weaved into her hair glowed menacingly and made her eyes shine with the same reflected light. The hair on Octus' forearms stood on end as he felt the air around him charge with power.

But it wasn't the kind he had become accustomed to since being forced to march alongside Isol. This power felt...foreign.

Screams rang out as, from above, purple streaks of light came shooting down at the troops gathered outside the city of Prommus. Cannons began to explode where they stood as the points of light slammed into them. Speakers dove from the wreckage and soldiers began to run this way and that. Some towards the purple lit craters that had been formed, others away from them.

The demons had returned.

"Get those cannons pointed at the beasts!" Yada was shouting. "The demons! Shoot them!"

Octus was having none of that. Even though such a strategy had worked against one, there were no less than twelve of the demons who had landed in their ranks. Perhaps they were all too aware of how the cannons were used against them and were ready to seek revenge.

A massive purple blade came down on a cannon that was powering up to fire at the new threat. As soon as the demon's weapon hit it, demon, cannon and all the Speakers who were around it were engulfed in a purple and orange explosion.

Octus felt the ground underneath his feet tremble. He crouched to better keep his feet underneath him and found that he wasn't the only one having trouble standing up. Yada fell backward onto him, losing her place next to the couch she had been sitting on, she ended up in his arms.

He had to restrain himself from snapping her neck as soon as she touched him. Of course, three blades came shakily down in his direction as soon as she had fallen. For a flash, he thought it might have been worth it to end himself to end Yada's miserable life.

But he thought of Olma. In that brief moment, her face flashed before his eyes, and he relented. Roughly, he stood Yada up on her own two feet. She must have felt his brashness because she shoved herself away from him as hard as her frail frame could.

Then he watched her as she observed the devastation all around her. The Isolian army was in disarray. Soldiers and Speakers were running in all directions. Prommus lay nearly defeated in front of them, but there was now a more pressing issue in their midst.

She huffed loudly, then looked over at one of her generals.

"Sound the retreat," she ordered. "Get the troops away from here. Leave me a team of Speakers."

"Your Holiness?" the general asked. Octus could see the confusion on her face.

"These demons have denied me my prize," Yada replied. "If you think I will sit by idly while they decimate my armies, you are mistaken."

With those words, an eruption of blue poured from her jewels as she reached out a hand towards the nearest demon.

Octus shielded his eyes as a blast of power shot toward the towering demon and another explosion shook his feet. He only had a small twinge of regret at being grateful he didn't kill Yada.

12: No Opportunity Wasted

The army of Isol was fleeing to the east. Just the sight of it pleased Silverwolf greatly. She found herself cheering the demons on to more destruction. The more they thwarted the plans of Yada and her armies, the easier their job became.

But there was something else about this as well.

And Silverwolf would not waste this chance.

"I suppose we should get ready to track them," Serinde said as she stood behind Silverwolf. From her crouching position, the assassin was glad that her elven companion was behind her. That way she could roll her eyes as much as she wanted.

"Of course we'll have to track the army," Silverwolf said, standing to her feet and stretching her limbs. From their vantage point behind a large grouping of rocks, the city of Prommus stood proudly against its mountainous anchor. Isol was fleeing in large groups, and the demons were being tormented by a group of Speakers who were casting a furious barrage of spells at them.

Silverwolf knew they couldn't keep this up forever. Even magic had its limits.

And that meant there was a slight possible chance that they could make a break for the gates.

"We need to get into the city," Silverwolf said, locking her eyes on the hole that was opening up in the lines between the gates and the army.

"Wait, what?" Serinde asked sluggishly.

Silverwolf should have known. The elf was not one to think on the fly when there was a plan already in place. Hopefully, she wouldn't take too much convincing.

"Holve's order," she replied. And with those words, she decided to walk towards the gates. The ground was hard beneath her feet. Shaking slightly, but hard. There were no shreds of grass or vegetation anywhere. The army had taken away every evidence of life on the plains in front. Fitting, Silverwolf thought. Isol wanted to take all life in Ladis. They nearly did.

If it weren't for the demons.

"Holve didn't say anything about..."

"He only told me," Silverwolf said. "Keep up."

"Something that important," Serinde began to argue.

"Is what we'll discuss later," she countered. "Right now we have demons to get around."

The purple beasts were still engaging Isol's remaining forces, which Silverwolf was keeping an eye on, but the majority of them were heading right for the middle of the explosions and blue spells that were erupting from the back of the camp.

Dawn was breaking and the last bits of the night were flying away before the suns began to peek out over the horizon. That gave them precious moments to cross the plains and get to the wall before any guards could see them.

Silverwolf was hoping the fireworks would provide enough distraction so that she and Serinde could crawl over the wall and get in. An army may not be able to find a way, but surely two competent females could.

"Holve wanted us to chase down Isol," Serinde said as they paused by another large outcropping of rocks. "He didn't know they were heading for Prommus for a fact."

"And if our journey did take us by the city, he gave me a job," Silverwolf said. "Now shut up. There's one of those things coming our way."

It wasn't entirely untrue. A hulking monstrosity was near them, but he wasn't paying attention. Silverwolf assumed it was a he, at least. How could one tell?

"It isn't looking this way," she said. "Let's go."

"Go where?" Serinde questioned.

"Into the city," Silverwolf answered as she pushed off the rock and began to sprint towards the stone walls of the capital. They were only about two good sprints away from the wall at this point. She felt the cold air bursting in and out of her lungs as her feet hit the ground and she continued to get as good a leg as she could.

Hopefully, the elf could keep up.

There was an abandoned wagon in front of her that she could hide behind. If she could just get there before the big demons got too curious in the pair running the opposite way of everyone else.

Isol was still in full retreat. There was still enough time to make it five more steps. Four. Three.

An explosion rocked the ground just in front of her feet. The air assaulted her face as a wave of blue energy rocked her. Her arms flew up in front of her face as her back hit something that grunted and then screamed.

The both of them hit the ground hard. Silverwolf felt the wind knocked out of her, but it would take more than that to keep her down. More out of instinct than anything else, she rolled herself away from where she thought the blast came from and got to her hands and feet.

Her head was spinning, the world was blurry, but she was not going to go down on her back that easily. A rumbling filled her ears after the high pitched hum died away. She tried to follow her senses to feel where it was coming from.

A large shape that was engulfed in purple came up from another blur that Silverwolf thought might be the wagon. When it also started to turn purple, she knew it had caught fire and that there was only a small window of opportunity.

Reaching for one of her swords, she stood to her feet and began to slowly walk backward. There wasn't much she could do to defeat this beast alone. She knew that full well from the times she had seen them attack. They were powerful demons that could rend houses in two with one swing of their blade.

Her vision was returning to her just enough to see that large purple shape raise a portion of itself into the air.

"Jump!" she shouted, hoping the elf could hear her and that she wasn't still laying on the ground where they had landed. The demon's blade came down with a crash, and the ground quivered beneath the force of it.

She rolled again, this time being more in control of herself and keeping her sword away from her body. Taking the first chance she got, she spun herself around hard and slashed with her blade. A terrifying, gut-clenching scream emerged from the air, which told her she had at least hit the thing. She didn't know where. And she didn't care.

She ran.

And much to her surprise, Serinde was right beside her.

"I think you took its foot off!" she shouted as she overtook Silverwolf and leaped onto a pile of rocks, then onto a pile of rubble that the Isolian cannons had created. The assassin wasn't too far behind the elf. Her vision was returning just enough so that she could get her footing and leap from the pile of rubble onto the wall of the city.

Well, a hole in the wall, but nonetheless, they were moments from being inside.

"Intruders! Invaders! Protect our city!"

"Ugh," Silverwolf groaned, before throwing herself flat against the rubble and dodging the first of many arrows that came shooting towards them.

"We can't get in this way!" Serinde shouted from behind a stone that served as her shield against the barrage of missiles.

A demon scream filled their ears as the arrows stopped just long enough for the archers below to reload and cover their faces in terror. The beast was coming closer.

"I'm not risking my life with that thing out there!" Silverwolf shouted back.

"We're risking our lives everywhere!" Serinde replied, just as loudly and with nearly as much frustration as Silverwolf felt. They were so close.

"Fine!" she said, before putting her sword into its sheath and picking up rocks. "These are the only weapons that'll work at the moment unless you have a better idea."

She didn't want Serinde to have a better idea. She wanted her to be as stuck as she was. Unless, of course, it meant they got into the city with more ease. TO her surprise, Serinde ran back to the wall's outer edge and began to wave her arms.

"Over here you big ugly brute!" she shouted.

"Are you insane!?" Silverwolf began to shout.

But the roar that followed must have drowned her out. Serinde turned back and shoved Silverwolf in the other direction, running through the opposite end of the hole and jumping out of it as quickly as they could. It was a good thing too. The hole collapsed as soon as they were clear of it.

The archers below were no longer concerned with two females coming at them. Instead, they directed their aim at the giant demon clambering over the wall, blade swinging and purple flames pouring out of its upturned hand.

Silverwolf looked back just in time to see that it was one of the demons who had a helmet covering its face, a large plate of otherworldly looking metal covering its chest, and a sword the size of a horse.

She didn't dare look for long as the demon had a giant wound on its leg and was furious about it. She and Serinde ran down an alley, into the streets of Prommus, and away from the wall that had kept an army out.

Prommus was open to them.

Silverwolf was not going to waste this opportunity.

13: Ice Cold

Serinde doubted very much that Holve would have actually sent them into Prommus. He wanted Blume's amulet back. And, if they could manage it, the other items that Yada held within her grasp as well. The old woman had stolen much from them, and they needed to get it back.

Why would Holve send them on some errand into Prommus? And why would he keep it a secret from her, as well?

It didn't make sense to her. But she wanted to see what Silverwolf was up to and had no real reason not to trust her.

Other than the fact that she was an assassin and a murderer and generally a spiteful person.

So the only thing Serinde really knew was not to cross Silverwolf, but to try to help her. In so doing, she may get more out of the bargain than she could have hoped for. Someone to have her back again.

It had been a difficult year without her sister. Indeed, for Serinde it was one of the hardest things she had ever experienced, even worse than losing her father.

She had never known how much she valued the companionship of Erilas until she was gone. So for now, all she had was Silverwolf. And that was almost like not having a traveling companion at all.

"This way," the assassin ordered as they made a turn and ran up a different alley in the large city of Prommus. Serinde would have liked to spend time observing the place. She had seen so much of the world traveling with this group. More than she ever thought possible. But there was no time. The city was still acting as if it were under siege.

Men ran this way and that, carrying pails of water to put out fires, stretchers that ferried the wounded from the front to the medics and tents of healing further into the city, and bundles of arrows to archers waiting along the walls. Cries of the injured filled the streets.

The city was both familiar and foreign to Serinde. She had spent a little time in it during their attempt to rescue Holve. The area they were currently in, however, was not one she had been through before. For that reason alone, she trusted Silverwolf's commands to turn, go straight, and then take a detour through what appeared to be a bakery. The assassin paused at the front of the store, looking out to the street beyond. A cloth covered a wide window save for one slit down the middle that allowed her to glimpse the outside. Serinde moved so that she could see as well.

This area of town was quieter than where they had come from. More than likely this was due to its distance from the wall and the castle towards the back of the city. Soldiers were at the walls. The civilians must have gathered as far away from it as possible.

Silverwolf turned and nodded as if her glance into the empty street answered any questions she may have had.

"Alright, it shouldn't take a long time," she muttered. Since she wasn't making eye contact, Serinde understood she was muttering to herself. But she wasn't going to just let it go.

"What shouldn't?" she asked, putting her hands on her hips. If she was going to risk her life for an errand of Silverwolf's, she at least wanted to know why.

Silverwolf turned, narrowed her eyes at her, and nodded.

"To find the high priest," she said.

Serinde cocked her head. That was not the answer she was expecting. To get some coins, sure. To kill a bounty she had become aware of, maybe. But to find the high priest? That didn't seem like the cold-blooded assassin she had known Silverwolf to be.

Unless...

"Did you say that the high priest was your," began to say.

"Yes, I did," Silverwolf answered quickly. "And he should be somewhere between here and the temple if I remember enough about Theocracy's siege strategies and the place priests and prophets fit into it."

"Why do you need to find him?" Serinde asked, a confusion of emotions assaulting her at once. She remembered their attempt to rescue Holve and what Silverwolf had said to the man who had ordered his execution. She had called him her father. She had also shot an arrow at him in what looked like a great effort to kill him.

Had she had missed? Or had Silverwolf pulled her shot on purpose?

And why did she want to see the High Priest now?

"Holve said..."

"I seriously doubt Holve said anything about this," Serinde cut in. "We're supposed to be getting back the amulet from Yada. Along with the rest of our things. How is this more important than what Holve sent us to do?"

"Holve sent me," Silverwolf said, turning and swelling up her chest. "I seem to remember you offering to come along."

Serinde could see that she was no longer dealing with someone thinking rationally. Silverwolf was a skilled killer. That wasn't someone she wanted to get into a fight with if she could avoid it. But she also wanted the truth. Serinde sighed.

"I'll go with you," she said. "But I want you to at least admit that being in Prommus right now has nothing to do with the task Holve sent us here for."

A group of shouting men came running up the street from what Serinde guessed was the city walls. It was hard to determine if the shouts were panicked or jubilant. Whichever they were, they were certainly loud.

Silverwolf had her sword out and ready as the voices came closer. Serinde didn't see any reason why she should question Silverwolf more at this point. But there were still things she wanted to know.

The men were now so close that they could hear some of their conversations.

"...the bleeding things can fight on our side anytime they want!" This was undoubtedly the loudest and most boisterous voice of the group. Some mild cheers followed this statement. Serinde felt sick. Were they cheering on the demons? Didn't they see how much death they brought with them? And how they didn't care who they killed?

"But did you see the one that destroyed the western tower? I thought that was going to make it through the battle until the brute tackled it."

This voice seemed a little more restrained. Wiser. The boisterous one responded.

"Whatever drives Isol back into the hole they came from is alright with me. They probably had those things angered with all of their sorcery and magic."

"So what now?"

"The captain says we'll be leaving to chase the Isolians out into the plains and run them down. Every man is to bring a week's supply of food on their backs before they can set up the caravans for us. Let's get going!"

The voices passed the bakery quickly, and Serinde let out a sigh of relief. If they were going to sneak around the city and find the high priest, the very last thing they wanted was to draw attention to themselves by getting into fights at every corner.

"This road leads up to the temple," Silverwolf said, not looking at Serinde, but out the curtains. "We follow this and see what they're up to. More than likely, the high priest won't travel with them. But he may offer up a blessing of the troops before they go. He may even send some of his guards to assist."

"The female guards?" Serinde asked.

Silverwolf didn't respond. Instead, she threw herself out of the curtains, barely making them rustle as she leaped through them. Serinde let out a quick huff of frustration before jumping out after her.

"No, wait!" Silverwolf began to say.

It was too late.

Serinde had already gone through the curtains and saw what the assassin must have known as soon as she entered the street.

"It's an elf, boys!" the boisterous voiced man shouted. "Just like they said at the wall! Get them!"

Silverwolf turned to give Serinde a look that made the elf's skin crawl and the breeze that blew through the street as cold as ice.

"You're more trouble than you're worth."

14: Uneasy Retreat

"Are you sure!?" the captain was shouting over the commotion of soldiers running in all directions. "A full retreat?"

"Her Holiness didn't misspeak!" General Cern shouted back. "Order your troops to the eastern rendezvous point and regroup there! If the demons assail you, continue until you reach the shores."

"Yes sir!" came the general reply as captains scattered to obey the orders.

Oberon turned to Cas and Rallet. The look she gave them told Cas that this was not a time to ask questions or second guess any order he was given. The demons had assaulted them far from the castle of Prommus.

Cas could still see the mountain range they had spent the last day running from. It loomed out ahead of them. In front of the castle, massive explosions still issued forth every so often, though not as many as during their frenzied retreat.

He had thought the army would fall back, regroup, and then continue with their assault of Prommus. They had been so close. The city walls could have only withstood a few more direct shots from the cannons of their Speakers.

Why had Yada commanded them to pull back now?

There wasn't any time to consider the alternatives, Cas knew. It was time to obey Oberon's orders or be left behind. He and Rallet tailed behind her as she strode swiftly through the ranks of soldiers who were scrambling to hear their captains.

They were not so bothered. Oberon had gathered her troops just as soon as she turned away from the general.

"Alright, scabs," she began in her usual encouraging tone. "We're being ordered east towards the shore of Ladis. Just keep your eyes in front and behind. I don't want any of those cursed demons on our tail as we make our way back to land."

She huffed once, not even taking the time to see who had shown up to her quick briefing. Cas turned to Rallet and shrugged.

"I guess there's not much else is there?" he asked, looking down at his remaining tent mate.

"I heard another soldier saying that Yada herself stayed behind to keep the demons at bay," the rounder man said. "Can you believe it? Her Holiness against those terrible beasts?"

Cas had a hard time believing it. Rallet often shared such wild stories. And only a few of them were true. Then again, there were some pretty large explosions behind them. Maybe some Speakers did stay behind with the cannons to ensure the army escape?

"Stop standing around and get moving!" Oberon ordered.

Cas realized he and Rallet had been looking back in the direction they had come while the rest of the army had begun to move east. A trumpet sounded, and the retreat was in full force. He and Rallet got in line. Their packs were long gone. The last things they had were on their bodies. Cas had a spear and a shield to his name. Rallet had only a sword, and it wasn't even his. Cas had let him use it since he had lost his own in the battle.

"Do you think we'll win?" Rallet asked as they fell into line within their company. The number of soldiers who marched alongside them had significantly diminished. The demons were relentless and had taken many of their number when they attacked without warning.

Isol had yet to see such a loss since coming onto the shores of Ladis from their island of exile.

Cas let out a deep breath.

"I don't know, Rallet. The captains keep talking about the southern forces marching up to help us. But I don't know if they sent for them in time. It's a long journey. And who knows if this is the only place the demons have attacked? What if they are down south too?"

"Aw don't say that, Cas," Rallet said, adjusting his slightly too small breastplate. "We can't lose after all we've done. This was supposed to be our great conquest. Right? Revenge for all the Theocracy has done to us?"

Cas shook his head.

All around them, the sky was darkening. Night would fall soon, but Cas doubted that would stop them from their retreat. They would march through the night and most of the next day. To regroup an army would take time. And every moment they spent falling back was time for Ladis to defend themselves against another attack. Could they discover a way to repel their invaders? They had been triumphant up to this moment. Now Cas felt like he had tripped and was falling unexpectedly.

Other soldiers must have felt the same way. The atmosphere around was gloomy. All of the faces he saw were somber. Captains, soldiers, speakers and all seemed like they had been punched in the gut. That's how Cas felt, at least.

He looked over his shoulder and saw a final, faint blue burst of light. Then the last sun dipped below the horizon, and the sky became darker still.

"I don't, Rallet," he said wearily. "I don't know."

15: Miracle

Miss Rivius had never before laid her eyes on such a pitiful creature as the one she was helping to carry over the walls of Meris. And she had worked with children who had been raised in the gutters and stables of Juttis.

This furry, filth covered animal seemed to be well mannered, but whatever she thought of his temperament or demeanor he smelled awful. She knew it shouldn't matter to her, and that she should treat the poor thing well. But it was hard to concentrate when the smell of years of neglect and imprisonment had undoubtedly seemed to embed itself into its skin.

Ferrin had, thankfully, cut into her line of thought with an excellent offer.

"I can take him from her, ma'am. He isn't all that heavy, and we won't be climbing any more stairs."

Rivius breathed out thankfully and took a step aside.

"Thank you, Master Ferrin," she said, hoping that the relief in her voice and face would only be perceived as gratefulness at the lightened load and not the change in proximity to the smell.

She looked around at the city behind her as Maccus and Tratta worked to get the rope back into position. It was their only escape. When she, Olma, Ferrin, and Galp, as the creature was called, climbed out of the rock tunnel, they were surprised to see the pair from Meris standing to greet them.

"All the soldiers went scurrying away after some explosion, ya know? I wonder if that's good news or bad," Tratta fretted.

Rivius hadn't taken any time to be thankful for their luck. She only pressed them forward and prayed that it would hold. And, up to this very moment, things seemed to have gone better than they could have hoped.

They made their way back to the stairs that led up to the wall without many difficulties. Tratta had aimed at one lone guard and dispatched him before she even knew there was danger. Other than that, their path back to the wall had been uneventful.

Now they needed to get down.

"I think I can carry you, Galp," Ferrin said as he took the rope in one hand and offered his other to the Skrilx.

"What about the dwarf?" Maccus asked. Rivius turned to see Olma helping Gorplin up the final step. He was grimacing, but walking on his own two legs.

"Bah. The dwarf will be fine," Gorplin muttered. Rivius had a distinct impression that Gorplin was much more hurt than his pride would allow him to say. "Just get yourselves over that wall and help the Skrilx."

Skrilx.

Rivius had heard of such creatures, but never in her wildest dreams thought she would meet one, let alone carry one.

"I would greatly appreciate you trying very hard not to drop me, sir," Galp said as Ferrin picked him up. "To die in a fall over this defensible position would be rather tragic considering I'm finally free of that dank dungeon."

"You talk a lot, ya know?" Tratta said as she checked the rope and looked back down over towards the castle grounds.

"I'm glad you've finally met your match, Tratta," Maccus fired back at her with a grin.

"Bloody chatterboxes," Gorplin muttered.

Rivius saw Galp grimace as Ferrin put him over his shoulder. The face was one of pain, she was sure of it. How many sores lingered on the poor beast's body? How weak could he be after such a long time underground?

"Don't pity me yet, dear lady," Galp said.

Miss Rivius shook herself, realizing that she had been staring.

"Let's save any feelings whether ill or not for after we've managed to escape Meris, shall we?"

***

Rivius dusted off her hands once they had climbed down the rope and made their way to the ground. She was relieved that it hadn't taken as much effort coming down as it had going up. Though she didn't think of herself as a particularly strong woman, she certainly hoped she could keep up with the group at large.

Maccus was the last one down from the wall. He and Tratta exchanged glances before nodding at each other and starting to walk along the edge of the defenses.

"Where did Gregory want us to meet?"

"The east side of Meris," Maccus replied.

"That'll be the trick," Tratta offered up. "If we can make it all the way around the city without being noticed. Maybe we could head out a little further onto the plains before making our way back, ya think?"

"No," Rivius said firmly.

Tratta and Maccus both gave her a puzzled look.

"Uh..." Maccus began.

Rivius didn't give him a chance to question her.

"If we cut out for the plains they'll likely spot us and maybe even send out troops to see who in their right mind would be out at night. Plus, hopefully, with all of their attention focused inward, we may be able to sneak close to the wall without being seen."

The two were silent for a time, only looking at each other once before back at her.

"Sounds good to me, mam," Ferrin said.

Miss Rivius inclined her head to him, but knew he would agree with her. He was still in her pay, after all.

"Perhaps, if I may," Galp said from atop Ferrin's shoulders. "Since I am a fugitive and will be recognized as the only Skrilx on the continent, perhaps it would be best if I were a bit less conspicuous?"

Tratta didn't say anything as she moved, but quickly took her bag off her shoulders and threw a thin blanket over Ferrin's shoulders, effectively hiding Galp from all onlookers.

"Thank you, miss," Galp said from underneath the blanket. "Perhaps a bit crude and not quite what I had in mind, but it'll do."

"Bah," Gorplin grunted. "If we're done chatting let's start walking. We don't want them to beat us there."

"No, we do not," Miss Rivius agreed. "Lead the way you two. You know the walls best."

Tratta and Maccus wasted no time setting out. Miss Rivius followed swiftly behind, with Olma and Gorplin behind her and Ferrin taking up the rear. The terrain was rocky and hard to maneuver. It felt exactly like the last few weeks of their journey, except this time it was next to a giant wall that surrounded a city in chaos.

The shouts and cries of the people inside became louder as they made their way over rocks and dirt. Miss Rivius allowed herself one shudder to repel the cold but otherwise tried to ignore it.

Maccus and Tratta were swift, and she needed to keep up. Both Olma and Gorplin stayed right behind her as well. She had feared that one of them might fall behind, but they were proving to be much more resilient than she had once thought. Dwarves were another race she wasn't as familiar with. Then again, when had Ladis ever had a large population of elves?

Men and their religion had always ruled the continent. This she knew quite well. She was an oddity among the country, and she knew it. She fought for every sale, every contract, and every scrap of clothing that she sold. In Juttis, she was a powerful woman who was taking over the city's business and trade one jacket at a time.

But now she was out in the country. Traveling to find more goods, according to the word she had given the man who was to run her shop in her absence. How long such a story would hold with the prince, she didn't know. Who was she when she wasn't running the largest fabrication store in the country? Was she still a powerful woman? Or was she hiding behind her work?

Something about this Holve Bravestead had made her curious. Could she be someone even more influential? Well, she was taking a lot of risks and going through several dangers to find out.

"Just around this buttress, I'm thinkin' we're gonna start seein' trouble," Maccus said as he stooped in front of one of the large stone outcroppings that helped to fortify the wall.

Rivius could hear the shouting grow louder as they all came to a stop behind Maccus. She looked up to see if any guards were moving along the wall. She couldn't see them, but perhaps she could hear them running back and forth.

No heavy footfalls seemed to make their way down to her ears, and she counted that a blessing. What made her nervous, though, was the intensity of the shouting and the smell of smoke in the air.

If the city were on fire, there would be much graver concerns to face.

"We're getting close to the place Gregory said to meet, ya know," Tratta said, looking out to the plains. "I just can't tell if there's something out there or not."

Miss Rivius scanned the horizon. There didn't seem to be anything out there that she could see. Perhaps a twinkle or two, but those must be stars coming into focus in the night sky. Surely no one would like a torch in such dire times.

She was squinting her eyes to see what might have been a spot that glowed differently than the others when her feet shook underneath her, and loud crash assaulted her ears.

"What's that!?" Tratta yelled, all sense of stealth obviously gone from her mind.

"Quiet!" Maccus said through his teeth. "Don't want the whole of the city knowin' we're out here!"

As it turned out, it didn't matter. A chunk of the wall just past where they had been walking blew outward in a fantastic crash and explosion of blue light. Stones and dust flew in all directions as the screams from within the city rose up into a crescendo and then went quiet.

"This way!" yelled a voice Rivius thought she recognized.

And then, out from the debris and dust clouds, Ealrin came running along as quickly as he could with another man Rivius didn't recognize leaning heavily on him. Gregory was walking backward, shooting arrows at a rapid pace as he navigated the fallen wall.

"Holve!?" Maccus shouted.

The figures didn't turn or slow their speed. Ealrin did look their way and wave with the other hand that they were to follow them. Rivius took three steps in that direction before her attention was diverted back to the breach.

The last figure to come out from the hole in the wall was glowing blue, wrapped in a circle of light and flame, Blume was shooting blast after magical blast back into the city.

Miss Rivius was reminded of the terrible scene that had unfolded within the walls of her own home when the Prince of Juttis had unleashed such unholy fury as she saw before her now. She did her very best not to cower or take cover as each blast issued from the girl's hands and went soaring back into the city. Explosions resonated from within the city walls as Rivius saw Blume screaming at the targets of her wrath.

She almost felt bad for them.

"Time to go!" Ferrin was shouting at her. "We need to go, Miss Rivius! Now!"

Rivius suddenly realized she had been rooted to the spot, instead of making good on their moment to escape the city. Tratta and Maccus had already followed the group running from the breach in the wall. Blume was beginning to turn as well, though Ealrin and the man he was supporting were waiting for her. Gregory still had his bow and arrows out, but it seemed laughable that he could do any more damage than she had already done.

So much for a quiet and stealthy getaway.

If the entire city didn't follow them out, it'd be a miracle.

16: Campfire

Ealrin was short on breath. The run through the city was more than he was ready for. A part of him had thought they would be able to get through the city by sneaking from house to house and using the chaos of the place to mask their leaving.

Once they hit the marketplace, however, he realized that it was going to be impossible to sneak through Meris. The collective city had lost its mind and was killing anything that moved: be it friend, foe, neighbor or family. The only ones safe from such violence seemed to be the very prophets and temple guards who Ealrin had hated since being arrested by them.

They moved through the city like wolves as they rounded up people and put them to the sword at random. Shouts and screams filled the air as people lost their loved ones right in front of their eyes. From what he could make out from the jumbled words of the people running wild in the streets, the temple guards were rounding up any-one they suspected of demon worship.

Meris had, apparently, been a recent target of a demon attack and the people had gone crazy in trying to repel such a terrible fate.

The temple guards were the ones who had sought to keep control of the city. In order to do so, they killed anyone who was brought to them with an accusation of demon worship or magic or witchcraft.

Pandemonium reigned.

Their group took all of this in within moments as they entered the marketplace. Ealrin was supporting Holve while Gregory walked ahead of them and Jurrin and Blume stood behind. Temple guards were running back and forth with swords and maces and bringing them down on any who were thrown at their feet. Stores were up in flames. Bodies lay in the street in all places.

The temple of Ladis guards were bringers of death and ruin, and it was too much for Ealrin.

It proved too much for Blume also.

As soon as she saw the extent of the destruction she had screamed and sent blast after blast of magical energy in every way she could muster. Far beyond trying to convince her to stop, Ealrin and the rest had merely walked behind her as she sent groups of guards screaming from the destruction they had caused.

And one point, they had made their way to the wall, and Blume sent a blast at what looked like the last group of assembled guards. They were trying to defend themselves, but again Blume and her magic, they didn't stand a chance.

The blast that shattered the wall took the guards with it. It also provided them with a way of escape. As the group fled through the opening, Blume continued to reign down destruction on the city of Meris.

Thanking the suns as they ran, Ealrin saw that Blume was leaving the city with them. Whether she wanted to be rid of the city as much as they did or whether she was just backing up without thinking, he didn't know.

But now they were on the plains outside of Meris, and Blume's magic was beginning to wane. Ealrin knew she would need to eat soon. There was only so much magic she could perform without requiring to rest and recover. They had meager supplies. There wasn't much they could offer her.

He hoped the other group had managed to find food along the way somewhere or they would have a very weak Speaker on their hands and the wrath of a city attacked once again by supernatural forces.

That was not a scenario Ealrin wanted to endure.

At last, the magical glow around Blume faded, and the area around them began to darken. It had been a blessing to have her lighting their path. On the other side of the coin, they had certainly been visible for anyone who cared to follow them.

"Gregory!" Ealrin called. "Help Holve!"

He let go of him sooner than he knew the older man was ready for. Holve had been coughing and gasping for the last few stretches since leaving the city. The last few weeks had not done him any favors.

But they couldn't leave Blume.

Ealrin ran and scooped her up in his arms just as she was about to fall over into the dust. She was light. Too light. That alone scared Ealrin enough to look around the scenery. They needed to find a place to hide and rest.

They needed somewhere where they could camp.

The city of Meris was still too close for them to stop safely, Ealrin knew this. But in their current state, they certainly couldn't keep going all night and into the next day.

"Tratta!" he called. "Is there a place we can stop for the night? Somewhere safe?"

In the darkness, Ealrin was fairly certain she had turned her head and nodded..

"There's an abandoned farm up ahead with a village that's been deserted for a month. We may deal with some other bandits who have taken up shelter there though, ya know?"

"We'll risk it," Ealrin called back, feeling the stitch in his side and knowing that he couldn't carry Blume all night, even as much as he wanted to.

Their group was tired, and they needed to rest.

Or risk burning themselves out before they even properly escaped.

***

The farm wasn't as far as Ealrin would have hoped from the city. If any guards were sent out after them, they would certainly look here first. But he couldn't go another step and had the feeling that he wasn't the only one in the group who felt that way.

Even Gorplin was heaving with great breaths when they came to the first structure of the abandoned village. It was a barn, just like Tratta had said. Gregory, the only one in their group who seemed not to be sucking wind, insisted that he go inside and check for other occupants before they entered.

Ealrin wanted to care and offer to go with him, but he knew he couldn't. At this point, he would be more of a hindrance than a help. He lay Blume down on the softest looking patch of dirt he could before sitting next to her, trying to breathe regularly again. They stood at the stone wall that must have at one time been a farmer's way of keeping wild animals away from his livestock.

Olma and Jurrin both fell at the base of the wall and tried to catch their breath. Holve collapsed in a heap but had the dignity to at least get to a sitting position. Gorplin refused to sit, which made Ealrin smile despite himself.

At least he was still the same belligerent dwarf.

Gregory came back only after a few moments.

"All clear," he said. "But we'll need to check the surrounding village before we rest easy."

"I doubt we'll rest easy regardless," Holve said, still breathing hard. "We're too close to Meris."

"Agreed," Miss Rivius said. "But we have few options. Let's go."

Once everyone had stopped moving, it seemed like it was more challenging to get up again and walk the last few paces than it was to run the length from Meris to here. Ealrin helped Holve to his feet and then picked up Blume again.

It was torture to hold her while standing upright, but he knew that she couldn't walk on her own. She had been utterly exhausted. He just hoped it wasn't as bad as the last time she had overexerted herself in such a way. She had been in a state of unconsciousness for months.

That was not something they could afford at this point.

They passed through the barn doors one at a time, only having it cracked open slightly. Once they were all in, Gregory closed the door behind them.

"Think we can risk a fire?" Maccus asked as he let his pack hit the ground. "I think there's some fire cloths in here we could use. That and maybe some oil."

"Make it small," Gregory said.

"And make sure the smoke is gone by dawn," Holve said. "We don't want to alert anyone to our presence."

Ealrin couldn't agree more, but he always wanted that fire to burn. It would help Blume recover. He laid her down, took off his jacket to cover her with, and then assisted Maccus with the fire.

The land of northern Ladis didn't have much in the way of wood. What little they did have was either too small to be built with or too precious to be wasted in fuel. So many of the residents of the north used cloth and the dry grasses woven into squares to light flames. He had seen this more in Juttis, but Meris was still far enough north that trees didn't grow in abundance.

Tratta cleared away some of the debris of the barn and made a circle of rocks. Those would be good to warm themselves later after they had been heated properly. Maccus arranged some of the fire-cloths while Ealrin found the old flint and some dry grass for fuel.

The command to make the fire small was unnecessary. They didn't have enough to make any more than this one meager fire. To-morrow night, if they stayed here, they would be cold for sure.

Once their fire was going, Ealrin could see the inside of the barn more clearly. The rocks were stacked up higher than he could stand. That made sense. Stone was the most readily available resource here. It looked like the rocks that had been dug out for the barn were from

the ground they were standing in. A small ramp had led them to the
ground they laid on now.

The roof was made of five wooden beams. They must have cost
the owner of the barn a fortune to buy. Across them lay the remnants
of the dry and brittlebushes from the surrounding area. Enough
cracks had been made in the roof for the smoke to filter through with
ease.

No one said much. There was the usual passing around of the
meager supplies, and people ate hungrily. But words weren't readily
exchanged. Not until after they had eaten and passed around their
water skins.

Thankfully, Tratta and Maccus had made sure to fill what they
could with water from the city and had taken time to stuff their
pockets with stolen food from the guard towers. It wasn't much, but
it was more than they had before they entered Meris.

Once everyone had eaten as much as they knew they could, saving things for the journey past this point, they sat around the fire and
warmed themselves by its gentle flames.

Ealrin, who had eaten just a few bites, took to making sure Blume
was comfortable. He felt her forehead and checked to see if the coat
he had laid on top of her was keeping her warm. She still felt cold to
the touch, so he used a cool rock to move one of the warmer ones
from the ring of fire over to her. Carefully wrapping it in another
cloth so as not to burn her, he laid it next to her stomach.

"That girl's somethin' else," Maccus said, breaking the silence that
filled the barn for the last hour or so.

"An extraordinary specimen," Galp said from his spot next to the
fire.

Ealrin nodded before looking over at the man. He and Tratta
were sitting with their backs against the wall of the barn. Gregory
was standing next to them looking out a crack he had left in the door.

"She's a skilled Speaker," Ealrin said, looking back at Blume admiringly. "But she can get a little ahead of herself sometimes."

Jurrin let out a chuckle.

"I think you're a little too kind, Mister Ealrin," he said with a grin. "She can do some mighty big magic when she has the mind to it. I just hope she's alright."

Ealrin looked at Jurrin with a knowing expression. They had both seen Blume exhausted to the point of unconsciousness. It was never an easy sight to take in.

"I'm just glad I'm not on the other side of one of her spells, ya know?" Tratta said, looking at Blume with awe. "She blasted half of the city away with her Speaking."

"Which brings us to our next steps," Miss Rivius said, sitting by the fire with Ferrin and Galp. The Skrilx had been awfully quiet as well but now seemed to perk up at the thought of sharing a conversation.

The woman turned to Holve and looked him in the eye.

"Holve Bravestead?" She asked, folding her arms and furrowing her brow.

"I am the one," Holve answered, inclining his head to her. "I take it you are Miss Rivius, whom I've been corresponding with in Juttis?"

"She is indeed," Ferrin replied, looking on her with pride. "Best fabric and cloth maker in Ladis. Best clothes maker too.

"Thank you, Ferrin," Miss Rivius said without looking over at him. "Well, I must say things have been quite a mess since your little crew showed up at my shops. Juttis has been turned on its head, and it seems Meris has gone much the same way. Demons and magic and Isol on our doorstep. I'd love an explanation as to what is goin' on."

Ealrin thought that he wouldn't mind being told what was going on either. Holve had been very secretive before they had managed to escape from Meris. Ealrin got the feeling that Holve was going to share more with him later. But that chance hadn't come. Yet.

Perhaps this was the moment when he would understand why they had stayed in Ladis so long when they could have left by now.

Then again, he felt, too, the tugging sense of trying to keep the peace between two groups of people who don't see eye to eye. He knew that feeling well. The question was, what was the sense in seeking it again after so many attempts at peace had gone wrong?

Holve let out a deep sigh.

"We were not supposed to have come here," he said wistfully. "But it appears fate had other plans. My group and I were taken hostage at an island the Theocracy claims and, unfortunately, was in the middle of inspecting when we arrived."

Ealrin still thought poorly of the priest, Jerius, and his prideful intolerance of them. He could still hear the man's whip cracking over his head.

"Since then I've been able to reconnect with some of my informants from the Rebellion Wars of Isol. I had hoped to stem Yada's fury, but it seems she's been building up an army for decades in preparation for this assault on Ladis. And she's winning, so far as I can tell."

"But why stay in Ladis?" Rivius countered. "You're a wanted man. You've been captured twice and nearly executed, from what your friends tell me. Why not just leave and allow it all to play out? As you said, fate may have other plans."

Holve signed at this. Blume stirred a bit in her sleep, and Ealrin put a hand on her shoulder. He noticed Olma out of the corner of his eye. She looked both concerned and nervous. She had her legs tucked in tight against her and was rocking back and forth slightly. Ealrin couldn't figure out what it was about Olma, but something had changed in her.

"Whatever fate has planned will happen," Holve admitted. "But I refuse to allow it to happen without my efforts to do what is right."

"And who gets to decide what is right?" Rivius said. "I'm sure Yada and those from Isol think they are right in invading Ladis. From what I understand, the Theocracy has done some terrible things to them and their people."

"Indeed," Holve answered. "Which is why..."

"But who is to say that the Theocracy is right, either?" Rivius said, throwing up a hand to stop Holve. "I just watched my Prince, whom I have always had the utmost respect for, turn into some sort of demon and attempt to kill the people he was sworn to protect."

Ealrin looked around at the room. Every single person had their eyes glued on Rivius. He was looking back and forth from Holve to her, trying to judge what was transpiring that was unsaid.

"Then there is you," she said. "This group of yours that you've banded together has certainly thrown a wrench into my life and the lives of several other people who have been living peacefully despite all that's gone on. This little girl has been uprooted from her family and livelihood."

Rivius motioned towards Olma, who looked like she was wishing to be much smaller than she was at the moment.

"Are you right, and the Theocracy wrong? Or is Yada right?" Rivius asked. "You all seem to believe wholeheartedly in doing what is right. Kill the Speaker. Glorify the rimstone. Kill those who would take the land. Take revenge over wrongs done to generations before you. If you're all so equally determined to be right, how could you possibly be able to convince the other side unless you just wipe them off the face of Gilia?"

Ealrin was aware that his mouth was slightly open. He closed it and shook himself. Everything he had believed about Miss Rivius he now took into consideration. She was not only a shrewd businesswoman. She was a philosopher at heart. And one who would challenge the whole world.

"The Theocracy worship the gods of old who drove out the Speakers of Isol. The Speakers believe they were unjustly eradicated after building a nation. Where do you stand, Holve Bravestead?"

Slowly, every eye turned to Holve, who was giving Rivius both an appraising look and looking quite taken aback himself.

"You are much more than you allow yourself to appear, Miss Rivius of Juttis."

"Flattery has gotten few very far with me," she replied. "Where do you stand?"

Holve nodded and adjusted himself.

"I believe in justice, Miss Rivius," he said plainly.

She looked like she was about to interrupt him again, but he held up his own hand.

"I listened to your questions. I beg you listen to my answers."

Miss Rivius scowled, but relented, nodding her head and settling back into a seated position, arms crossed and brow furrowed.

"I do not believe in taking life needlessly," Holve continued. "And I have spent a good deal of my life weighing whether or not such an act was needless or not. I believe that there cannot be peace achieved by war, but that war is needed when the other side has decided that they would spill the blood of any who get in their way. To defend oneself by killing another is honorable. To kill without cause is the greatest dishonor. When I was here in Ladis, helping Isol, I did not see that clearly. I do now. I must do what I can to help stop this tide of violence and bloodshed. And sometimes, I fear, the only way to do that is through bloodshed."

Miss Rivius looked like she wanted to respond, but instead, she pursed her lips tighter.

"A Speaker does nothing wrong when they communicate to the elements through rimstone. Decolos was a fool and a betrayer. He used the Speakers to build his empire and then cast them out when he feared they would overpower him. I'm afraid his actions have set us on this course. But we have more pressing matters to see to than he ever thought possible."

Rivius raised an eyebrow. Ealrin, however, nodded.

"The demons," he said, knowing what Holve was referring to. He had seen it before, on Ruyn. He had seen it here in Ladis too. "They are attracted to bloodshed and the loss of life. The more wars there are on Gilia, the more demons we have to fight back."

Miss Rivius took a deep breath.

"You mean that the prince of Juttis has aligned himself with some otherworldly creature?" she asked.

"If what you say is true," Holve replied. "Either that is the case or he has tapped into some other form of dark magic that he is twisting to cause harm to those around him. We cannot allow that to happen either."

Ealrin tried to take in the gravity of this conversation. They had spent so much of their time and effort trying to get to Juttis. Now that they had been there and back, this last convincing of Holve's contact seemed, almost unnecessary. But she was being won over. By the look in her eyes, she believed that Holve was genuine and that she felt the same way he did.

But there was something that was still not quite registering for him. A missing piece. Or, rather, a missing person.

"But if you're here with us, and the prince of Juttis suspects you of allying with us, how can you be a spy?"

The answer to that question would undoubtedly be an important one. Ealrin was curious, to say the least. Answers to that would have to wait, however.

Blume was awake.

And a blue flame had suddenly replaced their meager campfire.

17: Innocence

Olma leaped to her feet just as the fire turned blue. Looking over at Blume, she saw that her eyes were open and glowing the same deep, penetrating color as the flames.

She scrambled to her feet and ran to the other side of the barn. Looking back, she saw that Blume was slowly getting to her feet. Her movements were rigid, stiff, and didn't at all seem like the Blume Olma had spent time with.

The girl had scared her. She didn't know what to do with a Speaker. She had always been told they were evil. To be avoided. Shunned. Killed even. There had been a small part of her, a tiny part, that wanted to be friends with her.

But how could she be friends with someone who was so different? Whose very best part of her was something Olma had been told all her life was the reason her country was at war, why her friend's parents had gone off to fight, and why her family had been killed.

It all made sense now.

Seeing Blume in this way terrified Olma. She didn't know what was happening. And she was scared beyond speaking.

"Blume? Blume!" Ealrin was shouting over and again. "Blume what are you doing? Are you alright?"

Olma knew it was pointless. The face that stared back at them with glowing blue eyes didn't care. It didn't hear any of his pleas. It was passive and hard.

"Get a grip, ya know?" Tratta's voice came up over the general noise and confusion.

Gregory moved forward from the door and grabbed Ealrin by the arm and tried to pull him back.

"No gettin' any closer," Maccus said as he joined to help Gregory hold Ealrin back.

Then something changed in Blume. She turned her head slightly to the side and raised her hand. From it, a small, slow tendril of blue eased its way out. It split into two and parted in front of Ealrin, going to either side of him, and stopping right before Gregory and Maccus.

"Bow," came a voice so unlike Blume's that Olma had thought at first it was someone else doing the talking. But it had been Blume's mouth that had moved, she was sure of it. That same sickly blue light came from her mouth just as it did her eyes.

"She's losin' it!" Maccus said, his voice wavering a bit.

"What magic is this?" Gregory asked, inclining his head towards her.

He wouldn't get her answer.

The blue tendrils shot like lightning through both Maccus and Gregory. There was a breath, a moment where Olma could still see their hands holding onto Ealrin's shoulders. Then, with a blink, it passed. The pair of them fell limply to the floor.

Several things happened at once. Tratta wailed at the sight of Maccus on the ground. Miss Rivius let out a scream. Ferrin jumped in front of her, spreading his arms wide. Galp scampered away from the fire, and Gorplin picked up a piece of wood that lay next to him. Jurrin ran to Ealrin's side, yelling Blume's name. Olma tried to turn and to run. To flee. To save herself and escape this horrible place where magic had killed and she feared for her life. She barely heard Holve yelling at her to stop moving. She needed to get out, to escape.

A sickly black material began to swirl around Blume's body, adding to the flame that glowed around her. Olma turned around just in time to see it pouring from the ring she had used to cast her spells. It gathered in a long snake-like blob that circled Blume with ever increasing speed until it was nearly impossible to see where it began and where it ended.

Blume still looked uncaringly out in front of her. The two bodies of her victims lay on the floor at Ealrin's feet. She didn't even look down at them. She just stared ahead.

Olma couldn't believe it.

Blume had been scary. She had used magic to help them. Olma had thought it was frightening, but she had never dreamed that this girl would use her magic to kill their own. Blume rose her hand up to Ealrin's face. He just stood there, looking frozen to the spot. As if he couldn't believe what was happening either. Olma turned to face the wall again and began scrambling to get out. There was a hole for a window just out of her reach. If she could only jump up and grab it, she could climb out and get away.

"No, Miss Blume! Don't do it!" Jurrin was shouting. The little halfling was waving his arms up and down as if trying to distract her.

"Who is Blume?"

The voice spoke in a low, ominous tone. And though it came from the direction of Blume, her mouth did not move. It was like the sound was coming from another place.

"A wretch. A mortal. A powerless shade. A girl. A drifter. An orphan. A wretch."

Sounds bounced off the walls of the barn as Olma tried with ever increasing desperation to get out of the barn. She leaped up and grabbed a stone.

"My master requires her," the voice spoke in a tone that sent chills up Olma's spine.

She held on for just a breath, then the stone came loose, and she came crashing to the ground.

The stone landed beside her. As she looked up from the ground, she saw a figure leap from the window she had been trying to climb out of. It sprang into the barn, throwing something it held in its hands as it fell to the floor.

If the breath hadn't been knocked out of her body, she could have turned over to see what it was. But there wasn't any time for that.

Then the air around them exploded.

Olma felt her body lift off of the floor. Then there was the pain. Agony and pain unlike she had ever experienced before in her life. Her chest felt like it was going to cave in. Her teeth ground hard against themselves, and she clutched her body.

"You," the same ominous voice that had spoken before. "You will bring me what I want."

And then Olma felt nothing.

18: Questions

Coughing and spluttering, Ealrin picked himself up off the ground. He couldn't remember it, but he must have hit the back wall of the barn. He ached terribly as he tried to orient himself. He had been lying flat on his stomach. With great effort, he got himself to his knees.

People were talking. Voices he knew. But the ringing in his ears had not yet subsided. He shook his head. It was a bad idea. He felt he might split open from the movement.

"You alright? You were closest." came an unfamiliar voice.

Ealrin opened his eyes a fraction, just enough to see some standing, definitely standing in front of him. And yet he was looking him in the eyes.

A halfling?

"Jurrin?" Ealrin croaked.

"Over here, sir," came a voice from the other side of the room.

"It's been awhile since I've seen one of my own," the voice said again. "But we've got bigger problems here."

Ealrin blinked several times until the figure came into focus. It was indeed a halfling who stood before him. He had dark hair and a scarred and weathered face. This halfling had seen and experienced much, Ealrin could tell. From his clothes to the way he stood in the barn, surrounded by destruction and death but seemingly unbothered.

"Names Szabo," he said, turning to look at the crumpled heap where Blume had stood just a moment ago. "And you've got a demon problem."

Ealrin slowly got to his feet, steadying himself against the wall as he did so. Ambling over to the heap, he got back down on one knee to feel Blume's pulse.

He let out a great sigh of relief as he found that it was still beating strongly there. Closing his eyes, Ealrin felt the weight of their journey crushing down on him. How far had they come? What had he done to protect this girl?

And what dangers had he put her in by letting her follow them from fire to oven?

"Who are you?" Ealrin asked.

"Szabo," the halfling said again. "I'm seen my fair share of magic and demons. But this is something new."

"A girl half obliterating a barn is new?" Holve asked, looking at the halfling with a raised eyebrow. "You haven't seen as much as you might think."

"Bah," Gorplin spluttered from the corner. "Show off."

"Not her," Szabo said, looking down at Blume. "Though I must say, she's got a fire in her to pull off that kind of magic. Looks like her rimstone broke, though."

Looking down at her hand, Ealrin saw that her ring had in fact finally broken off of her finger. He picked up her hand. She looked a little burned along the finger, but it wasn't anything serious if they could treat it.

"No," Szabo said again. "I meant her."

He pointed at another heap along the wall of the barn. It wasn't Blume he was talking about. It was Olma.

Ealrin gasped and shuffled over to her. She looked... different.

"Her hair," he said, looking down at her with a puzzled expression. Olma had very blonde hair, just like the rest of the citizens of the Theocracy. But the flowing hair from her head was not a sun-soaked color anymore. It was red. Fire red. Ealrin then noticed the rest of her had changed as well.

"Look at her skin!"

"You'll notice those markings are moving, ever so slowly, but all the same, the surest sign of possession," Szabo said, almost like he was appraising a horse or other farm animal.

Ealrin felt for her heartbeat as well. It was strong but erratic and quick. He didn't know what that meant. He wished there was a healer on the continent. But knowing how Ladis had killed or exiled every Speaker they met, they had very few options.

"You say she's been possessed by a demon?" Holve said. "How can you know for sure?"

Szabo turned and looked up at Holve with a smirk.

"I"ve seen my case or two of those killed by demons. Sometimes they have very similar markings on them once they've been touched by one. But she's still kicking. Or at least she is for now."

"For now?" Ealrin said, turning to Szabo.

Szabo shrugged his shoulders.

"As I said, this is new territory for me. I've never seen anyone survive to this point."

It was at that moment that both Blume and Olma began to stir. Ealrin looked from one to the other. It was hard to tell.

Rivius, however, began moving to Olma. She skirted around Galp, who seemed fine, but unwilling to move at the moment. Ealrin nodded at her and got back over to Blume. Her eyes were no longer blue and glowing. In fact, they seemed unfocused and blurry. Ealrin tried to help her up to a sitting position gingerly.

"Blume?" he asked her in what he hoped was a calm voice. "Are you ok?"

She blinked, and her eyes began to come into focus. But she wasn't looking at Ealrin. She was looking past him. He turned his head and saw the two bodies of Gregory and Maccus. Tratta was weeping over Maccus' form, sobbing and saying his name over and over again.

Slowly, he brought his attention back to Blume.

Tears were welling in her eyes.

"I... I did that, didn't I?" she said, choking up.

There was no point in denying it. Ealrin sighed.

"You weren't... You weren't yourself, Blume," he said. "Something came over you. It's like you were..."

"Possessed," Olma replied.

Ealrin looked back at Olma. He knew it was her voice. It sounded like her. And then, it was different. Altered. He could see something in her eyes that made him shudder.

They glowed with a slight bluish tinge.

Blume looked at Olma and Ealrin could see something pass between the two girls. Something more than a look. A deep feeling. Whether it was understanding or hatred, he couldn't tell.

"How do you feel, Olma?" Holve asked. Ealrin could hear the reservation in his voice.

The girl looked down at her hands, now covered in markings Ealrin had never seen before. Markings that moved slightly, as she did. It was as if she had tattoos that were alive.

"Strong," she replied, jumping to her feet and making Rivius gasp in alarm.

The little girl flexed her arms and fingers as if trying them on for the first time. She scrutinized her hands and her hair, poking a bit and taking a lock into her fingers. Ealrin felt a sense of unease as she did it.

What was going on inside her mind? What was happening to her?

And was something she was going to survive?

Szabo spoke before anyone else could offer their opinion on the matter.

"Up in a cave nearby I have a contact who supplies me with... the necessities of my work," he said looking sideways. "He's a knowledgeable man. He may be able to discern what's going on with her. I trust him when it comes to anything dealing with these... demons.

Ealrin looked up at Holve. The old man stared down hard at Olma.

"Is it really you in there?" he asked her, sounding to Ealrin like he was talking to an enemy, rather than a little girl. "Or is there someone else we're dealing with?"

Olma spent a moment longer examining her own body before looking up at Holve with an innocent expression on her face. The atmosphere in the room grew tense.

"It's me," she answered.

Ealrin felt thoroughly unconvinced. But he also knew the right thing to do was to help her. No matter what it looked like or cost them. Hadn't and they helped Blume over and over again? What difference was it to help Olma now?

"Bah," Gorplin said. " I don't have a mind to trust anything tainted by a demon."

Miss Rivius is stood up and dusted herself off. She folded her arms and furrowed her brow down at the dwarf.

"So quick to abandon a friend?" she asked. Ealrin heard the disgust in her voice.

"Well... No... I'm not planning on leaving her soon," Gorplin muttered, losing himself in his beard.

A shade of shame covered his face, and he faltered.

"If I may," Galp said. Ealrin had nearly forgotten he was with them. "I recall before I was locked in that terrible dungeon, I heard tales of a man who was experienced in the lore of demons in this area. If our short friend here is telling the truth, we may benefit more than just to help our young Olma."

"What makes you think I need help?" Olma asked, looking over at him with a raised eyebrow.

That very question was all the reason Ealrin needed to seek out the man Szabo spoke of.

"And what makes us believe that you won't murder us in our sleep?" Holve asked.

Both Ealrin and Blume looked up that. Ealrin was startled. He wasn't sure he had ever heard Holve speak that way to anyone. Even his enemies.

"We have to help her," Ealrin said.

He felt like he was pleading with the man who had mentored him in what was right and wrong. The one who had led armies against the injustice of racism and genocide.

"You can't possibly mean to leave her to die?!" Ealrin shouted at Holve, standing to his feet and squaring up his chest. Surely Holve just wasn't thinking right. Well, he would change that.

Holve didn't return the glare Ealrin was giving him. He was looking down at Olma, covered in black markings that seemed so intimidating that Ealrin thought to take a step away from her. But he couldn't. He had to defend her.

"We cannot allow all of us to perish for the sake of a girl we hardly know," Holve said, his face hard and his eyes narrowed.

Ealrin couldn't believe his ears.

"We've done so a dozen times for Blume," he said. "What makes Olma any different?"

"She's been possessed by a demon!" Holve fired back. "Who knows what might happen?"

"Wasn't Blume carrying around that ring just as bad!" Ealrin shouted.

It seemed like Holve wanted to continue to yell at Ealrin. As far as he could remember, in the two years, they had known each other they had never had such a disagreement. Not this loud or this intense. Their argument was interrupted, however, by a sound by the wall.

There was a big sniffle from behind them. Ealrin turned to see Tratta looking out the barn door.

"Fellas," came her raspy, rugged voice. "I hate to have to cut this short, but we have a problem, ya know?"

Ealrin spun to see what Tratta was talking about. The haunted girl woman opened up the door to the barn just enough to let them see outside.

Along with the dawn, an army was coming over the horizon.

19: North

Pul was not impressed with the speed they were marching north towards Prommus. They had been attempting to get to the capital as quickly as possible. So far they had only been able to make it to Arranus. And even that had taken longer than it should have. The jungles were crawling with the lizards who had slept for generations. At every turn, they were fighting them off or being ambushed by the creatures who could blend in with their surroundings.

They had not lost many men to the beasts, but any losses at this point would be felt later down the road. This was supposed to be reinforcements for Her Holiness herself. Losing troops wouldn't do.

Captains and generals alike were anxious to keep moving north. But no matter how quickly they moved, an army would always need to restock and supply. They had cut off their supply lines from the south when they crossed the Rift. Rations were running low, and so were men's spirits. Pul had seen it time and time again in the Disputed Lands. When food was available, the soldiers fought with renewed vigor. When food was scarce, men didn't throw themselves at their enemies as readily.

And so they made to resupply and to set up enough food to last them until they reached Grellis. Then they would be where the Isolians had attacked. Pul wasn't sure on their information. Some seemed to believe that Grellis had fallen to Isol already and that Arranus was ripe to be attacked as well.

But since no Isol soldiers or Speakers had been seen anywhere near the city, Pul didn't know if that was true. He hoped it wasn't. They didn't have what they needed for a siege of a city. And if Isol had Grellis, where else might they have attacked? And would their attempt to come to Her Holiness' aid be futile?

Pul sniffed at his cup. The clay fired ware was not in the best shape. But that couldn't be helped. Every inn and pub inside Arranus had been taken over by the officers of the reserves. This was one where several of the captains had made a small claim. The "Vigilance Inn" seemed to be about anything but vigilance. Mud and leaves lined the edges where it had been eventually swept or kicked aside by patrons and those who worked at the inn alike. The table had crumbs all over it from the previous occupant. The cup Pul drank from had a small crack that he had overcome by placing his dirty napkin around it.

The building, like all the ones in Arranus, was made mostly of stone with some wood here and there. A long call back to the glory days of Ladis. The rafters were made of the long, heavy wood of the trees outside and they showed their age as well. Not a single step could be taken upstairs that didn't break or crack. It was not a nice inn.

The rooms upstairs were small and cramped. Pul shared one with three other men, despite there only being one bed. But since he out-ranked each of them in time served, they gave him the mattress.

It was odd.

The men slept just outside the city in tents. It felt strange not to be out there with the regular soldiers. He had to keep reminding himself that he had been promoted.

Sheerly by surviving longer than his battle brothers.

And by no other virtue.

He took a sip of the liquid the bartender had given him. He had never tasted it before and didn't really care to know what it was. His jungle village had been destroyed. His hopes of one day returning to his little quiet part of Ladis was destroyed. So until he was called on, he would drink this mixture and think about what the days he had left had in store for him.

It wasn't a pleasant experience.

"Captain Pul?" The call came from the door of the pub. Pul hadn't even recognized that it had opened. Looking up from his mug, he saw Tars. The young soldier had been given over to him and his company. There didn't seem to be anything that could quell his spirits or bring him down.

Pul both admired that and hated it at the same time. Not because he was jealous. But because he knew that in time, it would fade.

Just like it had with him.

"Yes, Tars?" he said, turning to face him.

"The Generals are meeting," Tars said. "They'd like the captains to be there as well."

***

Arranus had exactly one nice inn. That was the one the generals had taken over. Pul couldn't blame them. If he were such a high ranking official, he'd certainly want a few of the comforts that could be found in a city of this size.

Whereas the Vigilance Inn was falling apart, the Purity Bed and Breakfast at least looked like it was cleaned every so often. The high traffic of the soldiers and commanders could do little to keep the place immaculate, however.

Pul shuffled in with the other captains and officers in the army and found a spot towards the back of the room. He still felt like he didn't belong in this group. He asked Tars to come along with him, which he thought was going to be alright by the protocol. Several other soldiers milled around outside, waiting for their officers.

He at least would be able to discuss the meeting with one of his men. That gave him comfort. Looking out a window, he could see the man towering over the other recruits and nodded at him. At that moment, General Brand called the room to order.

General Brand had been in charge of Pul's battalion since he first came to the Disputed Lands. Despite all the odds and the number of other generals who were field promoted when they outlived their own commanding officers, General Brand was a man who was appointed by the king himself and had served alongside the great General Oranius.

Brand was man others respected and wished to be accepted by.

He was their leader, and Pul found himself with a large amount of respect for the man. He went into battle with his soldiers, not pushing them out ahead and hoping they made it. A charge with General Brand was one where you knew he had as much chance of surviving as the rest of his men.

Pul saluted along with the rest of the captains in the room.

"That will do," Brand said in his usual curt tone. He was not a man of many words.

"We have a few weeks left before we arrive at Prommus," he continued. "Intelligence says that Isol had been hard at work capturing the cities of the Theocracy. We have a long road ahead of us. Grellis and Meris have fallen to Isol."

Pul breathed in sharply. He had feared such a thing. There was a collective murmur at this news, which General Brand responded to by giving out hard stares. The noise died away quickly.

"But intelligence also tells us that in each city there are a good many survivors and that Isol left a skeleton crew behind to handle the city and see to its defenses. It does not yet know that we plan to come north. Whether word hasn't reached them or they feel they can invade Prommus before we arrive isn't known."

Pul nodded as thoughts invaded his mind of strategies and timelines. Perhaps he was a decent captain after all.

"Regardless, we're going to give them a beating once we meet up with them. The plan is to make it to Grellis, liberate the city and set up supply chains there, and then do it again with Ravus. From there, we head to Prommus and defend the king at any cost."

A small amount of shuffling and moving about ensued as captains and the other generals looked around to see the reactions of the others.

"We leave at first light," Brand said. "Prepare your men."

The clatter and scraping of chairs and dishes overtook the Purity and Pul got out as quickly as he could. He didn't need any clarification. The mission was clear, and Brand was sure not to add any unnecessary words.

Tars met him as soon as he walked out into the light of the suns.

"Did you hear everything?" Pul asked, walking with purpose to put some space between him and the crowd that was forming outside of the inn.

"Most of it," Tars replied. "We're heading north?"

"Through enemy territory," Pul finished. "We need to inform our company. There's still a difficult road ahead."

20: Snart in the Dark

After days of searching, Snart was surprised to have found evidence of something living deep within the caves.

The cool temperatures had slowed him down at first, but using his glowing stones, he created heat around himself that had allowed him to move as if he were standing in the sun.

This was a trick he had felt could be taught to two of his followers without fear of them understanding the stones better. They were blues, blues like he was. Cut and Trak were their names. They had been with him since the jungles of the south and had continued to follow him. Unlike the unlucky ones who had been standing close to him during the assault of the beasts, they had survived. They were strong.

Snart showed them how to think of heat instead of blending in and becoming invisible. With only a little practice, they managed to make warmth come from their rimstones, which allowed them to move faster than their colder brethren. They had created enough for themselves that they could move about the congregation, stirring the others on to search deeper into the caves.

Cut was the first to spot tracks that did not belong to them. These tracks were similar markings to their own. One difference stood out, however. Where the Veiled Ones had long slender toes and claws, these appeared to be more webbed and padded.

There was a chattering from below that Snart had begun to distinguish from the deep silence in the cave. They had followed water in order to sustain themselves.

Perhaps when they found where this water pooled, they would find the Webbed Ones, as Cut had referred to them already. Snart told his congregation to be ready. They all got their spears were out and used their stones to conceal them as best they could.

"Tracks go thissss way, way," said Cut. He pointed to a path that meandered down towards more darkness. Snart had felt like he had been able to light up the cave until this point. He didn't want to give their presence away before he had to. He also felt it was right, as the leader, to appoint scouts who would go down ahead of them.

"You three, three," he said pointing at a cluster of orange lizards. "Go down front, front."

They appeared like they wanted to protest. With a flinch of his clawed hand however, Snart made a ball of the cutting light appear in his hand.

"Now, now."

These three lizards had seen what he had done to the other with this light. Snart guessed they enjoyed having their bodies whole, because they turned to walk down the dark passage.

They didn't have to wait long for the three lizards to come back with a full report. There were definitely signs of a large group of creatures living alongside an underground lake.

The three unfortunate scouts had not gotten close enough to see more clearly how many there were or what this community was comprised of exactly. What they did tell Snart over and over again in great detail, was the fact that the lake was huge. Larger than any body of water they had ever seen before above ground.

This should have worried Snart. Such a large body of water underneath the mountains of Ladis could hold all manner of beasts. Instead of worrying him, however, he found himself thrilled.

What if he could control them? What if he could command them as their leader? Could there potentially be hundreds of reptiles whom he could call forth underneath his banner?

"New three," he said. "Come come. Show me the way. You there."

He motioned to a quarter of those he called his subjects. A few dozens.

"Follow follow."

Remembering his terrifying light and the way he had severed a lizard in half with only his hand, they followed.

The three scouts led them down a meandering path. It brought them to the lake which was, surprisingly to Snart, illuminated by massive rimstones lodged in the cavern ceiling. And here the blue glow filled the area. And the scouts were right.

The biggest body of water other than the big sea lay before them. Its depths were still and cold. Snart found himself shuttering at the thought of getting close to it and made his rimstone grow warmer.

"Down, down," he commanded. Several of his lizards, those who feared him the most, began to make their way down the path towards the glowing points of light down below.

All along the edges of the lake, smaller points of glowing rimstone illuminated caverns and what Snart assumed must be the dwelling places of those who lived in the deep. He continued to poke and prod those in front of him with a spear until they had walked up to the closest dwelling.

The sound of webbed feet running off down a path that connected to this one had Snart turn his head. He could hear the sounds of movement, but couldn't see anything. He made sure that he didn't show any fear. Whoever these creatures were, they would not scare him. He was the boss, boss.

The cave had stalactites and stalagmites that reached up so high in each direction that Snart was sure one touched both the ceiling and the floor. They were as thick around as any tree and surely helped support the massive cave ceiling that was above them.

He put his hand on one as he passed by. Something sticky and slimy came off onto his claws. He examined the goo for just a moment before slinging it off his hand. It was clear and runny.

Looking around the paths that lay before him, Snart saw one that passed by every dwelling that surrounded the lake. By each one, there was a small rimstone light. Further along, there was one dwelling that was encircled by the stones and seemed to be much higher than the others, though it was hard for Snart to tell from this distance.

He purposed to walk straight to that glowing circle of stones and speak with whatever tribe ruler these creatures had.

And to find out what these creatures even were.

"Stopping," a harsh, wet voice said right in front of Snart. The noise of caught him off guard, but he did not flinch cowardly. He had expected some type of greeting party.

"Take me to your boss, boss," Snart said to the darkness. His claws gripped his spear tightly, ready to lash out if the need arose.

In front of him there materialized a creature that looked similar to them, and yet there were very significant differences.

Standing with a stone-tipped spear was a Veiled One with large eyes, a clear bulbous sack under its mouth, and what Snart only knew to describe as scales covering its entire body. A simple rope held a skin that covered its loins. Those were its only clothes.

"Taking you to Great One," the creature said, its spear still pointed threateningly at Snart. "Coming with us."

"Us, us"? Snart asked looking around. He saw no other creatures like the one in front of him. And then suddenly, out of the darkness, several creatures resembling the first began to materialize. Forty or fifty of the creatures with stone-tipped spears and large eyes, all staring and pointing their weapons at Snart.

"Coming with us," the first creature said again, a sinister-looking grin crossing his face.

Snart resisted the urge to make a show of power here. Whoever this Great One was, he would wait to reveal his tricks when he was in front of it.

"We will follow, follow," he said.

The creature looked visibly relieved as it turned to lead them down the path. Snart kept a tight grip on his spear and, with a look, made sure those who had accompanied him did the same.

Walking down the path, Snart felt the stares of all of these odd creatures focused on him. He did his best to keep his magic only warming himself. There would be time for other shows soon enough.

The path was well-worn but wet and full of small stones. Snart found himself using more of his own padded parts of his feet, rather than his claws to move about. It was so different walking along the cave floor than moving from tree to tree in the dense jungles of Ladis. He was not going to show these lizards that he was inferior in any way. They would know that he was just fine in whatever circumstance they wanted to throw at him.

The glowing circle of rimstones came closer and closer as they walked towards the middle of the encampment. Snart saw the path take a steep incline. A poke in his back told him that they were to climb up first. He let out a low hiss to show his displeasure, then began to climb up towards the glowing circle of light.

Below on the lake, Snart though he caught a glimpse of a ripple on the surface. He looked back to see it, but it was gone long before he could convince himself it had been there. The surface of the lake was so still and smooth there couldn't possibly have been anything to disturb it. Yet, when he thought about it, water fell from the ceiling above him every few feet. The large rock formations there funneled water from above. Surely the lake had to have several drips falling into it.

He was probably too far away to tell.

With one glance over his shoulder at his group one more time, as well as a quick glance up at the path that had led them here, Snart returned his attention to the platform that was right in front of him.

Hopefully, his other followers were watching the scene unfold from a safe, but manageable distance. Brave as he felt, Snart didn't like the idea of facing this group without support from the much larger group of lizards he left behind.

The path leveled out as soon as Snart stepped into the circle of glowing rimstone. Each of the stones was as large as he was and was supported on a column of stone. These weren't things built by any hand, Snart saw, but rather a naturally occurring phenomenon, much like the stones that were embedded into the ceiling and giving off the light that kept the huge cavern in a state of almost darkness.

At the opposite end of the circle of glowing stones was a large mound of rock. Snart looked around for any other sign of why they might have been brought here. He began to finger his spear, thinking that this might be a sacrificial altar. He knew nothing of these lizards. The attack may come without any warning or notice.

He turned around, spinning to see what might be the purpose of bringing them up to this circle of stone. Perhaps they were going to wait for whoever the leader of this place was to show up? He looked at the lizard who had first spoken to them. Instead of looking down the stairs for someone to come, the lizard was kneeling on the spot.

And then Snart heard a deep voice from behind him.

"Explaining why you are here and who you are," it said in what Snart could only interpret as a menacing tone.

Turning around, Snart saw that the large mound of rock had big, red, penetrating eyes.

Snart grasped his spear, leaving all pretense of being casual behind. He was talking to a creature at least five times his size. Only the dreaded demons rivaled this thing in its size. The feature that really struck Snart, however, was its mouth.

Both of its red eyes were at least two spans apart. In between, moving slightly with the in-and-out gusts of wind that Snart assumed was its breath, was a giant mouth, one that could swallow him and ten of his lizards whole.

Trying not to flinch at the sight of such a monstrosity, Snart began to speak.

"We are Veiled Onessss," he said as confidently as he could. "I am Snart. Boss, Bossss. We seek man flesh, flesh. Tastes good. Fills us up. Makes us strong, strong."

The creature clicked its mouth several times. Snart was reminded of the sound of boulders crashing down on one another. The other underground lizards who had followed them here made similar noises with their own throats.

"Hearing about man flesh," the large creature said again. "Deep ones eating only fish and cave plants."

With a great gurgling noise, the creature spat out a wad of something at Snart's feet. He did his best not to look fazed by such a gesture. With a quick glance he saw a mixture of fish bones, green and purple rope-like plants, and some glittering scales. He adjusted his footing to be a bit further from it, but looked back up at the giant lizard creature.

"Man flesh is warm," Snart said. "Hot and juicy. Makessss Veiled Onesss tough, tough. Could make Deep Ones tough, tough, too."

The lizards who had brought them here shuffled their feet as Snart spoke. He wondered if they had ever eaten hot meat ever. It was nearly frigid down here. Surely the fish in the big lake were just as cold. Snart looked at his lizards behind him. They were licking their lips. If they were like him, just remembering the sweet taste of humans was creating a hunger in them that was hard to ignore.

Snart felt it. The hunger was in the air. They all felt it. Even the big creature stirred at it.

"Wanting to eat man flesh. Vallin is wanting to eat! Deep Claws wanting to eat man flesh."

The clicking noises grew louder as Vallin, who Snart guessed was the large creature in front of him, began to move. Its huge bulk rose up from the stone circle. It appeared to be some type of lizard that had eaten rocks and grown to become that which it ate. Vallin was huge.

"But first," it said as it stood up on its four legs. "Eating you."

Snart grabbed his spear and held it tightly as the other webbed lizards took their own stone-tipped weapons into their own claws.

He hoped his lizards were paying attention.

Or he wouldn't be boss boss for long.

21: Sacrifices

Jerius stepped over the mess that their ritual in the tower had created. Oranius' troops had apparently pleased the dark deities Decolos had said would come to the aid of those who opposed the rimstones. And from what he could see out on the plains, the last few remaining heretics of Isol who had stayed behind were now being rounded up by Theocracy soldiers.

There had certainly been some magic out on the field in an effort to stop the flow of demons that poured from the sky. Some of the beasts even turned on the city. But that was a calculated risk. Now that they had driven Isol away from Prommus, their own soldiers would be able to pursue them across the plains and seek to make sure the heretics never again invaded the land of the Theocracy.

Regis seemed pleased with himself.

"The king will finally see the power that the church has to offer him," he said, looking over the destruction in the field. "And the church will no longer have to play silly games in order to vie for power. We have power now. We will finally rule as Decolos meant for us to."

Jerius nodded.

Looking down at his robes, he saw streaks of blood from their grisly work.

"How many more times will we sacrifice to the dark ones?" he asked. This was a power that needed strong sacrifices. If the soldiers went off to war...

"We have all we need for now," Regis said. "But for the time being, we must return to the Temple and prepare the guards. The king will not march out to meet Isol without the guards of the Temple. We will show him our own strength."

Regis spun and moved towards the stairs, not once looking down at the carnage at his feet. Several of the temple guards followed him out. Jerius gave them time and space to walk down before he began his own trek.

Luca was walking right beside him.

"My priest?" she said as they began their descent down the stairs after Regis.

"What?" Jerius responded shortly. He did not enjoy being questioned by Luca. Nor did it ever impress him when she spoke first.

"The ritual that just took place."

"Yes?"

Luca paused for a moment. Jerius hoped that she might have lost her train of thought as they came down the stairs and into the chaos below. Soldiers were being called up all around and forming into their battalions. The pursuit of Isol was going to take place quickly, now that the demons seemed to have either vanished or gone off to chase the heretics.

Prommus was no longer on the defensive. It was poised for an attack. With any luck, the city to the east had been informed and sent troops to come to Prommus' aid during the siege. If they were already enroute, the two armies might catch Isol in the middle and deal them a decisive defeat.

Jerius smiled at the thought.

"Was that magic?" Luca asked, finishing her thought from before.

Jerius stopped mid step, causing Luca to nearly bump into him as he swirled around on her.

"How dare you!" he spat. "The church would never agree to such a detestable thing! Decolos, the almighty himself, declared that such a ritual may be used in order to repel those who seek to use magic! Of course it was not speaking or the use of rimstone! Do you think the high priest would ever condone such a thing? Put that heretical thought behind you!"

Luca looked shocked at his reaction at first. Her hands were raised to defend herself from his words, though they couldn't cause her not to hear them.

"Yes, my priest. Forgive me, my priest," she said, bowing her head.

Jerius spared her one more contemptuous look before turning briskly and continuing down the steps. How dare she make such an accusation. Magic. The high priest would never resort to using magic against the Isolians. Decolos had gifted them with the only thing that could stand to oppose the heretics. A dark rebuttal to the abomination that was Isol.

His mood was greatly disturbed now, due to Luca's meddling and inquiry. Instead of victory, he felt annoyed. The emotion carried him all the way to the Temple complex. He didn't spare Luca a single look of dismissal before storming off towards the high priest's chambers. He was going to inquire about whether or not he should stay behind while the high priest marched out with the troops.

Such a maneuver might enable him to find closer allies while no longer under the penetrating gaze of his master. Yes, these were the things he needed to focus on right now. Not the questioning of a lowly temple guard.

The long hallway that he had become accustomed to loomed before him as he made his way towards Regis' study. They had plotted and schemed here, thinking of a way to increase the power of the church and diminish the king's own hand in all matters of the Theocracy.

It had been like a drug to Jerius. Over and over he had read the sacred texts written by Decolos' own hand explaining how he had envisioned the Theocracy.

It was much different than it was in this day. Men wore the robes of the temple guard, as a start, and women were forced to do daily tasks, not see to the protection of the great temples of Ladis. The church was the ruling force in the kingdoms. Princes were lowly men who obeyed the orders of the church. Kings were figureheads, puppets of a strong and glorious Theocracy.

Such thoughts filled Jerius' head as he took the final few steps to the High Priest's door. It was much more quiet in the temple than it had been in recent weeks. Jerius imagined that the high priest would have cleared out most of the guard to take along with the king.

But then his steps slowed. There wasn't anyone in the halls at all. No priests, guards, or anyone. That was strange. Jerius looked up and down the long corridor. Even the guards who were always standing by the high priest's door were gone. He had never seen that door unmanned.

A sense of dread came over Jerius and he truly had no idea where it had come from, but now that it was here it clung to him like a mist. Taking his strides in more measured steps now, he continued his way toward the large doors of the high priest's study. Along the wall there was a spear, left by some guard who had apparently thought she had something better to do with her hands.

Jerius grabbed it in one hand as he shuffled the book of Decolos in the other. He cursed himself for leaving his whip down in his study. He always felt much more secure with that at his side.

"Lord Regis?" he asked as he came to the door. It remained as closed as it normally was. It had always been the guards who had opened the door for him up to this point. He was sure it would be locked, or secured in some manner.

Thene again, the high priest hadn't been too far ahead of him. Maybe he had been in a rush, like Jerius had been?

Resting the spear against his shoulder, he put a hand on the latch and it turned effortlessly. The heavy door, however, was a bit more difficult to manage. While still holding onto the books and balancing the spear, he pulled open the door and looked inside the large room.

Immediately, he lifted up the spear and shouted.

"Take your hands off the priest!"

Two figures in robes were at his desk. One had his hands around the high priest's neck. The other stood at his partner's side. Jerius didn't take the time to think. He knew he had to act. Taking up the spear in his hand, he threw it at the one who held the throat of the high priest. Flying true, the spear just barely missed the chest of the attacker. He expertly dodged the projectile.

And instead it went straight into the heart of High Priest Regis.

"Gaa!" the old man exclaimed. He looked down at his chest for just long enough to put a hand on the spear shaft. With a moan, he fell lifeless to the floor.

And the would be assailant screamed a horrible, piercing scream and ran at Jerius. But it wasn't the yell of a hard worn man. It was the screech of a woman. In her haste, her hood fell down and Jerius gasped.

"You!" he shouted at the white haired woman he had arrested on the island off the coast of Ladis.

"High Priest!" came a shout from behind Jerius. Seven of eight temple guards rushed in through the doors and towards the assailant. She killed one with a swift thrust of a blade Jerius hadn't even seen until just now. Her friend stepped forward and knocked another guard to the ground, before grabbing her companion and yanking her towards the window.

With one last tug, the white haired woman sniffed and ran towards it, throwing herself out of a pane that was missing and onto the ledge beyond. Her companion followed her and the two disappeared from sight.

"They've... They've murdered the high priest!" Jerius shouted, pointing a shaky finger at the pair. "Get them!"

"Yes, My priest!" said a few guards, who walked towards the window, spears drawn and pointed outward. They began to crawl out of the window cautiously, following whatever route the two had taken to get in.

Jerius was still breathing heavily. Looking at the high priest, dead on the floor with a spear in his heart, he felt a sudden rush of both fear and exultation.

He had witnesses of a pair of assassins attacking the high priest. They had seen them attacking him and would pursue them from the temple. A small part of him wished they would capture them. He hated that woman with the white hair more than he would ever admit to anyone.

But a much larger part of him hoped they would get away.

Because if they did, he would have his next change in station.

22: The Dark Prince

The howling winds scoured the landscape and the army that was marching south through it. The land had become much colder as of late, even for the changing seasons. Prince Dram gave it little thought. The only thing he cared for was claiming the throne he had been denied and trying to figure out how to outsmart a god among demons.

He rode up on his horse, surveying the countryside that he had ruled over since coming of age. It depressed him. Even his wrappings did little to keep him warm. He had always hated the cold. It had been a small bit of luck then, that he had kept his skin concealed from everyone who had ever encountered him. He had even refused attendants to help him dress and bathe, a luxury most of the lords and ladies in his small kingdom wouldn't have gone without.

Dram was different.

Prince Dram had a secret to hide. And unless he was careful, it would be a secret known all over the Theocracy. Once he came to power, it wouldn't matter. He would rule in such a way that would crush any opposition to his throne. None would stand against him. Not with his growing power.

The only thing that stood between him and total domination of the land of Ladis was the prince he had heard was dead riding in front of him.

Farnus had changed.

His hair was still as white as the snow that swirled around them, but other than that he had taken on a new demeanor. At least it was different from the man who had visited every realm as a younger man, Dram's included.

He remembered that visit vividly. It had been only after he had come of age and was given the authority to rule the wasted kingdom of the north. Striding through his palace, he had felt different. The stones hadn't seemed so bleak and dreary that day. He had been forced to live here with a single steward as his guide, mentor, and guardian.

Dram had hated that man.

But on the day he had turned eighteen, he was rid of him. His first official act had been to send the old fool back to Prommus to tell the king that his services were no longer needed. Dram would make his own decisions now. He would raise up the lords he felt had been loyal to him and tear down the ones who had pledged their allegiance to his frail steward.

Juttis was his kingdom. He would rule it as he saw fit.

So on that day when he had gone to the window to look down onto his court, the ones he now could command, and saw a carriage covered in the green and gold of the King he thought that his steward had forgotten something.

Or foolishly returned to the castle he had been banished from only hours before.

Walking down the stairs and into the halls of the front door, Dram felt powerful. He would handle this daring act of defiance with an iron fist. Servants bowed to him as he passed. Guards stood at attention. He would show them all.

He was a man worthy to be a prince.

The guards opened the door for him to exit and as his feet touched the gravel outside, he stopped in mid stride.

It wasn't an old foolish guardian who had come out of the carriage surrounded by guards. It was the King's Son. The White Prince.

Dram had never seen the man before, but there could be no mistaking it now. Wearing the King's golden crown on his chest and pushing his long white hair out of his face, Dram knew that this man was the king's son, the high priest's nephew, and the brother he must never admit to having.

"His Holiness and the King of Ladis introduces the prince of Ladis, Farnus, son of Gravis," cried a guard who had opened the carriage door and allowed the prince to exit. The prince rolled his eyes before placing his hands on his hips and looking down at Dram.

All of a sudden, he felt much more like a boy, than a prince of a kingdom.

He shook himself and stood, rather defiantly, and stared into the eyes of Prince Farnus.

"So you are the wrapped one I've heard so much about," he said. Prince Farnus kept his eyes on the young man, not turning them away or even blinking when the guards came out to join Dram in the courtyard.

Dram stood himself up to his full height.

"Welcome to Juttis," he said with a snarl. He was sure the prince could see his displeasure. A part of him wanted to dare the first prince of Ladis to accuse him of disloyalty. To tell him that he was a bastard and would never ascend to any throne.

He wanted Farnus to say that he knew who the prince standing in front of him was.

But there was no act of recognition, nor threat. No sign of any protest came from Farnus. He merely flicked his white hair over his shoulder and began to walk towards the door of Dram's castle.

"Pardon my unannounced visit, but the king thought it would be prudent for me to see the kingdoms of Ladis before I get much older. I doubt he thinks he'll ever die, but in case he does, I'll inherit the throne and it'll be best if I know the land I would rule."

Fanus said these words without looking at Dram at all. He had turned his eyes up to the castle of Juttis and its accompanying temple. Dram could tell by the look on the prince's face that he thought Juttis was not a land worth visiting. That he was only doing so because his father, the king, had suggested it.

"I accept your hospitality and the graces of this chilly kingdom."

There wasn't another word spoken between them for the entirety of his week long stay. Farnus moved about the kingdom as he wished and never made himself known to Dram, other than a cuseroy declaration of his intent for his day at the first meal and a snide report during the last.

Dram felt on edge the entire time. He could barely sleep, had no appetite, and felt increasingly paranoid. What was the prince really doing in his new kingdom? Was his visit just at the time of his ascension pure coincidence or was there something else that had motivated him to come?

On the day of his parting, they shared breakfast at the long table of the castle's main dining hall. There was nothing to show of the grandeur of the kingdom. There was very little grand about Juttis, other that its belonging to Dram.

Prince Farnus left the table after having eaten his fill of deer meat, eggs and bread. Dram had contented himself to sit and enjoy the food, knowing that it would be the last meal he would have to share with the Prince. Hopefully ever.

His meal complete, he threw a napkin at the first servant who walked by and demanded his horse. He would ride fast and far today, in an attempt to get himself away from the Prince as soon as he had left. Dram needed to breathe. He needed to feel the wind blow through his wrappings. It was a time when he felt like he was not the dark skinned prince none could know of.

Rounding the corner of the stables, he saw that his horse had been prepped for him. He spared no moments to pet the animal. He needed escape. Dram untied the rope that held his steed in place and moved to the side of it. Grabbing the reins and lifting his foot, he nearly tasted his freedom when a voice called from behind him.

"Prince Dram."

He stopped cold.

It was Farnus.

Dram wanted to reach for his dagger that was by his side. The prince had not threatened him once on his trip, nor had he given any indication that Dram should be fearful around him. Still. There was a sense of dread that Dram felt in his core.

"Yes?" he said, turning slowly and looking to see that Farnus had come alone. None of his guards accompanied him. He had spoken curtly. If Farnus had been looking for any reason to lash out, this could very well be all he needed. He was the high prince, after all. First in line to inherit the Theocracy of Ladis. This he had made plain. Dram stretched his fingers, remembering his dagger.

"The king wished me to deliver a message to you," he said, his face blank as he spoke words Dram had not expected to hear.

He blinked. For all the responses he had thought of to Farnus being in the stables alone with him, stunned silence had not been near the top of his thinking.

Farnus nodded.

"He wishes to convey his congratulations to you on your coming of age and inheritance of the kingdom of Juttis."

Dram held fast to his horse's rope. The beast kicked its back leg, impatient to get riding. Dram felt as if his legs had turned to solid stone.

"The king also wished me to tell you," Farnus said as he turned to the side. "That you are to stay in Juttis. There is no need for you to come south to Prommus in order to pay homage to the King for festivals or new years, nor for you to worship at the temple of Ladis found there. Juttis is your kingdom to rule as you see fit. But it is to be the kingdom where you stay."

Dram narrowed his eyes.

This was not a congratulatory message. It was a warning. A sentence of his term. He would rule a kingdom, but it would be his prison. Farnus looked back to him. His icy blue eyes stared right into

Dram's. Dram felt a chill he could not attribute to the lack of warm clothes.

But Farnus' next word cut to his bones.

"Have I made the king's wishes clear, brother?"

He knew. The king had told him.

Farnus knew.

Those were the last words Dram had ever heard from prince Farnus until he had arrived on his doorstep a few weeks ago. No official message from the king had ever come save for that one. Dram sent the yearly taxes south to Prommus by delegates and officials. He ensured that Juttis was represented whenever it was necessary. He even kept the temple funded, though he despised it and all of the Theocracy's hold of the empire.

But it was that moment that Dram had sworn that he would not only leave Juttis one day.

He would conquer Ladis as his own.

Thus had begun his years of research and studies. He knew of one thing and one thing only that the Theocracy loathed and that his lineage had helped eradicate. And therefore he would know everything he could about the subject.

He would be a Speaker of immense power.

"Halt!"

The command had come from the man who rode in front of him. It looked every bit as if it were Farnus, the High Prince of Ladis. Only he was now covered in plates of metal armor and he carried a sword he had never seen his half-brother wield. Dram knew this man was more than his family. He was changed. Different.

There was a power about him that had nothing to do with his parentage. Farnus turned to look at Dram and gave a wicked smile.

"This is where we will campt tonight," he said, his voice still distorted and rough. "And it is where I will make all things plain to you."

Dram gave no response, other than to raise a wrapped hand to slow his own troops. The men who had come with him called out their own command to stop their marching. In front of them, the horizon stretched out wide. Dram could see the road that went south, further and further along it until it reached the capital that all roads in Ladis led to: Prommus.

He had dreamed of this moment. Thought it might never come at times and been consumed with anger and fear. And never in his wildest imagination would he have thought that Farnus would be riding beside him as he sought the throne of his father.

"This is a great moment, brother," Farnus said. "Father has ruled long enough. It is time the empire was led by a powerful king. The Theocracy will fall and from its ashes will be reborn an empire that will conquer not just Ladis, but Ruyn, Redact, Irradan and Gallin."

His eyes narrowed as he turned back to survey the road. Dram followed his gaze. Farnus was looking towards Prommus. He clutched his reigns tightly and felt the power of his rimstones coursing through him. He had seen what this new Farnus was capable of.

And he wasn't sure he could match it. Not yet, at least. So he could little more than nod at his half-brother's next words.

"This will be an empire that will conquer a world."

23: Revenged

A wind whipped around the temple complex as Silverwolf and Serinde made their way down the same path they had come up. It had not been easy to find the route from the walls of the temple, to the spiraling tower, to the last window pane that had let them into the high priest's study.

Serinde knew that Silverwolf had a personal vendetta with the priest. Not least of all because she knew he was her father.

But she also knew that was not the outcome she had desired.

Her fingers ached as she moved across the sheer face of the temple walls. Climbing up had been much easier. Now it was perilous for them to climb down as each foothold and grip was below them, not above.

The guards who had come to the window had barely even tried to climb down the winding path of stone and iron. Serinde didn't blame them. The only reason she had come was to see what Silverwolf had planned for her father.

They had climbed the tower and broken into the high priest's study. Silverwolf had taken three steps into the chamber, turned to face Serinde as she made her way inside, and then grabbed her by the shoulder to shove her behind a long draping curtain. The elf had barely taken any time to observe her surroundings. What she had been able to see, however, told her that the position of High Priest was one that allowed several comforts and many opportunities for study. Books lined the walls, and there were several areas where one could sit and read in a comfortable chair or couch.

But the only thing she had been able to observe from her curtain was the desk of the high priest and the back of Silverwolf's head. Her ears were able to take in much more. Footsteps were approaching from outside the door that was opposite the desk. A bit of talking came through the wood, but it was barely distinguishable, even to her keen ears.

The door was pushed open, and a flurry of people came in.

"Yes I'll be arranging the guards myself," said a voice that sounded familiar to her. "And make sure the priests who are here in the castle know that they are not to make any rash decisions while I am gone."

"Gone, my Lord?" came a female reply. "Surely you don't mean to..."

"I mean to march with the troops at my brother's side, yes," the high priest replied curtly. "Now go and see that you've assembled the guards out on the lawn. I want to inspect them as soon as I can, but there is a matter I must attend to before that occurs. Go!"

Another scurry of footsteps and the sound of a door closing.

They waited. The high priest sat there, making notes with a quill on a piece of parchment that was laid out in front of him. Usually, as far as Serinde knew, when men did this, it was with furrowed brows and hard expressions. Like all of their mental faculties were being used to focus on that one sheet of paper.

Not this man.

He looked absolutely jubilant. Like everything he had ever wanted had come true.

Serinde didn't know the plan. She didn't know if Silverwolf had a plan to tell her. It didn't matter. Silverwolf had leaped from her hiding place and thrown her hands around the neck of the high priest before Serinde could even properly react.

"I want to know three things from you," she had said. "And I expect that every answer you give me will be a lie, but I'll ask them all the same."

A look of pure horror was covering the High Priest's face. His hands went immediately to his neck, trying to pull Silverwolf's away. Serinde had taken a step out of the curtains and drawn her knife. She wanted to make sure she was ready for any guards who might have come back through the door.

"Did you know I still had breath in my lungs? Who did you sell me to?"

Serinde paused as she had been moving from behind Silverwolf to the side so she could get a good look at both the priest, the door, and SIlverwolf's face. The assassin was a mask, devoid of emotion. Her words sounded angry and hurt, but her face was passive. Still.

"And why did you give away your own daughter, you sorry excuse for a man?"

Silverwolf's fingers tightened around the throat of her father. His eyes went wide as he gagged for breath.

"Answer me, father, and I may not kill you slowly. Call the guards, and I will definitely strangle you without a second thought of my own life. It's not been much to think of."

Relenting just enough to let him breathe, Serinde heard a terrible gasping sound as the man's airways opened back up.

"I..." spluttered the older man, looking much less pompous than he had just a moment ago. "I never sold you, Ella."

Ella? thought Serinde. So she had a real name.

Silverwolf's fingers wrapped around his throat again.

"That is not who they call me now," she said with a snarl in her voice. "They call me the Silverwolf. I am an assassin. I kill for coins, you old fool. I once slit a man's throat as he lay next to his wife heavy with child. For a king's ransom, mind you, but this is who I've become. A sellsword. A hired killer."

Serinde took a step closer. The priest was no longer fighting Silverwolf's fingers. Instead, his eyes were bulging, and pathetic gagging noises were coming out of his mouth. He couldn't breathe.

"Now answer my questions."

Another gag and cough followed as she let up on her grip and he took in life-giving breaths. The next time he spoke his words were so garbled that Serinde could barely understand him.

"I gave... Gave you away to hide you. To protect. To Gerriander Ottobon. A family friend who promised me he'd take you somewhere safe."

"You sold me as a slave, you wretch," Silverwolf replied. "I was on a ship headed for Galin as soon as the carriage left the castle."

"Galin!" the priest exclaimed. "No! That's not... But there must have been some mistake!"

"Give me one good reason to believe you."

"Gerrymander lives!" the priest gasped, as Serinde saw Silverwolf's muscle tighten and her fingers squeeze. "He told me you were safe! He lives in the east still. He can tell you what he told me!"

Serinde waited for Silverwolf to make the killing strike. To produce a knife or sword from a hidden sheath and end the old man's life. If he really had sold her into slavery, a fate which she said she only narrowly escaped, then even Serinde could see a need for revenge.

But the assassin didn't move.

Her fingers didn't close down harder, and she didn't take a hand away for a blade.

What was causing her to stop in her act of revenge?

"Lord Regis?" came a voice from the door. And before Serinde had turned around properly, a spear was flying past her ear and straight into the heart of the high priest.

As she climbed down from one perilous foothold to the next, Serinde replayed the scene over and over in her head. Silverwolf ready to choke her father to death for the sin of selling her off, freezing when he had offered a reason to believe him.

Not a reason, really, a name.

Serinde's hand slipped as a stone that she had been holding onto let loose from its mortar and fell a dizzying distance to the ground below. She felt a moment of terror before righting herself and grabbing onto a different stone. Praying it would hold, Serinde put her foot on the ledge that they had edged across to get to the high tower.

It would be balance and footwork from here on out.

"I'm sorry," she said, as she saw Silverwolf's back walking across a long stone path that was the top of a high roof. "About your father."

This had to be the roof of the magnificent temple sanctuary. Underneath them was a giant room with a great statute of the Ladis god: Decolos.

But thoughts of what lay beneath their feet drifted away as Serinde caught sight of Silverwolf. She had spun around at her words, a hand on a knife.

So she did have a few more blades hidden in her sleeves.

"Never mention what you saw to anyone," Silverwolf said through snarled teeth. "I have no father. I have no name but what you call me by."

Serinde looked at this woman she had traveled beside for so long. She saw red in those eyes. Not a rage-filled type of color that usually came with the desire to kill.

These eyes were red for other reasons.

Serinde nodded her head.

"As you wish," she said.

Silverwolf huffed and turned around, continuing on their journey. Serinde knew they would get out of Prommus without many problems. The city was now focused on the route of Isol and pursuing the army away from its borders. Together they would sneak out of the city and continue their quest to find Yada and retrieve their stolen goods.

And in the meantime, Serinde had many things to think over.

Not least of which was of Ella, the girl who turned into the Silverwolf.

24: Shoes of the Weary

Jurrin wasn't sure about everything that had been happening over the last two days. On the one hand, he was very concerned for Miss Olma and the new appearance she had taken on. With it came an attitude that seemed entirely not her own. While the Olma before the barn incident was quiet and reserved, this Olma was rambunctious, almost reckless.

She jumped from rock to rock, not appearing to tire or grow weary after a full day of walking. Jurrin felt like he had lead in his shoes. By contrast, Olma was restless and pacing the campfire at the end of the day. Jurrin could tell it made Holve anxious to have her so active. The older man hardly slept at all as he watched her moving and running about. Jurrin tried to keep his eyes open and help watch, but sleep overtook him.

He had slept next to Galp and Gorplin. The two seemed an unlikely pair, but they bantered back and forth often. Galp was a talker, even more than he was, which surprised Jurrin. He had known Urt to be quiet and reserved. Who knew a Skrilx could talk so much?

Gorplin argued with Galp every step of the way. He told him he talked too much, or that he was wrong about the rock types that they were encountering, or that his measure of a distance of a mountain was off by so many miles.

The two got on better than Gorplin did with most.

Jurrin felt a type of kinship with them as well. They were all members of a race that just didn't exist here on Ladis.

Well, Jurrin thought as he looked up at Szabo leading their group. All except him.

Jurrin had thought he might get along with Szabo, but the two hardly had any time to talk. Holve and Ealrin kept the halfling talking nearly nonstop about all the goings on of the Theocracy and Isol.

He was a wealth of knowledge and the two men lapped up every bit of it.

Miss Rivius and Ferrin kept to themselves at the back of the group, always within calling distance but not too close either. Jurrin wondered if Blume and Olma worried them. Blume had gotten a bit of her powers back at her disposal for a moment, but it had taken a heavy toll on the group.

"I'm sorry about Mister Maccus," Jurrin said as they picked their way through a rocky mountain trail. Szabo said his contact lived up in a cave high up on the side of the mountain. It had been a lucky circumstance that it was out of the way of the army. Jurrin could look out and see the banners of Juttis as they marched east and south, walking towards the city of Prommus. They were specks on the horizon now.

Jurrin turned back to look at Tratta as she climbed up behind him. She hadn't looked very well since the barn and Jurrin couldn't tell what seemed to be bothering her more. The woman had appeared to be so hard and well-traveled when they first encountered her. She was not a picture of defiance anymore. Her hair was unkempt, and her eyes were red and puffy. Jurrin could have sworn he heard sniffles the night before.

He couldn't blame her.

He had shed his own tears over friends he'd lost.

"Miss Tratta?" he asked again, trying to catch her eyes. "Are you alright? I know Maccus was a cousin of yours. I'm sorry that he's gone."

Tratta shook her head and focused her eyes on him. She blinked twice before swallowing and looking at him.

"Hmm? I couldn't hear you, ya know?"

"I'm sorry about Mister Maccus," Jurrin repeated. "He seemed brave and strong. I know he was family to you. Are you ok?"

Tratta sniffed once before continuing to climb up the hill past Jurrin.

"I'm fine," she said, patting Jurrin on the shoulder. "Thanks for askin' though."

She moved on ahead of him and continued to follow after Blume and Olma. Jurrin had a distinct feeling that she wasn't as well as she said she was.

"Keep an eye on her," a voice said from behind Jurrin. It made him jump a bit. Ferrin and Miss Rivius had closed the gap much more quickly than he had anticipated. "She's been a bit distraught."

"And not without cause," Miss Rivius said, her arms crossed. "That girl..."

Jurrin looked at them both with wide eyes.

"Miss Blume? She didn't mean any harm. Just that terrible ring from Isol. No wonder she's been a mess. And poor Miss Olma. Who knows what's gotten into her."

"I am precisely worried about what has gotten into her," Miss Rivius said.

Jurrin didn't quite know how to respond to that. He didn't have to. Szabo called them from further up the path.

"Just up here!" he said, motioning with his hands. Jurrin could see him waving down at them, just before he passed behind some rocks and a scrawny bush. Wrapping his arms around him and wishing his coat was a bit thicker, he continued walking up the path, thinking on Tratta and Miss Rivius' words.

Olma had changed.

Not least of her changes was the fire red hair that came down past her waist and the black markings that seemed almost alive on her skin. She jumped down from the rock she had been perched on and began walking the way Szabo had indicated. Miss Rivius and Ferrin gave her a wide berth, but Jurrin walked up to her.

"How are you feeling, Miss Olma?" he asked her while trying to get his feet to continue along the path. He was certainly feeling the day's climb and strain on his legs.

"I don't have a care in the world," Olma replied. "Not one. Did you know I could do this?"

Before Jurrin could respond, Olma had jumped up into the air and was almost as high as the men stood before coming back down gently onto her feet. She hardly even disturbed the rocks on the ground.

"Miss Olma!" Jurrin exclaimed. "How did you do that?"

Olma shrugged her shoulders and continued to walk up the path.

Jurrin closed his mouth. He had left it hanging open at her feat and followed behind. Whatever had come upon Olma was certainly something that needed more explanation than Jurrin could offer.

They were the last to arrive at the cliff Szabo had taken. All the other members of their party were looking back towards the plains they had come from. Jurrin didn't need to turn around to see what was on their minds. They all stood watching the army of Juttis.

"What do you think it means?" Jurrin finally asked. "Think Prince Dram is in charge of them?"

"Most definitely," Holve replied. "And it means he's going to claim the throne of Prommus. Whether or not he'll find one there is beyond me. Yada's forces should have made the trek there by now."

"And if they do find a Prommus under siege or one already occupied by Isol?" Miss Rivius asked. "What do you suppose then?"

Holve sighed.

"With what we saw in your own home, Miss Rivius," he replied. "I don't know the extent of the damage that could be done."

Jurrin took in a big breath. He had seen Prince Dram's magic. Or whatever it was. It was terrifying. And if he wasn't the only one who was capable of such feats, then the army of Prommus would have its work cut out for them.

And so would Isol.

"All this war," Jurrin said. "It hasn't really solved anything yet, has it?"

"What's that, Jurrin?" Holve asked.

"We've seen so many people go to fight. Androlion. Rophilborn. Now Prince Dram and Miss Yada."

He shook his head.

"So many people dying for little gains. Oh, the last two times have been alright in the end, but still, so many dying."

Jurrin imagined all the people who were marching off to war to fight others battles. What would it gain them? They had all they needed in Juttis. At least it appeared that way to him. Why take more when you had what was sufficient?

"So many deaths," he said again, shaking his head and failing to find words to describe what he felt adequately.

"Let's try to see if we can't save one then, shall we?" Szabo said, having already turned his back on the scene of Juttis' army marching south. "The cave is this way."

Szabo started walking, and the rest of the group followed him. Jurrin was just behind Ealrin and Holve.

"Think his friend will be able to help, Mister Ealrin?" Jurrin asked with real concern. He liked Olma. He hated to think about something going wrong with her. Something more wrong than what seemed to be going on around all of them, anyways.

The suns were finishing their descent after a long day's journey. Jurrin could feel the waking up mountains all in his legs. He hoped they could stop here for the night. Provided the lodgings were better than a bare patch of dirt, he may just be convinced he was staying in a lovely inn or even a palace.

"I hope so," Ealrin said, looking over at Holve. "I really hope so, Jurrin."

Jurrin looked over at Holve too but saw that the man kept this eyes on Szabo. Maybe he didn't trust him yet. Jurrin couldn't exactly blame him. They had only met the halfling two days ago. Then again, they had trusted others on much less.

The air began to cool significantly as they started walking not up, but down. Jurrin looked up and spotted an opening in the face of the mountain. A little cave entrance that was covered in vines. Jurrin wouldn't have been able to see that there was anything there at all behind the vines, save for the fact that they startled and moved slightly though there was no breeze on the mountain.

The cold air was coming from the cave.

Strange, Jurrin thought. The whole rest of the mountain side was utterly devoid of vegetation. How could those vines grow without any water or proper care?

"Mister Holve, remember those nasty creatures down south?" Jurrin asked, remembering being in a lake in a cave much like this.

"I do," Gorplin said, puffing out his chest and raising the dagger they had found for him. "And I'm keen to get some fighting in if I can. Galp hasn't stopped talking this whole way about rocks, and I need to break something."

"Not rocks," Galp corrected and pointing excitedly off to the side of the path they were on. "Indigenous species! Just look over there!"

"BAH!" Gorplin shouted. "I hope there's something to beat down in there."

"No monsters. An old man, maybe. Just in there," Szabo said, pointing inside the cave. "My friend Cecil."

"Cecil?" Ealrin asked, looking over at Szabo. "Seems like a proper name for someone who lives in a cave."

"Yeah, just make sure you look at his left eye," Szabo said, indicating his eye with his finger and giving a wink. "Ignore the right. It'll lie to you."

"I heard that!" came a shout from inside the cave. "And I've got company. Take your shoes off before you come in. Mind your manners!"

Szabo chuckled before turning back and heading inside the cave.

"Same ole' Cecil!" he said, taking care to remove his shoes before disappearing underneath the vines that covered the entrance of the cave almost completely.

"He was serious about the shoes, ya think?" Tratta asked as she stepped forward, looking at the undersides of her shoes as if examining them for dirt. All of their shoes were in the same condition: torn and dusty from the miles of walking they had done since arriving on Ladis.

"He was!" came a shout from within.

25: The Potion Master

The voice coming from inside the cave didn't sound old, Jurrin thought. Just grumpy.

With a shrug, he began to take off his shoes and watched as the rest of their group did the same. The only two who hesitated were Holve and Miss Rivius.

"Not very ladylike," she said under her breath as she removed her shoes and placed them neatly beside the pile everyone else was throwing theirs into.

Holve waited until everyone else had taken theirs off before removing his own. He sighed heavily upon doing it but removed his shoes quickly before turning to walk into the wall of vines.

Gorplin and Galp followed Ealrin, and Jurrin followed them, with Blume and Olma right behind him. The smell that assaulted him must have hit everyone harder because they all slowed their steps as soon as they walked into the cave. Jurrin kept going, but he raised a hand to his nose to waft away the odor.

It was overpowering.

The entire cave was filled with a haze that had both color and seemed transparent all at once. Jurrin could barely make out the top of the cavern, but only just. Some stalactites poked down through the fog, while stalagmites reached up to meet them.

Everyone seemed to either grow accustomed to the smell or resigned themselves to it, as they moved forward down the path and towards the light that issued from within. The walls of the cave were lined almost entirely with shelves. Both natural shelves that had been formed out of hollows in the cave wall and humanmade, or rather carved, shelves that didn't seem to follow any particular order.

They were just everywhere and held everything.

Jurrin couldn't take it all in fast enough as they walked past it all. Books, bottles, skulls, feathers, jars, scrolls, parchments, rocks of every color imaginable and much more beyond that.

"Don't touch a thing!" came the voice again, this time Szabo joined it.

"Oh give it a rest, Cecil. They need help."

"And you need to pay me!" Cecil's voice replied.

Jurrin felt the crunch of the cave floor more distinctly with just his bare feet touching the ground. It was smooth and worn, but also a little damp. It was undoubtedly leading downwards, however. After a few more steps, it became clear that they weren't walking towards one light, but several.

The back and forth between Szabo and Cecil grew louder as the group finally came to what must be the primary study or, Jurrin thought for a moment to find the right word, workshop, of the man.

A table carved from stone lay in the middle of the largest room of the cave. On top of that were several deep pots. Some of them had fires underneath them, while others sat right on the cold stone. Jurrin was trying to see what some of the cauldrons that had steam pouring out of the top of them held within them when Szabo and Cecil came into view.

They were still arguing.

"I paid you half that last time!" Szabo said, looking up at the older man.

"Well, times have changed, and I can't get the Manu roots like I used to. So it'll be double."

"What if I have the roots for you?"

"You can't have gotten the roots!" Cecil argued. "They are way too far south for you to get them and then bring them up to me here in time!"

Szabo reached down into his pockets and filled out a bundle of dirty, stubby roots.

"Picked two weeks ago by the half moon," he said, a look of pride on his face. "Just like you like them."

Cecil's face grimaced and simultaneously smirked.

The old man was indeed eccentric. He wore no shirt, and his body had scars all over it. Jurrin could only assume it from boiling pots overflowing or the mark of a flame gone haywire. His face full of stubble, but his hair was wrapped up in a bun and matted down with mud and dirt. Jurrin supposed the man could have had dark hair, but it was hard to tell.

He had mismatched eyes. One was larger and almost green in tint. The other was a stark blue. That one was on the right. Neither eye seemed to be looking forward or any direction that would be helpful to him as he gathered supplies from around the shelves and table.

Even though he rubbed his hands on the root that Szabo had given him, his eyes were looking over the group that has come into his cave.

"I remember telling you expressly that my prices had changed," he said, putting the roots down on the table and throwing the halfling a scowl.

Szabo just chuckled.

"I don't think you'll remember the last three conversations we have had!" he said checking the contents of the pouch. He looked up with what Jurrin thought was mock horror. "You shorted me by at least half."

Cecil scowled.

"Ungrateful," he muttered under his breath, moving to another series of shelves and rifling through the objects there. "Sit down if you must, but don't touch anything! Especially you, missy."

Tratta pulled her hand away from a book she had almost touched. She turned and looked down at Jurrin with wide eyes. He smiled cautiously.

"I think he saw you, Miss Tratta," he said, looking back at the man who definitely was not looking in their direction.

Jurrin looked around and saw that there was not a single chair in the entire cave. Not any that he could see at least. Finding nothing better, he sat himself down on the cavern floor between a barrel full of something that smelled rotten and a shelf of things floating in jars.

He stopped trying to see what it was inside the dirty jars when he caught sight of something floating that also appeared to be looking back at him. Others in the room had put themselves down on different areas on the cave floor or else leaned against the wall, resting as best as they could.

Everyone sat except Olma, who seemed to be fascinated with a cauldron that was bubbling under a hot flame. Jurrin thought he might scoot himself closer to it. The cave was cold everywhere that there wasn't a fire glowing.

Cecil's words cut him off short from moving, however.

"So, you've brought me someone to fix, eh?"

Szabo looked at Olma and then back at Cecil, shrugging his shoulders.

"I figured if there was anyone who could help us out it would be you."

Another scoff escaped Cecil's mouth before he turned back towards the group and looked in Olma's direction. At least, Jurrin was reasonably sure that's where he was looking.

The girl didn't look up from the mixture that boiled in front of her. Instead, she continued to be transfixed on the substance that was inside it.

"She's much more resilient than any I've ever seen so afflicted and apparently in full control of herself. Well, until it started to smell my Dark Bane potion. Always good to keep some on hand."

Cecil walked up to Olma and then began to circle her. He reached into a pouch that hung around his neck and shoulder by a thin string. Jurrin got up off the floor and stood so that he could see what Cecil was doing. The older man threw something into the pot that turned the smoke first blue, then red, then green.

Olma breathed it in deeply. It appeared to Jurrin that she was in some type of trance, though her eyes were fully open and staring.

"Now. Now. Now," Cecil said, throwing one more handful of something that looked like dirt into the pot. "Let's get some answers before we proceed."

The fires around the room began to dim. Jurrin saw Ealrin stand next to Blume, whose face was full of worry. Ealrin put a hand on her shoulder, but she didn't look much relieved by the act. Holve was standing just behind them, arms crossed, a sour expression on his face.

Cecil stood right in front of Olma and, again, reached his hands into his pouch. This time, he pulled out a mushroom type plant and held it in his hand out in front of him. He was standing much closer to Olma than he was while he was circling her.

"Why don't you tell me who you are?" Cecil asked, still holding up the mushroom.

"Olma of Fray," the girl said quietly, though she still kept her eyes focused forward.

"Try again, missy," Cecil said. With a quick movement, he slapped one hand on top of the other, and the mushroom disappeared in a cloud of dust.

Jurrin closed his eyes as a bright flash of light filled the cave for a moment. He threw his hands up to his ears as he heard a terrible screech. Looking through the haze and the smoke, he saw the outline of a great beast. It was gone before he could blink twice.

The whole company was up in arms. Gorplin and Galp were standing looking around wildly. Tratta had her bow drawn, and Holve was holding out a sword.

Cecil, however, was over by a shelf, pulling off various packets and plants and handfuls of everything.

"Ah!" he said with a voice that sounded triumphant. "We've got a feisty one!"

Another puff of smoke cleared the room of the green colored fog. A distinctly burning smell filled Jurrin's nose. He gagged only a bit before he found he could control his stomach.

Olma still stood in the same spot, but the black markings that now covered her body were lined with purple light. Her arms were moving up and down quickly as if she were trying to shake off an annoying insect.

Cecil came close once again.

"Now that we've gotten a look at you might as well do a little talking you great beasty."

A snarl escaped Olma's mouth as a noise that sounded otherworldly echoed through the cave.

"Leave me be," the voice said. "I've work to accomplish, and this vessel will do nicely."

"You've other vessels more usable than this, I know from all that your kind have been up to lately. Taking villages. Killing all who dare walk around you. I'm surprised you haven't eaten up this whole group."

Olma began to lunge forward, but Cecil threw something in the pot that exploded with an orange flame. Jurrin covered his eyes as he saw Olma recoil.

"Not so fast there, demon," he roared. "I've got more questions for you before you terrorize this girl more."

Jurrin thought he had heard wrong, but he could have sworn he heard Cecil say demon. Did he really think there was a demon afflicting the poor girl? And what word did he keep using? Vessel?

Jurrin had more questions than he had time to ask.

"Why haven't you devoured the vessel and her companions?" Cecil yelled in a demanding voice. "What is your purpose?"

"Death," the shrill voice said again. "Pain. Blood. All of these things my master desires. But more so, he wants this one who has stood in his way before and is doing so again. He wants death. But he wants to do it on his own. The pleasure of the act fills him."

"Who?" Cecil asked. "Who is your master?"

Another scream, followed by two short blasts of orange from the cauldron.

"The one who has traveled the darkness beyond. The one who filled the light with dark. The one who they sealed away. The one who has come to destroy the refugees and fugitives. Darkness and fear in form unknowable."

The purple lines that glowed along her black markings grew brighter and brighter. Olma seemed like she was in pain. Jurrin couldn't help but call out.

"Miss Olma! Hang in there, Miss Olma! Don't give in!"

She turned to face him and screamed long and loud. Jurrin covered his ears. The sheer volume of it broke several of the glass jars beside him. Their contents spilled onto the cavern floor, and Jurrin nearly did throw up this time.

A violent blast shook the cave.

Jurrin found himself thrown to the floor of the cave, his hands over his head. It felt like a powerful tremor traveled through the cave, making the books and jars rattle on their shelves.

The halfling hoped it would be over shortly. More dust and debris fell on his head, and he remembered the giant stalactites. To afraid to see if there any above his head, he interlocked his fingers and waited for the shaking to stop.

An uneasy calm filled the cave.

Jurrin heard coughing and movement as some of their party returned to their feet. He peeked out from between his fingers to see Holve still on one knee, looking at Cecil and a little girl.

Olma lay still on the floor in front of him. Cecil moved over to her quickly, and Jurrin saw him pour something down her mouth. Tilting her head back, Cecil looked at her intently until she swallowed it. When she opened her mouth again to take a breath, he moved away and sighed heavily.

"She's a feisty one."

26: The Plan of The Exiled

The uneasiness of the men outside the tent was palpable. Demons were walking along the edges of the camp. Even though they were ensured that they would not attack the armies of Juttis, there was still a feeling of dread that surrounded the whole area.

Dram could feel it too.

He stood at his tent flap and thought about how he was going to proceed from here. The suns had set, and the three moons of Gilia had been rising all night long. He took a deep breath and felt his chest stretch against his wrappings. He held his dagger tightly, even though there was no threat present to him at the time.

Holding it made him feel at peace. He felt like he was in charge.

Set into the hilt of his trusted dagger was a rimstone piece. It glowed slightly at his touch, and he felt the warmth coming through his hands. Another deep breath steadied him. He was a prince. He would soon be asking if all went according to plan.

He had nothing to fear.

A glowing orb of purple came close to his tent. Dram looked at it as it approached. He didn't know what it was, but he had a feeling he knew where it had come from.

"Dram," a voice said from within the glowing orb. "You are required at the tent of Farnus."

Dram nodded and began to walk in the direction of the prince's tent. The orb led the way, though Dram felt it was unnecessary. Possibly, if he had turned away or refused, the globe would have persuaded him more forcefully.

He wasn't ready to test his suspicions.

The tents of the army had been set in neat rows, as Dram had made sure his generals had prepared his men. Dram was a man of order and desired that his army appear royal, organized, and able to attack at will.

The only thing that made the camp seem off were the glowing purple lights that surrounded it. Each of them was a demon of terrifying size. He knew they were on the same side. But the way they patrolled the perimeter made him feel as if they were ensuring the men stayed inside as guards would, rather than traveling with them as brothers-in-arms.

Dram continued to walk towards the tents in the middle of the camp. His own had been placed at the front at his request. He never enjoyed being surrounded, even by his own forces. There was a part of him that wanted to be free to roam if need. In Juttis, such luxuries had been offered to him.

He was a dark prince, but he was no prisoner in his own kingdom.

The ball of purple flame moved ahead of him as he entered into a circle of tents in the very middle of the camp. It hovered outside one of the larger structures, then closed in on itself and went out.

Dram knew this must be the one he was supposed to enter. Steeling himself, he stepped purposefully inside. The tent was massive and had one large area in the middle, with four smaller sections off to the side.

Farnus was already standing in the large section, covered in the huge metal plates that had appeared when he first revealed himself to Dram and looking down at a table with several maps and parchments.

There was no need to announce his entrance.

"Come in, Dram," Farnus said, keeping his eyes on the map at his table. Dram did as he was bidden, though he thought it seemed unnecessary. Taking three steps over the rug that had been placed on the ground, Dram stopped short of the table when someone came out from one of the flaps.

Really, Dram thought. It was more like a something than a someone.

The demon who had appeared at the same time as Farnus came into the meeting area. Dram would have ventured to call it female, though he wasn't sure such things mattered to these creatures. It seemed to have a feminine body. But its face and chest were the least of his concerns.

She had wicked claws on her hands, and her hoofed feet were covered in metal similar to Farnus' plate armor.

"What is the mortal doing here?" she asked as she placed a pointed claw on the map.

"The mortal is key in this, and it will be not be discussed, Graxxin," Farnus replied, finally looking up from the parchment at the demon named Graxxin.

Dram looked from the man he believed to be his brother, or at least mostly his brother, to the demon with horns and wicked claws. The two stared at one another for a time, before Graxxin shrugged her shoulders and crossed her arms.

"Makes little difference to me."

"Good," Farnus said. "I trust the warriors you've assembled will meet us at Prommus?"

"What ones survive will," Graxxin answered. "There are surprisingly few who have been able to live past the first few days."

Farnus shook his head.

"You do not ease them into your service," he said.

Graxxin licked her lips.

"And you would never desire me to, Rayg."

That name again. Dram had heard that name. The demon had spoken it when he had shown himself for the first time. What did that name have to do with Farnus?

"We have a small window of opportunity to work with," the man Dram knew as Farnus said, pointing at the table. Dram saw that it was a map and that careful drawings had been made around Prommus. "Isol is on the run, from what our sources have told us. Prommus is pursuing them, leaving their castle in a weakened state we can take advantage of. Once we've established ourselves there, it'll be easy to make our claim on the first continent of Gilia."

Dram had been looking down at the map where Farnus was pointing, but now his eyes shot back up to meet his brother's. They had a shine of purple to them that began to glow brighter with each passing moment.

"The first continent?" Dram asked, unsure of what Farnus meant. "Surely you don't mean..."

A wicked smile crossed the man's face. It was then that Dram knew he had not misheard him. His intentions were clear.

"I told you this would be a day to be remembered," Farnus said, spreading his hands wide over the table. "This is the day we begin our conquest of not just Ladis, but all of Gilia."

Dram looked down to get a better look at the papers laid out on the table. Taking the last few steps, he could see that it was not only Ladis drawn on the map but Irradan, Ruyn, Redact and even Galin.

Every continent on Gilia, with crosses, circles, and arrows drawn over them. An elaborate plan was unfolding before him. Dram could see that many markings had been removed from Ruyn and then redrawn.

"What are you planning, Farnus?" Dram asked, looking down at the map.

"To test your strength," he replied.

Dram looked up quickly. He was just in time to see Farnus grab the sword from behind his back and bring it flying over the table in a wide sweeping arc. Reacting instinctively, Dram threw up both of his hands, and a burst of blue light came up in front of him, stopping the sword just inches from his face.

Farnus smiled.

"Good," he said. "Now, give me more!"

He pulled back his sword and swung again. This time, Dram jumped back towards the tent entrance. He heard the crash of the table from behind him and the laughter of Farnus. It filled his ears, but he tried to remain focused.

The first bit of magic had been a reaction. Turning to look back at the damage Farnus had done, Dram let the power he had come to learn flow through him freely. If his brother wanted a fight, he would give him one.

Blue light began to fill his vision as he felt the rimstones in his bracers grow hot. He had always worn his magical rocks there, on his forearms and covered in cloth. They were close and yet concealed. He had always felt prepared for any attack, no matter where it came from.

The girl in Juttis had been a surprise. Just like his half-brother's assault.

But he was no weakling.

His hands grew hot as swirls of magic flowed through him. He knew Farnus was testing his strength. He would not hold back.

Jumping backward, he allowed the two blasts of energy to escape his hands. The tent crackled with magic and fire. Dram could no longer see Graxxin. Where she had gone bothered him, but not as much as the direct threat of Farnus. The sword came slicing towards him again from overhead. He opened his palms and let another blast of energy repel the sword.

"Ha!" he heard Farnus yell. "Is that all you've got, brother?"

Dram felt hot with growing fury. He had waited years for his rise to power. The ability to see it to its fruition was close at hand. He would be king of Prommus and rule over Ladis. There would be no reason to hold back.

The blade swung again, and Dram did not bat it away with the force of his magic. He grabbed it. Dust and smoke swirled around him, and Farnus came into full view. A whirlwind of power was emanating from the pair.

An expression of hunger lit up Farnus' face. Dram met it with a look of fury.

"You've not seen all that I am capable of, brother!" he shouted.

Twisting the blade with an magical blast from his hands, Dram threw his elbow at Farnus' face. A surge of blue came from behind his blow. The force of his energy took him forward. In a flash, Dram found that his elbow slid through the air. Farnus had dodged the blast and was rolling away from Dram, even as he felt his balance lost in the momentum.

He wasn't about to let that stop him, however.

Turning on the spot, Dram sent another blast of magic behind him. The force propelled him forward and gave him back his balance. With the force behind him, Dram broke into a run, trying to catch Farnus, who had exited the tent.

As soon as he was past the flap, he saw his brother, sword at his side and hand outstretched. The same wicked smile was on his face. Dram could feel the energy in the air as it gathered right in front of Farnus. He ignited his own magic, drawing out everything the stones in his bracers could offer him.

For years he had practiced in secret. Only a select few knew of his heretical sorcery and the devotion he gave to the craft. He knew how rimstone drained a person. How the magic could bring him to the point of starvation and unconsciousness. He knew his limits and what he had to do to control the magic flowing through him.

The blade flew through the air. Reacting more than anything, Dram threw his forearms out in front of him and formed a magical shield. The force of the blade still hit him hard enough to push him backwards a few paces. Hovering in midair, the blade continued its unrelenting approach.

Dram heard a laugh coming from in front of him. Farnus stood with his hand outstretched, a look of triumph on his face. Dram could feel the sword continuing to try to force itself through his shield of magic.

He refused to allow it to happen. The rimstones in his bracers glowed fiercely as blue magic continued to flow from him. The shield out in front of him took shape into a large, man-sized shield of Juttis. Dram could feel sweat beginning to pour down his brow. It was taking too much energy to maintain the shield.

Farnus' hand shook with what Dram hoped was the same amount of effort it was taking him to keep the blade at bay.

"You're strong, half-brother!" he said through gritted teeth. "The deity is pleased!"

Dropping to the ground and sinking several hands into the dirt, the sword disappeared from view. He wanted so bad to fall to his knees, but Dram summoned up every bit of strength he had left to continue to stand in place.

"D...deity?" Dram asked, steadying his breath with great effort.

Farnus took deep breaths as well. That brought Dram a bit of comfort.

"There is at work something much greater than the both of us," he said. "Something that goes back to the very foundations of the Theocracy and beyond. I have seen visions of Decolos himself."

Dram tilted his head. Did he hear Farnus correctly? Had something indeed been revealed to him that was over a thousand years old? The Theocracy was the seat of humanity on Gilia. It was where all men had sailed from and settled the other continents. It was the throne of old. The very place where living memory ended.

Had his brother really seen the ancient god of the Theocracy?

He looked into the eyes that shone purple and hoped his confusion did not betray him. Farnus smirked at him in response to his stare.

"I shall inform you what I know. But only if it pleases Rayg. All must be done to please him. I am his servant, a vessel of the living god of demons."

27: Scouts

Ragged, weary, and exhausted, the Isolian army came to a halt just beyond the rocky cliffs of the Theocracy, not far from Tremus, the easternmost city in the empire. But certainly not near enough to it to cause alarm.

Octus set down his pack as the rest of the soldiers around him groaned with the effort of carrying their supplies a week's journey east of Isol. He wasn't sure why they had to march so far to the east. The supply ships should have been able to gather them right at the mouth of the Rift.

Something must have delayed them.

Serving at the beck and call of Her Holiness should have given him all the information he needed, but even during times like these, when he was just a few short paces away from her, he still didn't know all of the information that was kept in that wooden palanquin.

The reality was that the army of Isol was tired. No man who was a part of the invading force was feeling ready to fight again. They had conquered city after city when they had first arrived, giving them so much momentum. Now that the demons had intervened in the battles, they were weary.

Octus could see it in the faces of the soldiers and speakers who surrounded him. They were strong, but they were tired.

"Slave," said a voice from Octus' right. Being the only man with no shirt or shoes within calling distance, Octus knew he was the one being called.

Still, he chose to pretend, just for a minute, that he did not hear the command.

The voice rang out much louder in his ear as a tall, muscular woman came over and shouted at him again.

"Slave! Pick up this pack! You're coming with me!"

The short-haired woman barely looked him in the eye when she gave the command. That was what bothered Octus the most about this whole situation. Granted, he was a servant of the enemy and separated from the one girl he had sworn to his brother he would protect if needed, but the fact that no one ever looked him in the eye grated him.

He was a servant, yes, but he was still human.

Getting his bag on his back was no small feat. Having felt the relief of taking it off, he had relished the possibility of respite. It was not to be. The back of the female soldier was already disappearing into the crowd when Octus began to walk in her direction. He was a servant to Yada, but he was also a servant to any who was in her army.

He didn't know what would face him as he obeyed the orders of Captain Oberon.

"Get these two set up with their tent!" she yelled, pointing a finger at two men whom Octus had seen before. They were the same ones who had ventured into Yada's tent when there had been a group of thieves who stole a few jewels and some weapons.

Yada had been terribly furious with them. Octus had seen her personally put one to death.

Now, these two soldiers needed help with their tent. Octus couldn't find the strength to be belligerent at the moment, so he decided he may as well help with the shelter and then return to find his own lodging for the night.

The evening sky was turning from bright orange to a pale purple. Night time was coming.

A stack of sticks and rope hit Octus in the chest. He caught the pile and furrowed his brow at the soldier who had thrown it. He could be no more than seventeen or eighteen.

"Who are you?" Octus asked as he threw the fabric and poles on the ground. He was familiar with how they set up their tents. Having been a part of her holiness' personal guard, however, he had not yet been set this particular task.

"Cas and Rallet," the young man said. His friend next to him was older. Not quite Octus' age, but certainly no new recruit.

The trio began to set up the tent as the rest of the army from Isol did the same. The suns were starting to set past the horizon, giving them just enough light to see by. Fires would go up soon, and the generals from the army would meet with Yada to form a plan.

Octus wanted to be a part of that. He knew that in the chaos of the retreat, he could have gotten lost or pretended to be dead and fled. Something held him back, however. Whether it was a desire to bring the killing blow to her holiness or, though he hated to think it, the growing fear that Olma had not survived the siege that had separated them, he didn't know.

The tent went up without much hassle. The other two soldiers didn't say another word to him during the process. Octus had expected that. Everyone felt tired. Besides, in a war, what was the need for introductions?

The people he was meeting might well be dead tomorrow.

Driving the last stake into the ground and tying a rope around it to secure the tent, Octus prepared to leave and report back to Yada's palanquin. He stood up to bid farewell to the two soldiers but found them staring at a fixed spot. Neither of them was moving.

"It's a little too early for ghosts," Octus said, turning his head to try to see what they were looking at. He found himself in awe as well. The familiar flash of white hair ran past a tent and up towards where the generals were gathering.

"Well, I'll be," Octus said under his breath. He had seen that flash of hair before. No one he had ever met had such starkly white hair and could sprint like that.

The two soldiers had grabbed their spears and were already heading in that direction before Octus could make a move. He remembered that they knew her as well as he did.

"Careful boys," he said as he began walking with them. "This is not a woman you want to cross idly."

Soldiers instinct made Octus reach for a knife that he didn't have. He knew he was a slave, but in the war, he certainly wished they would give him something to defend himself when needed. Oh well. He had gone into other situations weaponless before. This would just be another time for him to improvise. The three of them crept through the tents, not wanting to make too much noise, lest they scare her away. Octus new that she had traveled with a group before. This time he only saw her. That gave him enough pause to realize they should be looking for more than one.

"Rallet," he said looking at the younger boy. "You've seen her before. You know she doesn't work alone. Keep an eye out."

The words were hardly out of his mouth when a dagger soared past his nose and landed squarely in the neck of the older soldier. A gargled gasp escaped his lips before he fell to the ground, dead.

"Cas!" the younger called, going to his friend.

Octus took the spear out of the dying man's hand and turned to face the direction the knife had come from. Wearing a dark cloak, one of the white-haired woman's companions came flying at them a sword in one hand, and an ax in the other. Octus made a quick stab with his spear, narrowly missing the elf's head. She was quick.

A shout and a trumpet called rang up from the tent of Yada. The elf did not bat an eye before she dodged another stab from Octus, slicing down on his spear with her blade. The weapon lodged itself into the wood of his spear shaft and, before he could respond, she ripped it from his hands. Then, she turned and fled away.

Octus saw a blast of magic scatter dirt and rock from a short distance away. A cry of anger let him know that Yada had missed.

If he had thought there was going to be any rest tonight, he knew now he was wrong.

***

Yada and her generals were furious. Whatever scouts had been placed in the area where the two assassins had infiltrated the camp were executed publicly. The entire army was forced to watch. Octus was still not used to the amount of magic the old woman could produce from the stones woven into her hair.

Everyone near Yada's tent was placed on guard duty. He had been instructed not to sleep upon pain of death. He also knew everyone was in a tense enough mood to see those orders carried out.

Whenever he had seen Her Holiness, she had been caressing a green jewel that she had not let out of her sight. It hung it on a leather band around her neck and was held by a crude metal claw. He knew the group that had invaded her campsite before had tried to steal it. He just didn't know why.

"Speakers and their rocks," he said under his breath as he patrolled the south side of the royal palanquin. Half of the army had been instructed to patrol while the other half slept. Yada was now braiding her generals from inside her wooden throne.

Octus could hear most every word.

"How dare you allow them to get so close to me!" she was yelling.

With a small bit of satisfaction, Octus imagined the worried looks on her generals' faces.

"Forgive us, your holiness," Octus heard one of the generals begging. "Our forces are far too spread out. The demons who attacked us were too strong, and our army is scattered over the beaches of the Theocracy. Perhaps if we were able to regroup, we would be able to protect you better and returned to our domination of our homeland."

Octus heard a very satisfying slap. The general managed to contain his grunt of pain. Yada may be old, but Octus knew it was foolish to question her strength when she was angry.

"Should I perform even the simplest of tasks for you!?" Yada yelled. "Why have you been unable to gather your own soldiers from the four corners of the Theocracy? Is that not the job that I had given you!?"

As much as Octus hated Yada, he could not fault her. She was right.

From his own days of leading men, he knew whose responsibility it was to keep track of them. Her generals were nervous in her presence, but they were potentially terrified of the demons they had encountered. Instead of trying to find the best way to react to the new threat, they had run. Perhaps their campaign had been too easy up to this point. They had taken over cities without much of a fight.

Had they really thought it would be so easy?

Their magical cannons had been most effective against the demons. Last time, Isol had used them with great results. However, during the recent demon attack, they had come upon them too quickly. There wasn't the time they needed to employ their powerful weapons. The armies of Isol were scattered. Octus took that to heart. If they stayed scattered, perhaps the Theocracy would be able to take them out piece by piece. It was much easier to dispatch an army in small groups.

Octus heard Yada muttering under her breath before a cry echoed outside her shelter. He knew too well the words were a speaker's magic spell.

Instinctively, he readied himself for a blast. Small magical bursts of energy had long been the favored weapon of the speakers he had fought before.

Instead of a blast of magic, however, Octus saw a giant pillar of light erupt from Yada's palanquin and pierce the dark night sky. A blue column of flame that never flickered reached up to the stars. It pulsed brightly every few moments, sending a shimmering circle of light that went up alongside it. Octus looked around and knew that no other light from a city or campfire could extinguish such a light. He heard Yada cackle with glee inside.

"If you say my armies are scattered and I need to bring them to me, then let this beacon bring them to me."

For a moment there was only stunned silence from the generals Yada had assembled. Octs wondered if they could see the entirety of the light from within her throne. Perhaps Yada had disintegrated its roof with her magic.

Then Octus heard the voice of Captain Oberon speak out. He had never known her to be timid or shy. He wondered if she understood the full implications of questioning a divine plan of Yada's.

"Your holiness," she said. Octus could see her bowing in his mind's eye. "All of your armies will indeed see this beacon and know that it is you who is calling them."

There was a pause. Octus wondered if Oberon was going to say the thing he was thinking. She might lose her tongue for it if she did.

"Your enemies," she said, her voice faltering ever so slightly. "Will see this beacon as well. They will come for us. Perhaps even the demons will follow it."

To Octus' surprise, he did not hear another slap, nor a blast of magic ending the faithful captain's life. Instead, he heard another more dangerous laugh than the cackle that had echoed when she had first cast the spell.

It turned his blood cold.

"Let them come," Yada said.

28: Failure

Serinde was cursing herself. She had known better than to allow Silverwolf a moment's peace. Before she could stop her, the assassin had abandoned their camp outside a small rock formation and ventured off into the Isolian ranks.

They had discussed the possibility of sneaking in to steal the amulet. No plan they had been able to come up with seemed to work better than another. Perhaps it was Silverwolf's desire to close herself off to Serinde that had stalled them. Ever since they had fled the city of Prommus after watching her father killed by the priest who had brought them into this forsaken continent, Silverwolf had hardly spoken a word.

Serinde wasn't sure which she liked better. A sarcastic, snarky assassin, or a killer who only communicated with her eyes and deadly silence.

At the moment, she preferred her to be dead, but she also knew she could not survive on her own.

They ran as fast as their feet could carry them. Several guards had given them chase, but a few quick maneuvers with Holve's spear and Ealrin's oddly shaped sword had dispatched them.

Whether or not more were coming was yet to be seen. Neither female had looked back to check, and both of them could hear well enough to tell if a hunting party had come after them.

Not an hour had gone by after Silverwolf's failed attempt to steal the amulet when a giant blue light appeared in the sky behind them. It came from the center of the Isolian camp and lit up the entire area around it. Serinde could see small shadows of men and their tents. The light of this beacon rivaled the moons.

"Well the old hag is certainly off her throne now," Silverwolf said. The words took Serinde by surprise. She hadn't heard Silverwolf's voice in a full week.

"What's the purpose of that?" she asked, pointing at the light, though she knew it was quite evident to the assassin.

"Beats me," Silverwolf replied. "But I can tell you every army on Ladis is going to be able to see it. And most of them will head straight for it."

"Do you think Ealrin and the others will see it too?" Serinde asked. She wanted to get back with the group they had departed from. Even though they had plans to meet them at the fishing port just to the east, she hoped not to have to take that journey with only Silverwolf at her side.

Silverwolf shrugged her shoulders.

Serinde nodded. That was probably the end of the assassin's words for the day. Or the week, more likely.

She was wrong.

"Do you think about your sister much?"

Serinde was not only caught off guard by the question Silverwolf asked, but she was also struck with the sincerity she heard in her voice.

Of course she thought about her sister. She thought about her every single day. How she had been unable to save her. How she had led her out into a battle she did not want to fight. How Erilas had only come because she wanted to protect her sister.

"Yes," was all Serinde could manage to say in answer. She found that her throat was constricted and that tears were welling in her eyes.

The truth of the matter was that the death of her sister haunted her. The only time she had felt any type of joy or connection with someone else since coming on this trip was with the girl, Olma. Serenity didn't know why, but she felt something for the little human. She worried about her. She had a terrible feeling that something awful was going to happen to her.

Serinde shook herself. She would not fail Olma. There would not be another named so tied to her in death.

And then a question formed in her mind. Silverwolf had been so sincere when she had voiced her own. She hoped she could communicate the same in her query.

"Your father," she began tentatively. "Do you imagine you'll think about him?"

The question was odd. Silverwolf had threatened her father. She told him she planned to end his life. Serinde was almost sure that the assassin would have. What was one more dead man to her?

And yet Silverwolf had not acted as quickly as her blade could fly. Serinde held her breath, not thinking that she would receive an answer.

"I've thought about that man every single day since I was sold into slavery," Silverwolf replied.

Serinde blinked. She looked over at the assassin and saw a line of tears running down her cheeks.

"I wanted answers," she said. Her teeth were clenched, and her fists were balled so tightly Serinde saw her knuckles turn white.

They looked out from the same outcropping they had camped behind earlier that day. The same outcropping Serinde had chased her from. The Isolian camp was in chaos. A bright shining blue beacon of light shot up from the middle of it, illuminating the countryside. If there were any allies of Isol or enemies of them, they would all head for that one point.

"Instead of answers," Silverwolf said, her eyes reflecting the brilliant blue light ahead of them. "I have more questions."

Serinde let the chill of the night air wash over her as she considered the words of a fearless, doubtful assassin.

29: Priestly Ambitions

"What new unholy tricks have the heretics come up with now?" Jerius asked as he peered over the top of his tent.

The army of the Theocracy had marched out of Prommus victorious. Jerius knew that they had not won the battle based on the strength of their men, but rather on the wisdom of Decolos.

It had been his doing. He had been courageous enough to summon a demon to fight back the speakers. That demon had wreaked havoc on their enemies. Because of this, he was a hero. And he should be treated as such.

Now that the high priest was dead, Jerius was the natural successor. Having no other priests within the city, he had effectively become the high priest without vote or contention. No Voice could oppose him and no priest was near enough in such a time of crisis to run against him. The only thing that stood in the way of him gaining ultimate authority was the king.

King Gravus was a man who could now celebrate the victory of his nation, and question the motives of this new priest. Jerius knew the king would doubt at least some parts of the story that had been told to him. How his brother had been killed by an assassin who fled from his best guards down what was supposed to be the unscalable walls of the temple.

How even though they had chased them through the mountains, the king's own guards had come up with no tracks or any trace of people at all.

There were witnesses. Guards who swore they had seen the priest die at the hands of a white-haired woman. That last piece was the greatest gift to Jerius. As much as he hated them, the band he had arrested on that island had become infamous in the theocracy. How much he found himself regretting that he had brought them here. A small part of that was knowing that he owed his current status to that unfortunate encounter.

Having obtained something along the lines of a folklore status, they were both an easy target and a convenient alibi.

Still, some questions were yet to be answered.

The Theocracy had come after the armies of Isol for revenge. What they saw now on the shores of the east was a reason for concern.

"Do you see this, my priest?" Luca said as she appeared next to Jerius.

"Inform the king," Jerius commanded.

Luca saluted and began to walk in the direction of the king's tent. Jerius called her back, looking over at a captain who was also observing the phenomena.

"Inform the king of this," Jerius commanded the man in a louder, more domineering voice than he had used with Luca.

For a moment, it seemed as if the captain might question the authority Jerius had.

He looked down at the robe Jerius was wearing. The skull with a double line on its forehead, sewn in gold thread told him who he was speaking to:

The High Priest of the Theocracy.

Bowing his head, the captain ran off. Jerius thought he saw a small glance of contempt, but no matter. He sniffed and found that he had already become accustomed to this new power.

This had been the thing he had worked for his entire life. Respect. Honor. Authority. But most importantly, power.

He allowed a smile to cross his lips. As he heard the king returning with his guards at his side, however, he adjusted his expression to one of somber concern.

"My Lord," he said inclining his head. "The heretics call us."

Jerius watched closely as he observed the face of the king. He was as hard as ever, if not even more so at the news of the passing of his brother.

"What is this?"

"Your majesty," the insignificant captain said. "Perhaps it's a trap, something the heretics are hoping will draw us in? Perhaps we should send scouts to see what lies ahead?"

Another captain butted into the conversation.

"Scouts are already ahead and reporting, my king," he said rather indignantly. "The army of heretics has continued flying east. We'll trap them between Prommus and Tremus. They have nowhere else to go."

The king continued to watch the beacon, examining it.

Jerius thought to stoke the controversy.

"Unless it is a sign calling their ships to them," he said.

More than one pair of eyes turned to him. Jerius allowed himself to feel a moment of pride. It was short lived. He saw that the king remained steadfastly staring forward.

Having spent so much time in the capital, Jerius knew this tactic. The king was not listening to him. Doing so would make him appear weak. The king would only listen to his military officers and advisers, not the head of the church.

Jerius has learned this tactic well and would use it against King Gravus.

"May the king do what he thinks is best," he said making another bow in Gravus' direction. "The church had reported to me that several Isolian ships were seen departing from the coasts of their island. I suppose it may be to resupply the main lines with food and soldiers. But it may also be to resupply them with men. Suppose that beacon is for them?"

His words had not been mainly for the king to hear. He wanted the captains to know of this possibility. All he needed to do was to sow doubt in their eyes. As one who had led the faithful for most of his life, he knew the power of doubt. Used correctly, it could lead to fear. And those who were afraid would do whatever they were told would bring them peace.

"Send our scouts down through the beaches," the king commanded. Two captains saluted and moved away quickly.

The king was still looking at the beacon of light.

"Whether they are calling their ships to them or taunting us towards them,' the king said. "I will know the truth before we move."

Jerius bowed to the king along with the remaining captains and walked off.

"What does it really mean?" Luca asked Jerius.

He looked over his shoulder at her, sniffing his long nose.

"It means that the church will reign over the Theocracy sooner rather than later," he said. "You are dismissed."

Waving his hand at her, Jerius retired to his tent where he had commanded a small desk be placed. He sat down with a sigh and opened the book of Decolos.

There was still much more he needed to learn. If the next demon he planned to summon was going to do what he desired, he needed to know more.

And he was confident he had sown just enough doubt to accomplish the task.

30: Capital City

Prince Dram could see the capital city on the horizon. They had marched for days, and now they were finally within sight of the grand capital. They had come upon no scouts for armies. That made Dram feel at ease and gave him pause.

On the one hand, it meant that their army could proceed forward without any difficulties or obstacles. The weather was becoming colder, but that did not seem to bother Farnus in the least. They continued to march east until they were right within sight of the capital. But knowing that the land was still at war made prince grandma feel like they should have run into someone along the way. But, for all he could tell, the western part of the empire was quiet.

Farnus had not yet made mention of their fight since it had happened. In fact, he seemed all too pleased with Dram. Farnus had not summoned him to his tent again. He appeared not to mind to allow Dram whatever freedoms he desired, be it inspecting his troops, observing the demons who walked beside them, or riding up ahead of their forces. He moved about the army without impediment. Perhaps prince Farnus really did trust him now.

He knew his magical skill was still needing to be developed. But whatever it was, he knew that Rayg still had the upper hand. There would come a time when they would fight again. Dram knew this. So he studied and practiced as they marched.

That was another benefit of the change that had occurred. Now that Juttis was free of the Theocracies rule, Dram did not have to hide in the shadows. Instead, he walked along and didn't care who saw his magic. The cloth he had always worn he kept wrapped around himself, however. For years it had been his secret. Now it was his badge of honor.

A trumpet sounded and the army came to a halt. Dram pulled his horse to a stop and looked in several directions for Farnus. Surely he would be close by.

As the thought crossed his mind, the prince rode by on his horse, his metal plates still surrounding his body and his enormous sword slung over his back. How both sword and armor did not entirely way down Farnus' horse was beyond Dram. He knew there was other magic at work here.

"It's time to claim the throne brother," Farnus said as he looked out towards the city. "Father has ruled weakly as of late, and it's time for him to be replaced."

Dram was all too willing to see his father replaced. He had lived in the shadows for so long that he desired nothing more than to come into the light and rule more than a forgotten kingdom of the north. What Dram had never considered, however, was that his rise to power would involve his half-brother.

"You are most familiar with the city and its defense," Dram said to Farnus. He had never been allowed to visit promise. "What obstacles stand in our path?"

Farnus only laughed at this statement.

"None that can hinder us," he said. He looked over at Dram with a gleam of purple in his eye. "Do you see how the walls have already suffered greatly?"

Dram looked out and saw that the shining walls of Prommus he had always envisioned were not in the greatest repair. They were hundreds of years old, this he knew. But what he saw in front of him seemed to be damage from a terrible siege.

Was the city already taken?

No, he could still see the flag of the theocracy flying from the towers that lined the wall.

Perhaps the city had survived the siege from Isol, but just barely.

"The way has been made for us," Farnus said. "All we must do now is show the survivors what we are capable of."

Now it made sense why Farnus had allowed him to rest and recover. There was work to be done.

"I know you have power beyond what you have shown me," Farnus said. "Reveal to me what you are truly capable of."

Farnus indicated the far-off city of Prommus. It was still a day's march away at least. They would need to set up ranks and determine the best possible solution to invade the grand city. In order to conquer it with just one of the great empire's nation, it would take strategy and determination.

Unless Farnus had a different idea.

Dram felt magic coursing through him. He channeled it into his hands as he let go of the reins of his horses and stared at the city gates.

His horse reared as magical energy flowed all around him. As the beast came down to the ground Dram let loose all the power he had stored within him at the center of the gates of Prommus. The blast flew straight and true. A solid blue line of energy soared through the air. When it found its target, an explosion of light assaulted their eyes before they heard the cracking of stone echoing around them.

A cheer rose up from the ranks as Dram breathed deeply, wondering if he had spent too much energy. He could feel sweat beading on his forehead. His muscles ached, but he was ready for more. He looked over at Farnus.

The man only laughed.

"Well done," he said with a look of appraisal. "Now watch me."

In one smooth motion, Farnus began to float off of his horse as waves upon waves of magical energy filled the air around them. Dram could feel the skin under his wrappings tingle as waves of energy overcame him. His horse reared again and threatened to run off with or without him.

Dram did his best to stay the beast. As he did so, he looked up at his half-brother who had his arms stretched out as if inviting the waves of energy to come to him. Five balls of light appeared and encircled him. They grew so bright that Dram struggled to look at the point Farnus now occupied in the air.

And then, with a sudden jerk of his arms, the five magical bolts sped towards the city of Prommus and, as Dram's had done, assaulted the walls of the city. But the amount of his destruction that they caused made his efforts look feeble by comparison.

Another cheer rose up from the ranks of Juttis as Farnus came down to the ground and touched his foot to the earth. His horse had stayed still and obedient the entire time he had worked his magic.

When he looked back at Dram, it was plain that he had not even exerted his full strength. He wasn't even breathing heavily.

"In the morning," Farnus said, looking out over the plains. "We take the city."

31: Snart and the Underlings

Snart thought the most annoying thing about the Webbed Ones they had come upon was their fear of the light.

He would have led them out of the caves and onto the plains past Prommus a few days ago, had they not been so irritated by the suns.

Though the underground cave city was lit up several rimstones, each of the new lizards claimed that the burning sky lights were like a fire to their skin. Because of this, they had only gradually made their way into more and more brightly lit portions of the cavern.

It hadn't taken that long to get up to the ground above their cavernous dwellings. Snart was surprised to find that these lizards had lived so close to the surface without ever venturing out.

"Stupid," he hissed under his breath.

"Saying what?" he heard behind him.

Snart had thought he was by himself. The only good thing that had come out of the fear these Webbed Ones had was moments where he did not have to be in their presence. Snart was standing in the brightest area of the cave he could find. The mouth of the tunnel was just a few paces away from him.

He looked back to see that the monstrosity known as Vallin was making his way towards him. The great lizard creature still bore the mark of the scar Snart had given him. The leader of the Veiled Ones did not take kindly to being threatened to be eaten. He had, at that moment, decided that not getting eaten was more important than preserving a relationship with the leader of the Webbed Ones.

He had blasted Vallin with a burst of his magic. The effect was immediate. Vallin had stopped threatening to eat their party, perhaps wrongly assuming that all of their lizards were as skilled with rimstone as Snart was. As far as Snart knew, he was the only Veiled One to wield magic in such a way. Still, it had been enough to have the

Webbed Ones concede to follow him. And that was all he really cared about.

Snart could think of all manner of curses he could wish upon the great beast who waddled up beside him, but for now, he simply nodded his head towards the opening.

"Smell man flessssh," he said. This was not altogether a lie. As soon as they had come to this area, Snart had definitely tasted the presence of men. He had sent several scouts out ahead to investigate. They had come back to report that the armies of the island and the mainland had indeed passed this way only a few days ago.

For one who had never smelled a man before, Snart hoped Vallin would not be able to distinguish how far away they were.

The large creature took in several deep breaths. His eyes were closed in concentration. Snart impatiently tapped his spear on the rock he was standing on.

"Eating man," Valon said softly licking his enormous lips a tongue equally as large. "Tasting warm?"

"Yessss," Snart replied. Perhaps if Vallin could be persuaded about how delicious a fresh man could taste, they could speed up this agonizing process of gaining only a few yards a day.

"They taste best warm, warm. Not good cold. Makes you strong, strong."

Snart beat his chest for good measure. It was true. Whenever his kind could feast on the flesh of men, they did grow stronger. Whatever ancient law or magic was at work within that, Snart didn't care. All he wanted was to be strong.

"Webbed Ones become strong, strong too," he said. "Vallin convinces his lizardssss. It's time, time. We must march to eat, eat."

Vallin opened his eyes and narrowed them. Snart could tell the lizard beast was not as convinced as he was about the taste of men.

That would change.

"Sending a few for you," Valon said after a considerable time had passed.

Snart picked up his head a little at this prospect. It was something.

"Yesssss," he said thankfully. "Send them to taste man, man. Tell you about the tassssste."

Vallin nodded his massive figure.

"If tasting good," he said. "The rest of us will be coming. "

"Good," Snart said, taking the few paces required to get to the mouth of the cave. "Send your best, best lizardssss.

Before Vallin could respond, Snart was out of the mouth of the cave. He had been underground too long. He wanted to feel the suns.

"Stupid," he muttered under his breath.

"Saying what what?"

Snart ignored the question and threw his spear straight at the heart of a nearby bird. An explosion of feathers told him he had hit true. It wasn't the flesh of men, he thought as he bit into the fowl. But it was warm.

32: Throne of Their Fathers

Prince Dram looked at the gates of Prommus that lay in ruins before him. They had marched up to the wall of the capital city without so much as an arrow being flung in their direction. Farnus had no good reason to know why this had been the case. There were soldiers on the walls. They did not fire on them. Perhaps it was because of the banner of Juttis they had flying in front of them.

Perhaps it was because of the brutal fight they had experienced when Isol had attacked them. During their day of marching, Dram had seen so much devastation that looked like it was caused by magic. The walls of Prommus were in even worse condition than he had first realized. Large chunks of it were blown completely away.

It was the condition of the plains in front of the city that had confused him. It looked like magical destruction had happened there as well, but that could not have of been the case. The Theocracy had no way of dealing a magical blow to the Island nation.

Had there been a rebellion in the ranks of the speakers of Isol?

It was not until they had reached the gates of the city that Dram would get his answers.

A captain rode out to meet them with a few of his guard. Dram couldn't tell if the look on the captain's face was one of relief or worry. It was likely to be both.

"We thought the blasted heretics had returned," he said, looking at Prince Farnus and the others who were around him. His gaze lingered on Dram's cloaked visage for a just a fraction longer than the others. "Those two blasts yesterday were very much like the cannons they used on us during the siege."

The captain inclined his head from on top of his horse.

"Prince Farnus," he said indicating the white-haired man. "You are certainly a sight for the eyes. And this must be Prince Dram of

Juttis? I do not believe I have ever laid eyes on you, my lord, but I will admit another prince of the Theocracy is welcome here."

Dram very much doubted that would be the case for long.

The captain swallowed hard as he looked back and forth between Dram and Farnus. He had apparently run out of things to say. Dram noticed that they were not being offered to come into the city of Prommus. Were they, perhaps, being stopped?

"Is something wrong?" Farnus asked.

Dram could feel the magic coursing through the air. He wondered if the captain could tell that something has shifted too, because he begin to look uncomfortable in the saddle of his horse.

"My..." the captain standard. "Forgive me, Prince Farnus. It is strange to see you. We spent a full week mourning your death. There had been many reports that you had died in a siege fighting the heretics."

Dram wondered what else have been reported.

This was not the relieved face of a captain seeing a prince returned from the dead. This was a man who was trying to stay calm in what he understood to be a dangerous situation.

"Then by all means, invite us in for a feast," Farnus said. He motioned to the army that stood behind he and Dram.

"My men are hungry. They could use a good night's rest before we continue onward."

The captain cleared his throat.

A shadowy moving above Dram showed him that the city of Prommus was not as unguarded in the streets as he had thought.

A cloak shifted overhead to his left and on his right, dust moved as if someone had just changed where they were standing. Farnus was looking up as well.

The prince brought his attention down to the captain and clicked his tongue.

"Tut-tut, Captain," he said, sounding more dangerous with every syllable. "Is this a way to welcome a prince?"

Farnus raised his hand into the air and shot several small bursts of magic out from his outstretched fingers. Four spread out to the top of the wall and exploded there. Shouts of pain that were quickly cut off echoed down to them.

Before the captain could even draw his blade, a magical burst ended his life and knocked his dead body off his horse.

The guards who had accompanied him on foot put their hands on their blades, but Farnus directed his palm at them.

"Bow before me," he said, magical energy filling the air. "Or die before me."

***

The city of Prommus had not put up much of a fight after their entrance. Word of the return of Prince Farnus was met with jubilation by some, but most of the city greeted their return with fear. Word of his aligning himself with the heretics spread quickly. It was understood that the White Lion had returned. It was also known that he had become that which the Theocracy had hated.

A Speaker.

Dram knew it to be much more complicated than that, but, the men who remained in Prommus needed a little more explanation. The men who were left in the city, as well as their wives and children, bowed before Farnus as their prince. Dram knew that soon they would bow before him as their king.

Dram walked into the throne room of the King with Farnus out in front of him. The two had walked right past the guards of the city. Not a single man dared defy them. News of Farnus' new power and the man covered in wrappings who was a prince from the north spread quickly.

Farnus had always been the favorite prince. Whereas he had once been treated with reverence and respect, those feelings were now replaced with fear and terror. With just a few guards behind them, the two men climbed the tall dais of the throne room up to the very top, where the throne of the king sat under the watchful gaze of previous kings and the gods of the theocracy.

Dram stopped to look down at where he guessed his father had sat for decades. He had never seen the throne room before and the place gave him both chills and an elated sense of purpose. This was the throne from which he ought to rule.

Farnus spent much less time taking in the moment. He sat on the throne and looked well at ease.

"This is the seat from which I will rule," he said, looking at Dram.

There was no 'we' mentioned at all this time. Dram had come to expect that. He knew that only one could sit upon the throne. For a thousand years the Theocracy had been ruled by a High Priest, the Voice and the King.

But everyone knew who the power truly belonged to.

At least, that's what Dram always believed. What could the church do but instill fear of the afterlife in its adherents? What could the Voice do without the blessing of the king? It was from the throne that a man could rule one of the mightiest nations on Gilia.

And Farnus had placed himself on it without a second thought.

"The people will recognize my rule," Farnus said. "They will turn from my father as soon as he is defeated in battle by his own son."

"You fear no words of rebellion or dissension?" Dram asked. The words left his mouth before he had fully thought them over.

Farnus snapped his fingers and a magical bolt of lightning sailed from his hand to the nearest idol of the god of war. It disintegrated into powder as soon as the bolt hit it. Dram did his best not to flinch, knowing full well that the bolt could have been intended for his own head.

"I think the people should fear me before they do any rebelling," Farnus said with a smirk. "For I am not only king of the Theocracy. Rayg has granted me a great power and responsibility within the ranks of the demons. He has named me the king of those who dance in purple flames."

Dram looked at the statue of the god of war whose head was now a pile of rubble and dust on the ground. Who could possibly be the king of the demons?

"Farnus..." he began to say. He was cut off by the entrance of a handful of guards.

"My Lord Farnus," he said, bowing as he came inside. "There's something you need to see out here."

Farnus took his time standing from the throne. It seemed that he loathed leaving the seat of power to inspect some nuisance. Dram allowed him to walk down first and followed in his footsteps.

The guards led them to the nearest balcony that overlooked the city.

"There My Lord and Prince," the guard said, pointing east. It was quite unnecessary.

A giant beam of light pierced the sky. Though it was midday, there was no mistaking the brilliant beacon of light that shot up past the clouds.

"When did this appear?" Farnus asked.

"The guards noticed it this morning," the guard said again. "It's been growing steadily brighter as the day has gone on."

Farnus nodded.

"Then call the captains and the generals," he said. "It seems we are being summoned to war."

33: The Lost

David walked, though his feet bled and the suns had long since set, through the plains of the Theocracy. He had lost all sense of where he was weeks ago. Every traveler unfortunate enough to cross his path had met the same fate.

In his wake, he left a trail of blood and pain.

But he continued to walk.

His lips were caked and dry. A trail of blood ran from his mouth down his chin. Some animal that had wandered too close had become a meal. Whether it was a week ago or a day ago, David could no longer remember. Each day and night was the same. He walked until he fell over from exhaustion. Then he woke feeling a little rested and much more tired. Yet he continued to walk.

The voice of his goddess called him. Graxxin called him to her. She needed him. If he didn't come, his mother would die. Like so many he had killed. She was all he had left. A vision of a past he could hardly recall.

David would fight for the vision of the woman he kept in his mind. He could no longer remember her voice. It was only her screams that he could hear. Whenever he wandered too far in the wrong direction, her screams would echo in his mind until he found his way. Whenever he fell to the ground, too tired to walk another step, her tormented cries would keep him awake until he had crawled enough to satisfy the goddess of blood.

So he walked.

It was this night that was different than others he had encountered.

The trampled ground beneath his feet was no longer dirt, but an ancient road. The stones were smooth, but uneven. He continued on.

Something hard grazed his foot. A metal thing. He didn't stop, but he did look down to see what it was.

The thing appeared to be a helmet or a shield. Something a soldier of the Theocracy would carry. He didn't bend to pick it up to protect his own sunscorched head. It would mean he would hear the screams again.

He hated the screams.

Men must have come this way.

David continued to walk.

After a few hours, or maybe days, he couldn't tell, other shambling feet joined his own. Instead of feeling the need to lash out and destroy these travelers as a sacrifice of blood, the overwhelming need to not look at them at all came over him.

David didn't want to see who belonged to those shambling feet. He didn't want to see. They all walked as he did. It wasn't just one pair of feet, or even four. It was several dozens. Even though he desired to look away, David turned his head, only once, to see who was behind him.

Hollow, sunken-eyed youths followed in his wake. One who could be only a year younger than he was carrying a shovel caked with blood. Another had a sickle in two hands. A girl whose hair was long and matted had arms covered in blood up to her elbows. Long nails had grown from her hands and were the darkest of reds.

Many more came behind them. All wore clothes that were ragged and hung off of them in hunger. David turned his eyes forward again. He felt no pity or fear. He only understood one thing.

They were all marching for the goddess of blood. For Graxxin. They would all do her bidding.

These were his family now.

An army of blood.

34: The Light

Snart felt his body acclimating to the light of the suns. He felt alive again. It had been far too long since he had not had to use his energy to create heat through the stones. Now he could use his mind to think of other pursuits.

Like how he might be rid of the giant Vallin and his great complaining.

"Burning, burning," the lizard said infuriatingly.

Snart wished he had brought the underlings out from the caves in the summer, rather than in this beginnings of winter that appeared to be coming over the land.

Yet the suns still came down on them with warm beams of light. Snart's lizards all appeared in the highest of spirits. They could feel the suns and smell the flesh of men nearby. This was certainly all they needed to survive.

Sun and flesh.

Yet the Webbed Ones moved with a slowness that irked at Snart's being. He wanted nothing more than for the lizards to follow him without complaint and Vallin to burn up under the heat of the suns he complained for days on end about.

"Men close, closssse," he said impatiently. "We could be closssser if Webbed Ones moved fast, fast."

"It's burning," Vallin said again. "Lizards need resting."

Snart hissed. He was sick of resting. He wanted to see the armies of men and to taste their spoils of war. Once they had done so, he was sure the Underlings would give up their desire to stay out of the suns' rays in order to feast.

His mouth was becoming wet just thinking of the desire to eat the flesh of men. Snart would be strong, this he knew. All he needed was to use the desire to eat to help both the lizards he commanded and the underlings to rally to him. To call him leader.

"Very burning."

Snart whipped out his tongue twice in irritation. Hopefully every lizard would deny Vallin his next breath. That was certainly his greatest desire.

"We musssst march on, on," Snart ordered. The men were gathering somewhere. He was sure of it. The tracks of the armies from the south went further and further on than he realized. They would continue on until they reached the cities of the north. If the lizards hated the suns, Snart thought, he would certainly not want to see them get under the cold winds of the north. They would turn around and defect if they didn't taste meat soon.

They had to taste the flesh of men before such a time came.

Snart moved forward again, ignoring Vallin's continued strains of complaints. If only there was a village somewhere within the range of their marching. If only some of the underlings could taste flesh. That would have them moving forward.

And then, he saw it. In the sky over the horizon, growing brighter with each blink. A beacon of light. A bright blue pillar in the sky. Snart could see it, but he could also feel it. There was some type of magic at work. Something very powerful and strong. It called to him. It told him to come. He desired to come and feel the light on his skin.

He began to move towards it without even knowing that he was telling his claws to walk. Yet they did.

Looking behind him, Snart could see that the two groups of lizards he commanded, lizards of all colors from both above and below, were coming to follow after him. They too had seen this beacon and were being called to it. Even Vallin had began a slow, steady march towards the light ahead of him.

This was better than Snart could have hoped for. They needed the light. He would bring his lizards to the light.

And there they would taste the flesh of men.

35: Pul and His Men

After several days marching, Pul was finally getting used to the plains of Prommus. They looked much more like the Disputed Lands than he cared to remember. His jungle homeland was far behind them now. It seemed to suit the others who had been marching with them for such a long time to not be as close to the trees where menacing lizards and other beasts of the forest lived.

Although they felt it was better, Pul knew the landscape was certainly not ideal. In every large town they found caravans of supplies willing to follow them for a week or two, but then they would tighten their belts and hope that they could last until they made it to the next larger city.

After weeks of following the King's command to march north, the next city they would encounter was the capital of the Theocracy.

Pul had only heard stories about the famous city. He had even seen a drawing once, but he wondered how true it could have been. In the artist's rendition, the city looked like it was not only built into the side of a mountain, but was the size of a mountain. Surely no place could hold so many people? To Pul it it seemed like the city the Prommus could hold the entire population of the rest of the Theocracy. Could itt really have so many within its walls?

There wasn't much wondering to do now. They would soon find themselves in the protective fortress that was there capital an under the guidance of the king.

Pul wondered if he would be able to see his face. If they would get so close so that he would be able to actually look at their ruler. Perhaps they would even receive a blessing from the high priest? There was once a time when he thought he would never step a foot outside of his jungle home. Pul had traveled much farther than he ever thought possible. He was a soldier and veteran of this terrible war against the speakers. There wasn't much that he could show for it. Nothing except for the experience of fighting against warriors who could speak fire into existence.

"They're saying we'll be there in only a day or two," Tars said. "Are you excited?"

Pul didn't know how to answer that. He wasn't excited per se. He didn't want to be so far from home again, after seeing it in its ruined state. What he wanted to do was rebuild his community and establish a city there once again.

But perhaps that was a dream of a younger man.

"I don't think excited is the right word," Pul said.

He looked over and saw Tars was no longer paying attention. A group of scouts was coming out from the direction of the city they were marching towards. They were carrying the green flag of the Theocracy.

Beside it was the white flag of surrender.

The call came for the army to hold as the riders came closer. Pul wondered what bad omen this might mean.

Being a captain, he knew that it was his duty to stay next to his men. As General Brand rode by however, he motioned that Pul should follow him.

"Keep them in line," he told Tars.

"Sure thing."

Pul shook his head. He didn't think Tars would ever get the hang of chain of command and respect.

Pul jogged after the general who rode ahead on his horse. He waved at other captains to invite them to join as they made their way to the front of the line.

The riders had stopped several paces behind the front line of the army. Pul wondered if that was out of fear or respect. Or maybe something else.

"Where do you hail from?" the ride next to the man with the green flag of Theocracy asked as they came closer.

General Brand tried to stop to his horse in a cloud of dust before replying.

"The king called the armies of the Theocracy out of the Disputed Lands and our struggles against the island invaders to come and assist him with the war. We are that army."

The face of the man who had called out to them did not change at this information. Pul had thought that perhaps he would at least show relief. They were the promised reinforcements. Was that not good news?

"And to which king do you pledge allegiance?" the rider asked.

That was a question Pul had not been expecting.

He could tell that the general had been caught off guard by it as well.

"King Gratis of the Theocracy," General Brand answered with what Pul guessed was indignity. "To what other king would we owe allegiance to as faithful servants?"

It was this response that made the rider put his face at ease. The men around him exchanged looks and nods that seemed to say that this was a correct answer.

"Forgive me," he said. "There has been a coup in the city of Prommus. The King has marched east with the army in order to fight the heretics who have fled there. In his absence, Prince Farnus and an army from Juttis have claimed the throne. I fear we are living in trouble times."

Pul was shocked. He had thought they were living in trouble times before this moment.

What had the reinforcements from the south gotten themselves into?

36: Close at Hand

The dust had hardly settled on the cave floor when Ealrin heard a commotion outside. He knew that something was wrong, but he wasn't sure which case was more dire. Olma lay on the floor in front of him and Blume seemed in a panic.

He decided the more pressing issue was the one right in front of him, and so he ran up next next to Blume.

"What's wrong," he asked.

Blume was breathing heavily and looking around her in all directions.

"It's him," she said, becoming more and more panicked with each passing breath. "It's here. It's him! He's back!

"Who are you talking about?" Ealrin asked. "Who's back? No one's here. It's just us."

Although, Ealrin thought to himself, they weren't exactly the safest group of traveling companions.

Szabo was up and conversing with Cecil the potion master in hushed tones. Galp had made his way over to Olma and was inspecting her. Holve was at his side. The old man seemed wary and cautious. Olma's eyes were fluttering slightly.

Ealrin grabbed Blume by the shoulders and forced her to look at him.

"You are okay!" he shouted at her. "You are fine. Nothing is wrong. No one's going to come after you."

Blume was shaking her head wildly.

"I know he's back," she said weekly. "He called to me."

With those last words, Blume seemed to calm down. Instead of a state of panic, her eyes became unfocused and her breathing slowed.

Ealrin wondered if that was a good sign or a bad one. Seeing that she was at least calm for the moment, Ealrin stood up and looked out towards the entrance of the cave. Gorplin and Tratta were coming back from inspecting it. He didn't have to ask them to receive a report.

"Bah, there's definitely something you'll need to see out here."

"It's like nothing I've ever seen before, you know," Tratta said.

"Is it an immediate problem?" Ealrin asked.

Gorplin shrugged his shoulders.

"If it suits you it can wait," he said. "Bloody crazy, though."

Ealrin nodded and looked over at Holve and the others. They were still tending to Olma. Ealrin could handle 'bloody crazy' in just a minute. For now, he needed to see how Olma was.

"What's wrong with her?"" he asked no one in particular. He didn't mind who would answer, so long as someone who knew what was going on did.

"She's recovering," said the old potion master.

"From what?" Ealrin asked.

Szabo chuckled.

"A very heavy dose of sedatives and mind calming herbs," he said. "I've seen much stronger men put on their back for days by the same kind of work. She's a tough one."

"I've never seen someone so possessed," Galp said. "How does it work? Is the demon inside of her or is it controlling her from the outside? Does the demon have to be female like her, or could it be a male demon? Or do demons have male and female and they're all just demons? That's a particular question I haven't yet researched..."

Holve shook his head in response to most of Galp's questions.

"More like than not, the demon inside of her is mixed within her spirit," Cecil said. "I've seen my fair share of these ones in smaller form or power. Whoever has taken hold of her is no small worker. She'll be in for it when she wakes."

"In for what?" Olma said, her eyes coming open with a snap. Holve, Galp and Szabo took a step back. Ealrin stayed steadfastly close to her. He knew what was coming. Or at least he guessed at it.

"How do you feel?" he asked, knowing that the wide variety of answers she could give would not exactly answer any of his questions.

Olma looked down at the ground and felt her chest. Her fire red hair fell over her shoulder.

"Dizzy," she said. "But most okay. Have I been alright since the barn? What happened to the others?"

She looked around the room. Ealrin did his best to keep his eyes on her as well. He didn't want to know what the possible outcome might be if Olma knew that some of them didn't make it out because of her own actions. They had gone over this with her once before. Had the demon affected her mind?

"Not all of us made it, ya know?" Tratta answered sadly.

"But you," Miss Rivius said from the back corner. "Are...different."

"What do you mean different?" Olma said, looking down at her hands. Her eyes became wide as she saw the markings there. A lock of hair feel in front of her face and she gasped.

"What's wrong with my hair?"

Ealrin breathed a sigh of relief. If Olma had enough sense of mind to worry over her hair, he was content for now.

"What's happening outside?" Ealrin asked Gorplin, turning to the dwarf.

He grunted and turned in response. Ealrin could handle that. He rose and followed the dwarf out of the cave. The suns were setting and darkness was creeping out over the land. The darkening horizon, however, was a bright blue. In the east, a giant pillar of light shot into the air.

"Bloody wild," Gorplin said. "Any ideas what it might be?"

Ealrin shook his head. Away from the mountains and from Prommus, closer to where Holve had said they should meet if they got separated, was a blue beacon. It called to him. It felt like he should go to it.

And he feared what would happen if he did.

"Holve," he shouted back into the cave. "You'll want to come see this."

***

The whole company sat outside of the cave entrance, looking at the beacon that lit up the night sky. They didn't worry about lighting a fire. Anyone close enough to spy a blaze would be much more concerned about the blue pillar that was far away. They warmed themselves by the flames as they looked at the blue tower.

"What do you think it means?" Miss Rivius asked.

"It has to be Isol," Holve answered. "The work of Yada I'd wager."

"And what do ya think it means?" Tratta asked.

They kept going in circles around that very same question. They mostly agreed that the light could be the work of a very gifted speaker, though Szabo did point out a demon might be at work in it. Whether Isol or demon, however, the question was what to do about it.

"There's no denying it's in the direction we told Serinde and the others to meet us," Holve said. "If they've been able to get back our weapons, the books and Blume's amulet, we'll have to head that direction."

"Then let's get going that direction!" Gorplin said, obviously irritated with the slow going of the conversation. He sat with his arms folded, looking cross.

Ealrin was sure that would be what they had to do. At least at some point. But with the armies marching behind them and the unknown and unseen troubles ahead of them, would it be the right choice to go headlong into the unknown? It wouldn't be the first time.

"We should go," Holve said with a tone of finality. "Gather what supplies we can and head there. If Silverwolf and the others have been successful, they may have all we need in order to get off this continent."

"I thought you wanted to do something about the Theocracy?" Miss Rivius said.

"I do," Holve nodded. "And if they've managed to do the task I set them, both can happen."

Ealrin took a deep breath. He felt like they were making a plan that would end poorly. He had no reason to think this, but something inside of him caused him concern.

"Let's get goin' then," Tratta said. "The sooner we can put a cap on ole' Yada the better."

"Everyone goes," Holve said again, turning around and crossing his arms. "But Olma should stay here with someone. Anyone willing to volunteer."

Ealrin felt an immediate desire to fight this proclamation. He was not alone, apparently.

"Leave the girl here?" Miss Rivius said, crossing her own arms. "That's not a very wise thing to do, Holve. Not with the armies of the Theocracy out and about."

"We can't have her come with us," Holve said again. Ealrin heard the tone in Holve's voice that said that he was not willing to negotiate this.

Ealrin had known Holve to consider Blume important to any endeavor they undertook. He was surprised by the finality of his mentor. It hurt him.

"Why?" he asked.

He hadn't meant for his voice to sound so accusing and angry, but he couldn't help it. He was upset. The companions around the fire fell silent and shifted themselves. Ealrin could tell they were looking from him to Holve, but he didn't meet any of their eyes. He was looking at the older man he called his friend and guide.

"Why can't we take her? We've got to protect her. Like we do for Blume. Like we do for everyone we've taken with us. That's what we do. We take care of people. We look for peace, not to abandon someone."

Holve shook his head.

"This is different," He said.

Ealrin looked defiantly at Holve.

"What makes this any different than Blume? Or Jurrin?"

"Oh don't bother about me Mister Ealrin..." Jurrin said feebly from beside the fire.

Holve's eye reflected the firelight in them. Ealrin saw his brow furrow and expression harden.

"Blume is a speaker," Holve said, pointing to her as she sat warming herself by the fire. She had been quiet for much of the evening. "She channels the magic of the rimstone by speaking to it and bringing out the elements it controls. She can manage her magic. She can control it."

Ealrin thought there was something to argue about the controlling part since coming to Ladis, but he didn't want to fight. Not yet.

"Olma," Holve said, pointing to her as she stood by, looking placid and calm. "Is possessed by a demon. An ancient foe who may be able to see everything she sees and hear everything she hears. It may very well be telling its foul allies every word of this conversation! Olma is now a spy for them! We cannot risk having those things know what we're doing and see what we're seeing. It risks too much!"

Holve took a deep breath. His eyes softened, but only slightly.

"We can come back when it's over and make sure she's safe."

Ealrin finally broke his stare with Holve to look at Olma. The girl they had found in the jungles of Ladis and had brought all the way here. The one who had endured so much in such a little time. The one who was possessed by a demon.

She looked between Ealrin and Holve, a look of apprehension in her face. Ealrin blinked. Had he seen something in her eyes? Surely it was a trick of the fire. But their fire was not a shade of blue.

He shook himself.

"We can't leave her behind," Ealrin said, making up his mind. "I'll take her myself if I have to. We'll split up. But we can't just leave her."

"We won't just be leaving her," Holve said. "The potion master will be here with her along with anyone else who volunteers."

It was at that moment that Szabo and Cecil came out of the cave. The Potion Master had several bags around his hips and over his shoulders. He was also wearing a large and heavy cloak.

"The Potion Master is leaving," Szabo announced. "Too much going on for him around here. What with the demons and the beacon, we'll be heading south soon. Probably to Arranus."

Holve put his hand up to the bridge of his nose and closed his eyes.

"We can't leave her," Ealrin said again, more forcefully this time.

Ferrin stood up. He had been sitting dutifully at Miss Rivius' feet.

"I have to agree with the lad on this one," he said before bowing to Rivius. "Of course, I will go where Miss Rivius does. But leaving such a young one behind seems cruel at best."

Jurrin stood up, though the effect was more muted than Ferrin's gesture.

"I'm with Mister Ealrin."

Tratta shook her head and went to stand behind Holve.

"I can't stand it, but it's the facts, ya know? A demon with us is a bad deal. Plus, remember what happened in the barn, ya know? Leave her and come back later to get her. She'll have enough food and what not."

Miss Rivius shook her head.

"I'll not travel with demons," she said.

Ealrin looked at Ferrin, who swallowed, but made no argument.

"Bah," Gorplin said, looking between Blume and Olma. "I can't make up my mind. I've seen demons. I've fought the devils. I don't want them spying on us, but, if they hurt such a wee one."

"She's only a few years younger than me," Blume said, not standing but looking defiant. "The same age I was when I came with you all in the first place."

"Do I have a say?" Olma asked.

The entire group turned to her. Ealrin hadn't wondered what she might want. He had assumed she wouldn't want to be left alone. Was he wrong?

She stood up solemnly and looked at them all.

"You've all been very kind to me," she said. "I don't know what would have happened to me if you hadn't helped me. But I don't want to be a hindrance to you or the fight ahead. I should be with my uncle. If he's still alive. Maybe it'd be best if I went back to Arranus. I could go with Szabo and Cecil."

"No," Ealrin heard himself say before he even had finished the thought. It wasn't right. She was their responsibility. It should be them who took care of her. Who helped her. After the war calmed down they could find her uncle. She shouldn't have to leave with Szabo. They had just met him. And the potion master, Cecil? He was wild at best.

"She wants to go," Holve said, looking at Ealrin. He couldn't stand to meet his eyes. All he was worried about was making sure Olma was safe. Like the rest of them.

He was just about to say so.

When the trumpets behind them rang out clear through the night.

And a blaze of purple flame erupted just above the cave entrance.

37: Battle Lines

Wind whipped through her hair as she listened to the sound of the ocean's tides. The early morning suns began to warm her skin and she looked proudly over her army. They had come. She knew they would. Her beacon in the sky had let the surrounding countryside know where Isol was and had called her troops back to her. They were running to serve their holy queen.

Yada felt exultant. She had taken what was certainly meant to have been a defeat and was going to turn it around into a victory for her island nation.

Those who had taken their gifts for granted, called them devils, and dismissed them from the very castles they had built would now feel her wrath. She would show them the great power of the speakers. She was Yada, the Holy Queen of Isol, and she was not to be crossed.

There were others who were beginning to gather around them as well. Those who are not allied with her.

"Your holiness," General Cern said bowing before her. "The armies of Prommus have come out against us."

Yada nodded her head at this and then waved the general away. She would not be troubled with such nonsense. Looking over her shoulder she saw that several of her magical cannons were being set up to rain destruction down on those who would come out against them.

These had been saved from the chaos of the demons. It had been her quick-thinking generals and their fear of her that had ensured the cannons were saved.

It would be only an hour or two before they were operational. Once they were ready, her enemies would be decimated beyond recovery.

Yada took another breath and allowed pride to swell within her. She was going to be the ruler of not just the forsaken island nation, but of a massive empire. Those who did not yet fear her soon would.

One of her speakers came near and bowed down to her.

"Your holiness," he said. "There should be one cannon ready by the time I return to them. In an hour, all will be operational. We will be able to repel the attacks of our enemies."

Shouts came up from the camp as the flags of Prommus came marching over the horizon. Yada nodded at the speaker and sent him away.

"Tell them they are to fire as quickly as they can," she said.

There would be the need for cannons in order to repel these attacks.

Yada again felt powerful. If this was the army of Prommus approaching them, they had their moment to strike. If the Isolians ships bearing reinforcements and supplies came now, they would be able to crush the army of Prommus without giving them a chance to resupply.

Where they were was right where they needed to be: beside the beacon of light calling their ships to them.

More and more soldiers dressed in the green of the theocracy came into view in the morning light. Yada dismissed them in her mind. What were they? A few ten thousands of soldiers?

On her ships she carried every single speaker and soldier that they had given to the fight in the Disputed Lands. They had pulled them back for this purpose and this assault. If she could conquer the north Theocracy, she will be able to take the entire continent.

She looked over at the slave she had taken from the city. He stood there, hands behind his back and shirtless. Octus. The hero of the south they had called him. A man who had fought against the lizards and her own soldiers. The hero who was now her personal slave.

Yada smiled to herself. It would not be the last time she did so. All of these who had taken advantage of the speakers would feel a similar fate. They would be forced to work. Forced to rebuild the castles they had not taken care of. Her speakers could do the same job in a half cycle of the moons. She would force the men and women of the Theocracy to toil over the task for a century. They would feel the humiliation they had caused. They would pay dearly for what they had done to the speakers of Isol.

Trumpets blew in the distance and Yada watched as the army of Prommus lined up against the horizon. Foolish. They would die on these beaches. The survivors would be marched back in humiliation. She would be victorious. She was sure of it. Yada stroked the amulet at her neck, feeling its power. This artifact alone would secure their victory. Her hair flowed with the other rimstones she kept there. A smile widened on her face.

This thought of victory was cut off by her captains coming to her again.

Bowing before her, it was Oberon who spoke first.

"We await your orders, your holiness," she said bowing down.

Yada looked out over the plains of Prommus. To her left there were the ocean tides, promising her the arrival of her reinforcements. They would come.

"Send in our soldiers," she said. "Repel the traitors until our cannons are ready. When I remove the beacon of light, retreat. For when the beacon disappears, hell will rain down upon the armies of Prommus."

38: Power Unleashed

Jerius looked out over the army of the theocracy. They were comparable at least to the speakers and heretics who lined up their ranks out in front of them. With the beach to their south, they would be cut off from any maneuvers in that direction. He looked behind him, knowing that the king had ordered the southern troops to join them in the defense of the theocracy from the speakers. Would they come?

Jerius clenched tight to the book that was in his arms. The words of Decolos.

It had been because of these words that they had driven the speakers away from Prommus.

Perhaps, before the day was over, he would read the words held therein again.

The previous High Priest had been too cautious. He had warned Jerius that Decolos had hidden the power to call forth terrible beings in this book, but that he had only ever done it once. And in his efforts to remove the speakers from the mainland of the theocracy, Decolos had summoned forth an army of demons.

They had come and destroyed the speakers, but they had also mercilessly ravaged the armies of the Theocracy's budding empire as well.

The former high priest had warned him that to summon the demons again would be to summon upon themselves the potential for such losses.

Jerius scoffed. Such a cautious approach had been why the speakers had been allowed to exist. If they wanted it to be fully rid of the heretics, such drastic measures would be necessary.

No matter the cost.

Captains and soldiers jostled each other to form the ranks they had been instructed to. Jerius sat on his horse, watching the ordeal.

He would act when it was necessary. No matter the orders of a dead priest or a living king.

"Jerius!" he heard from behind him. It irked him that he should be called by his name only. He was High Priest of the Theocracy now. He should be addressed as such.

Then again, he knew the voice of the one who called.

Turning in his saddle, he inclined his head as he addressed the king.

"Yes, my lord?" he asked with as much respect as he could muster.

"Can you see those cannons they have used against us?" the king asked, looking out over the battlefield.

Jerius pointed to a far hill where it looked like the magical monstrosities were being assembled. If anything was going to stop them from being successful today, it was this.

"It seems like they are not yet prepared to fire them," Jerius said. He was sure the speakers would have unleashed their fury the moment they saw them if they were.

The king nodded.

"No signs of the demons either?" he asked looking around the plains and beaches before them.

The king was wary of another attack. He had cautioned his army against the demons, not knowing that it had been Jerius himself who had summoned them.

"No sign, my Lord."

There was no need for Jerius to show what he was capable of just yet. The strike must be purposeful and timely in order to have the effect Jerius intended. The high priest was a position of power. But in order to secure such authority, one more test must be set.

The king rode off away from Jerius and towards another group of generals.

"What would you have me do, My Priest?" Luca asked at Jerius' side.

Jerius looked down at his faithful guard. She had served him well. Perhaps she had served him long enough?

"There is a battle before us," he said, returning his gaze to the king. "Go and find a captain to put yourself in the service of. Fight well."

"But.." Luca stammered. "But my Priest!"

Jerius waved his hand.

"War is no place for a woman," he said dismissively. "I should have left you in the camp. Either return to the tent or fight in the battle. The choice is yours. But if you survive, I expect your services once again."

He did not look down at her. There was a sniffing sound he ignored. Looking down to his side, he saw that Luca had vanished. A smile creased his lips. It soon went away as he heard the voice of Gravis.

"Men of the Theocracy!" the king shouted to the line as he turned around to face the army. "We will strike down the heretics here on this beach! We will drive them into the ocean and drown them in their robes! Fight today and we'll be rid of the Speakers of Isol now and forever! Fight and we will never again know their apostasy! Forward, men of the Theocracy! For the cleansing of Ladis!"

A cheer rose up from the army as they began to march forward.

Good, thought Jerius. Now he had room to work.

Taking the book off his chest he opened it in front of him. At that moment, the trumpet from the island heretics' side blasted over the plains. They had seen the advance of the Theocracy.

The battle was about to begin.

Jerius began to run his finger over the ancient words, speaking them aloud as he did so. He hesitated on the last word, leaving it in his throat.

He shook his head and shut the book.

No, he thought. *Not yet.*

He would wait for the Theocracy troops to lose heart. He would show them that Jerius the High Priest was the one who had saved them from ruin. He clutched the book to his chest again. With another hand, he removed his whip from his side and spurred his horse forward.

Several companies of soldiers had already marched past him. He would join the battle, but from a safe distance.

There was still work to do.

***

Clashing into the ranks of Isol, the army of the Theocracy fought with a vengeance. Jerius knew that they felt like they were fighting to rid the land of the heretics. They had been stirred by the king's words. They would fight for him and the chance to be rid of the speakers who had attacked their city. Jerius knew they were seeking revenge.

But he had seen the power of the magical cannons that were, thankfully, not yet operating. They would rain destruction down on the army. That would be when he would act.

At the proper time, he would reveal his salvation of them all.

Men with spears rallied around him. A host of temple priests wielding maces surrounded his horse. He was the High Priest, after all. He was worth protecting.

Flashing his whip above his head, Jerius let out a shout.

It was followed by the screams of the warriors of Isol. A flash of magical blasts shot from the hands of the speakers on the front lines of Isol.

Soldiers went flying in an explosion of dirt and blood. Jerius' horse reared and panicked, throwing the priest from his saddle. He landed in a sprawled out in a heap. Groaning with pain, he became very aware of what was in his hands, and what was not. His whip was still tight in his grasp. He was grateful for the weapon.

But the tome of Decolos was nowhere to be seen. Jerius scrambled to his feet, his whip in his hand. The protective line of soldiers that had covered him from the front line of Isol was now gone. In its place, there was a crater of bodies.

Before an Isolian soldier who was rushing around the crater could confront him, Jerius let his whip fly around his neck. With a jerk of his arm, the soldier crashed to the ground, his neck broken.

As he fell, Jerius watched him fall on top of the book of Decolos.

Rushing to where the body of the soldier was, Jerius shoved his lifeless form off the ancient text and grabbed it up off of the ground. The battle continued to swirl around him. Men fell and died, both from Isol and from the Theocracy. The front had shifted slightly away from him. There was no time to be grateful, however. Turning around, he saw a group of three soldiers running for him. He held his whip overhead, ready to let it fly again.

There was no need.

A group of temple prophets crashed into the soldiers, their maces careening down on their foes with a vengeance.

Jerius was immediately thankful for their service and their sacrifice. Once the threat was over, they turned and bowed at him. They were exactly what he needed.

"Follow me," he commanded.

Dutifully, they followed him away from the fighting and the crashing of bodies.

Jerius found a rock that was wedged into the sandy dirt and laid the book on top of it. Pulling it open, he flipped through it to the page he had read before.

"Stand before me and defend me!" he said, pointing at the ground ahead of him. The men did as they were told, holding their maces and turning away from him to look at the battle in front of them.

This time, Jerius read every word in the incantation loud. Pulling a knife from his belt, he thrust it into the back of the prophet standing directly in front of him, allowing his blood to spill out over the ground in front of him. Quickly he pulled a knife out and shoved it into the neck of the man standing to his left.

Groans and painful moans escaped the first man as the second fell dead to the ground. The third man turned around with his mace. Jerius pointed a finger at him and commanded with as much authority in his voice as he could.

"In this body may you dwell for my service!"

What had once been confusion and anger turned to pain as the man's eyes exploded with a purple flame.

His body twisted with contortions, growing in size and emanating a thin purple glow. Blades grew from his hands and reached down to the ground. His face twisted into a combination of metal and flesh with the helmet he had been wearing.

It had worked.

Jerius looked at the demon who now resided in the body of the prophet. Then he gave his order.

"Rain devastation down on my enemies and the enemies of the Theocracy. Destroy them all. Then find King Gravis," he said, his fist clenched around the bloody knife. War and death surrounded them again as the lines came close to the spot where he had summoned the demon. Jerius had found his new power. This would be what would take him to the throne and be the undoing of King Gravis.

"Find him and Kill him. "

39: David's Last Battle

The sound of battle and war invaded David's ears. It had been a few days since he had heard anything except for the tide going in and out and the constant marching of feet beside him. They had moved as one. Falling over from exhaustion as a unit, waking to feed from the ocean and drink from whatever stream they could find that feed into the waters there, and then walking on again.

Now, after weeks of walking, they were close.

David had felt her presence nearby. He had known that the orders of Graxxin had grown louder in his mind and driven him forward. The cold on his skin no longer bothered him. Nor did the grit under his feet.

The only thing that mattered were the screams in his head.

One voice was of a woman he loved, though he wasn't sure why.

The other was the commands of Graxxin to march. To come to her aid. To battle for her.

He knew they all felt it too. The calls of the goddess of blood. Dozens of them had joined his unrelenting march. They all obeyed the same call. They all heard the same scream.

"East!" it said over and over again.

It echoed in his mind until the only desire he had was to see the point on the horizon where the suns woke him from his march everyday. And now he had arrived.

Looking out over the horizon, he saw two armies at war. A sea of green fighting a sea of silver and blue. They fought and they died on the beaches. Many bodies floated in the water, staining the tide red.

David only knew one final scream in his mind.

"Kill!"

The desire to see blood spilled by his own hands overcame him. It was the only thing in the world that mattered. He took the blade he had dragged for the last weeks and raised it above his head. The others did the same with their own weapons. As one, the army of those who had marched and given their lives for Graxxin, the goddess of blood, charged towards the rear of the soldiers in green.

Some turned to see the beleaguered and bloody mob come at them. David even saw some men laugh at their approach. That was the first one he killed. The soldier died with a look of confusion on his face, not knowing that he had been met with the power of the demons.

They were unstoppable. Moving far more quickly than any man who came against them, the army of Graxxin cleared a swath of blood and bodies out from the rear of the army of green. All the while, in his mind, David heard the cry of pleasure.

"YES!" it wailed. "More! MORE!"

He shoved his blade into the stomach of a man who coughed red into his face. He didn't care. It was for her.

"Why does she scream?" he asked in a scratchy voice. He couldn't remember the last time he had used it. The man did not answer him. He only died on his blade. So David charged another.

"Why does the woman scream?" he asked the next man he slammed his blade into.

Again, no answer came from him.

He died too quickly.

The man slid off of his blade and he turned to stab another. More and more fell to his blade as he killed and spilled blood for Graxxin.

"MORE!" Graxxin yelled in his head. "More blood, or you'll hear her screams forever! She'll scream until you've spilled enough sacrifice for me! More! MORE!"

David obeyed.

For the goddess of blood was his mistress.

He obeyed and feared no other.

40: The Prince Arrives

The army of Juttis marched over the hill until it came to its crest. Dram could see the armies fighting below. This was why they had come. It was now that they would act. The Theocracy and Isol would tear each other apart.

And then, after they had fought and killed and worn each other down to the end of their armies, Juttis would overtake them both.

That was Farnus' plan. To remove both of his enemies with just a wave of his hands after they had killed each other and died fruitlessly on the beach below.

"Look at them squabble," Farnus said, riding his horse up next to Dram's. "They fight a battle they will both lose! And we will step in to claim the spoils!"

Dram couldn't help but agree. The fight below was brutal. Isol sent blast after blast towards the line of the Theocracy. Soldiers marched into death over and over again. But the green of Ladis was not deterred. They had fought the ones they called heretics before. They would continue to fight until the Speakers lost all energy and gave in to the fatigue that would take them.

It was then that the Theocracy would make its killing blow.

And it was then that Juttis would come down on them and kill them all, taking both the Theocracy and the island of Isol for its own. Neither side realized the doom that awaited them, even if they became the victors in this battle.

"This is how an empire begins," Farnus said.

Dram was sure he wasn't talking to him specifically. If he was, Dram nodded anyway. There would be time to secure his own throne. Time to discover who and what Farnus had really become. There would be time to understand and to act.

But now it was time to watch their enemies undo each other.

As they watched, the lines of Juttis formed behind them, ready to charge down the hill when given the signal. The captains and generals rallied around their troops. Some of them were recently enlisted from Prommus, being told that to deny Farnus would mean death for them and their families.

It was a messy affair, but one that must take place.

Dram took in a deep breath. As he did so, he felt something change. A spark of energy. A movement of power.

Graxxin stepped out from the shadows of the troops beside him and Farnus. The demon still unnerved him. The other demons began to appear beside the troops as well. Great horned and four-legged beasts that had patrolled alongside them since the long march from the north. When they had come upon Prommus, the demons had stayed behind or disappeared.

Now that battle was upon them, they came back in force.

"The old hag still lives," Graxxin said, pointing at a spot behind the lines of the Isolian army. It appeared to Dram that this was the place where the beacon of light had originated from. There was a group of soldiers there, holding banners and flags that must be the personal guard of Yada.

"So she does," Farnus agreed. Dram could see a sneer on his face. Apparently Farnus was just as displeased to see Yada as the rest of the Theocracy.

From the middle of the front lines of the battle, a burst of purple arose. Both Graxxin and Farnus spotted it and turned their gaze down to it. Dram saw it too.

"That's not one of ours," Farnus said. "Rayg has not called it."

"Then who did?" Graxxin asked. "Mine are there."

She pointed to a spot of devastation behind the lines of the Theocracy, where Dram saw that several in no uniform or marking carved a trail of destruction, overwhelming the rear of the army of Ladis.

"Then what has called it and why is it here?" Farnus said, looking up to the sky.

Dram tried to follow his gaze. He saw that, to his bewilderment, that the Dark Comet had turned from a deep purple to a bright orange glow. It had done so two years previous. It appeared to do the same as it had done then, pulsing out a steady glow.

"Rayg says it is time," Farnus said. He held up his hand and reached for the comet. As he did so, he began to glow a ghostly white.

On the comet above them, trails of purple began to soar to the ground

Dram watched as these hit the area around the fighting. Some to the north, others into the water below. One by one they appeared with their weapons in hand. The ranks of the Theocracy and Isol recoiled as the demons began to wreak havoc on them.

Then, with a pulsating blast, the blue beacon of light shot up into the sky and then receded. The landscape changed almost immediately as the blue colors that had saturated the view disappeared.

"What the..." Farnus began to ask. He was cut short by the blast of some type of magical cannon.

Two sent shots directly into the lines of the Theocracy, decimating their lines into ruin. Another fired a shot through the chest of a demon to their right. The great beast yelled out in pain, and then exploded into a blast of purple.

Dram could not hear Farnus' shouts. His ears were filled with the cries of men and the yells of the dying from below. Graxxin's shrieks of rage, however, filled the sky around them. She leapt into the air and flew towards the place where the beacon had gone out.

In its place, a glowing blue orb had appeared, sending tendrils of magic out from it. The soldiers who had stood beside the beacon now fled from it. Graxxin burst into the orb and a shower of sparks erupted from her claws.

Dram managed to keep his horse in place. Farnus had dismounted.

"Hold the line!" Farnus ordered. "Wait for my signal to charge!"

"What signal?" Dram asked.

In reply, Farnus shot a burst of purple flame into the sky, as he himself began to glow with a purple light.

"Do not fail me, half-brother," Farnus said as he turned to face him.

Dram could see the glow of purple in his eyes and the look of power that had overcome him.

"Rayg is not pleased with failure."

41: Unrevoked

The battle was growing more intense with each passing moment. Jerius' arm was growing weary from wielding his whip and dagger. Several faithful prophets had rallied around him, unaware that the last few who had done so had suffered a terrible fate.

He didn't care.

It was his own safety that mattered. If he didn't survive the battle, how could he gain more power? And who would lead the Theocracy and its church then? If hundreds more prophets died protecting him, their sacrifice would be remembered as preserving the Theocracy's hope.

With another stroke of his arm, another heretic in blue let out a yell of pain that would be his last. The prophets around him fought with a fury. They were defending their high priest. At least they were loyal to their religion even when its nation was crumbling around them.

Jerius looked over and saw a multitude of purple spots on the horizon. He paused just long enough to consider them. He had only called one demon, and a small one at that. What were all of these doing here?

He looked down at the tome of Decolos that was still tucked into his satchel. It was where he had left it and no telltale signs of magic leaked from it.

Then he saw it. Up above them on the hills. An army gathering and preparing to charge. But something was wrong. It was not holding up the skull of the Theocracy, but a different banner. The banner of Juttis.

"Reinforcements?" he said aloud.

The words had no longer escaped his lips than he saw the blue beacon that had lit up the plains grow bright and then fade away completely. The light's absence had an eerie effect on the landscape.

Then the blasts began to ring out. To his right and left, two magical explosions hit the Theocracy lines. Along with sand and rocks, men scattered and died as the magical barrage continued. The demons that he had not called ran forward, threatening the lines of the Theocracy from the rear.

Jerius saw the end playing out before him.

"We must escape!" he shouted.

"There is no retreat!" came an angry shout from behind him.

Jerius looked around and scowled. It was the king and his guard. They had been narrowly missed by the first salvo from Isol. Where was the demon he had summoned and why was it not doing the job he had tasked it with?

"We must wait for the reinforcements from the Disputed Lands!" the king shouted as his soldiers and guards joined with those who defends Jerius. "We must hold them until they arrive!"

A burst of blue erupted behind the Isolian lines, followed by a screeching wail that made Jerius throw his hands over his ears. Another blast and explosion rang out. Blue light again filled the land.

"We cannot fight demons and magic!" Jerius replied. "Not on this scale!"

"It was done for us once before," the king replied. His guards looked grim as the battle lines continued to close in around them. "Perhaps the gods who gave us their blessing before will do so again."

"The gods have nothing to do with this!" Jerius shouted.

King Gravis stood to his full height and looked down his nose at Jerius.

"Such words of doubt from a man of faith!" he said.

He would have replied. But his focus had been taken elsewhere. The king was standing in front of him in his regal armor and plate. And yet, behind him came a rush of purple and fire.

Jerius turned to flee, but found his way blocked by the prophets who had defended him from the line. Looking left and right, the king's guards stood resolute against the tide of Isol that was swarming down on them.

The demon whom he had summoned was crashing into any soldier it encountered, Theocracy and Isol alike. It did not discriminate between army or faction. It killed with reckless abandon.

It destroyed everything in its path as it came for that which it was summoned for. The blades that extended from its hands flew in a dance of death. Jerius raised his whip, ready to defend himself. Gravis, not seeing what was behind him, put up his own sword.

"You dare threaten a king!?" he bellowed.

The terrified shouts and screams of the soldiers behind him must have finally reached his ears. Just as he began to turn around, the demon leapt into the air and sliced wildly with his blades. The king fell before he had time to even pull back his sword.

Jerius was still attempting to get away from the beast who he had summoned. There seemed to be no stopping him. Standing up from his latest kill, the demon man looked Jerius in the eye. Soldiers who had come near to defend the king lay dead at his feet. Prophets who had been rallying around Jerius had fled or died in the melee to avenge the king.

"I summoned you!" Jerius shrieked. "I command you now! Destroy my enemies! Kill the soldiers of Isol!"

Words made no impact upon the demon. No soldiers from either Isol or the Theocracy moved to engage it or to attack Jerius. The battle had shifted away from this pair after so much death. Jerius still clutched the book of Decolos in one hand and his whip in the other. His palms were sweating as he realized what was happening.

He had sought power. He had wanted authority. He had done anything it would take to attain more and more. He had called from the depths of the darkness a powerful being over which he had no control.

The battle had stopped around the demon who now stared down the high priest of Ladis.

"Blood for the goddess of blood," it said with a mournful voice, it's bladed hands reaching out for the one who had summoned it.

Jerius raised his whip.

It was the last thing he ever did.

42: Pul's Last Charge

The Beacon disappeared from the sky just as Pul thought they were coming close to the place where it had originated. He wasn't sure if he should take the disappearance as a good sign or a bad omen.

Whatever the case, the tale tale signs of war were unmistakable.

Birds of prey circled up ahead, waiting to feast on the remains of the battle. Large tracts of footprints where previous armies had marched lined the beaches and dry soil all around.

They would soon come upon the decisive battle in this war.

Pul thought it strange.

He had spent most of his life fighting down in the south, convinced that he was making a difference. Or at the very least that their battle had been worth something.

And yet it was going to be in the north where the war was decided. Far away from the Disputed Lands the Theocracy and Isol warred over. If Pul had time to consider it more, he would have questioned whether or not it had been worth the effort in the south at all. But such thoughts were the luxuries of those who were less involved or far away in libraries or palaces.

Pul was a captain. He had to think like one.

Looking back over his troops, he saw they were anxiously preparing. It was easy to see on a man's face if he was ready for the battle or trying to convince himself he was.

Pul had never been excited for war. The men who were made him uneasy. It was natural to see looks of determination on some faces of the soldiers. Those men who knew they had no choice but to fight. Those who decided they would fight well, even if it was not something they desired to do. It was the men who desired combat that Pul stayed away from. He only wanted to serve well and play his part.

And, if the gods saw fit, live to see another day before he was greeted at death's door.

Trumpets rang out and told them all to stop. Pul put up his hand to command his troops. So often he had been the one to obey the orders. Now he was giving them.

A messenger was riding down the lines of soldiers, stopping at each captain and commander to relay the battle plans. When he rode up to Pul, he saluted and relayed the message.

"Scouts ahead say the battle is already in progress," he said quickly. "Those are your commands: to remain focused on supporting the rear of the Theocracy line. The companies are to offer support against Isol and Juttis."

"It really is Juttis?" Pul asked. The scout messenger nodded and rode away. Pul shook his head. There had been a part of him that had hoped it had been a misunderstanding. A coup within the theocracy. Who had ever imagined such a thing?

The war was more complicated then he had first thought.

If the heretics had allied themself with a northernmost province of the theocracy, then there would be more trouble for the remaining army of the Theocracy.

Pul turned to his men and relayed the message.

"We have an enemy on two fronts," he said. "Speakers on one and a rebellion on the other."

There was more he needed to say. More that ought to be explained. He wasn't sure he understood it all himself.

"We fought the heretics in the south. We fight them now in our own territory in order to stop them from invading the capital of our nation."

He swallowed hard as he looked into the eyes of his soldiers. Some were young. Younger than even he was when he first began to serve. Some were older. Not many though. The Disputed Lands had claimed many lives.

"I've suffered loss at the hands of the speakers," he said. "It's time for us to avenge those we've lost and show these heretics we are not afraid."

Grim faces nodded at him in return. He needed no tears or shouts of affirmation.

War was not some grand affair.

It was terrible and bloody.

And they were going to charge right into.

43: Flight of the Companions

Earlin ran down the mountain while his companions fought back the demons that had appeared at the mouth of the potion master's cave. In front of him ran those he was trying to help. They were all trying not to fall, but also to put as much distance between themselves and the wolf-like creatures who had come to engage them. Holve, Gorplin, and Master Ferrin were the ones who had engaged with the demons.

Ealrin and and the others were trying to get their companions away safely. Blume was still weak, but managed all right. Jurrin was helping her walk is quickly as they could. Miss Rivius had Olma by the hand while trying to help her navigate the rocky terrain.

"Do you think they'll be okay?" Jurrin asked as he looked behind him.

"Don't look back!" Ealrin ordered. He knew that those three had given them the opportunity to escape. They needed to take advantage of it.

The potion master and Szabo came shambling down beside them.

"Give it up old man!" the halfling was yelling. "There's no use in you keeping it!"

"It's been in my family for decades!" Cecil was wailing. "I'll not give it up to some strange girl!"

Ealrin had no idea what they were talking about, but the halfling was forcing the potion master closer to Blume and pointing at her with every step.

"Give it to her!" he shouted once again. "It might be the only way we make it out of this alive! All of my potions and tricks are inside that cave that's blocked! You don't have time to mix up anything new so give her the rimstone!"

Ealrin whipped his head around at that last word.

"You have some!?" he shouted.

An explosion rang out behind them and Gorplin came rolling down the hill, swearing with every turn.

Ealrin looked back to see Holve and Master Ferrin holding off two demons by themselves.

"What are you waiting for! All of us to die?" Szabo shouted.

Ealrin could see both fear and resentment on the face of the potion master as he reached into one bag and handed Blume what looked like a silver bracelet. Worked into the metal, he saw, was a glowing piece of red rimstone. No black smoke tainted this one. Still, Ealrin nearly reached out to smack it away from Blume's hand. The last time she had used magic it had been disastrous. But before he could do so, she had snatched it up and put it on her wrist.

Words of speaking flowed out of her mouth immediately as she threw a magic blast towards the demon that was rearing up to attack Holve. The blast of the impact scattered the other two demons along with Holve and Ferrin. Ealrin looked to see which way they were going when he felt a body rush past him.

At first he thought it was Blume, rushing up to help with the other two demons. But then he heard her speaking more words of magic right next to him. It was then that he heard Tratta.

"You're going to get yourself killed, you know!" she shouted.

Then it made sense who that fiery red blur had been.

"Olma!" Ealrin called.

It was too late. The girl had already made her way up the mountain towards the fighting and was engaging with the demons alongside Master Ferrin. Arcs of red light shot from her hands as she began to wrestle with the demon itself. It was like her limbs had been extended by the red light. No part of Olma's skin touched the beast, even though it looked as if she was wrestling with it.

Ealrin's jaw hung open as another magical blast soared passed him and landed squarely on the demon who was approaching a crumpled mess on the mountain side. The blast did away with the demon, but not before Ealrin recognized that the crumpled mass was Holve. He must be hurt!

Ealrin rushed back up to Holve's side, sword in hand and puffing the whole way. The old man shook his head as Ealrin tried to rouse him. He quickly got to his feet, shaken but seemingly unscathed.

"I'm glad you're okay," Ealrin said. It was true. He had lost Holve once. He did not want to experience that again.

Holve didn't appear to hear him.

He was shouting and pointing at the last struggle going on just a bit away from them.

"Blume! The both of them! Use your magic!"

Ealrin saw that Holve was pointing in the direction of Olma and the demon. But there was only one, not two. What does Holve mean?

It dawned on him with a terrible shock.

"No!" he shouted. "Don't do it Blume!"

Before his words had escaped his mouth, a third blast of magic hit the spot where Olma and the demon were wrestling. The wolf exploded into a thousand particles of light. Olma flew through the air and hit the ground hard beside Master Ferrin.

Ealrin cast one last shot look at Holve before trying to run towards Olma. Holve caught him by the arm.

"You don't know what she's capable of! Or what she's become!" he said with a snarl.

Ealrin shook his arm free.

"And I won't let her be sacrificed for it!" he shot back. Ealrin ran forward and kneeled down at Olma's side. Her eyes were open with a shocked expression on her face.

"I didn't know," she said weakly. "I didn't know I could do that."

"It's all right," Ealrin said. "You're going to be okay."

He found himself saying those words a lot today. Helping her up into a sitting position, he looked over and down at the armies marching below them.

He saw that most of them had begun to engage with one another. Had they seen the magical explosions that had happened up on the mountain nearby? Would they worry about such a thing with enemies so close? He didn't know. He didn't know if he could afford to care.

Looking over his shoulder, Ealrin already knew there was only one thing he had to concern himself with.

Holve had told Blume to attack Olma. Had he meant for her to kill the young girl? The old man had his arms crossed and was looking at them both with a stern expression. Ealrin couldn't tell.

"We've gotta get out of here, ya know!" Tratta said. "There are some scouts coming up this way now!

Ealrin whipped his head down and saw that she was right. A dozen or so soldiers in green were heading up the mountain. Apparently enough of a magical commotion had happened to warrant the attention of the Theocracy.

"We can't get over the mountain!" Szabo said. "There's no good path around it. We're going to have to fight her way down and through!"

Ealrin was tired of fighting. He also knew that he did not have the capacity to argue with the halfling. Szabo knew the area better than he did.

"Then we'll fight our way down," Holve said.

Everyone did their best to stand and recover.

"Ealrin, Gorplin, Ferrin and myself will take the front," Holve said. "Tratta, Szabo, Cecil, you three watch over Blume and Olma."

Ealrin wasn't sure you like that idea. He wanted to be the one who was watching over them. He wanted to make sure Holve's intentions were pure.

"What about us, Mr. Holve?" Jurrin asked, standing next to Galp. The poor Skrilx looked a little worse for the wear he had experienced.

"Take up the rear and help Miss Rivius. Make sure everyone keeps moving forward. That's gonna take a lot if we're going to get out of this alive."

44: Down the Mountain

The company made their way down the mountain as quickly as they could. Ealrin was at least glad to know that they had the high ground and that this alone would give them the advantage over the scouts. What he didn't like was that between them they only had two bows with a few dozen arrows. If the scouts who were coming up to engage them had any projectiles, they would have to rely on Blume's magic and Master Ferrin's one shield to protect them.

They didn't have to worry for long.

"Everyone on your guard!" Holve shouted as the first barrage of arrows came flying at them.

Blume sent up a wave of magic that disrupted the arrows just enough to throw them off course. Ealrin could feel the force of the wind she had commanded and it nearly knocked him over as well.

"If you could do something about them so we don't have to engage them," Holve shouted at Blume. "I think that would be best."

Before Blume could act however, Olma was throwing out her hands.

Sparks of red energy arced from her hands towards the scouts who were only a stone's throw away. When the magical energy touched them they shuddered and fell to the ground. Arc after arc Olma sent at the approaching scouts. One by one they fell to her magic.

Ealrin, who had traveled with Blume across three continents, was not surprised by the magic. But he did find himself intimidated. Blume's magic looked nothing like this. Everything she had done was either a blast of energy or a use of the elements around her. Something about all of this looked and felt otherworldly.

He could see the markings on her skin moving in dizzying patterns as she continued to throw energy at the approaching scouts. He wondered if, like Blume, she would need to rest soon. She was using so much magic! Only two of the dozen or so scouts remained. Olma's magical arcs began slowing down.

"I've got it!" Blume said with a wave of her hand. Several rocks flew up from around them and hurled themselves toward the scouts. Try as they might, they could not deflect or dodge the projectiles fast enough. The last few fell with a thud as Blume's rocks hit them one by one.

Ealrin wondered if this was how the island nation had engaged the continent. Throwing magic around on any who advanced upon them. No wonder the Theocracy had thrown all of its people towards the conflict. There was no way they could overpower them. Their only hope was to outnumber them.

Step after dusty step, they passed the soldiers they had disposed of and found themselves at the base of the mountain and on the plains just before the beach.

The only problem was now they were dangerously close to the battle going on below.

Just as they reached the bottom, the giant blue beacon that had lit up the sky disappeared from sight. Almost immediately, Ealrin felt the shuddering power of the magical cannons ringing out their destructive blasts.

Holve shouted something, but Ealrin couldn't hear it over the noise of the battle.

Looking up, Ealrin saw to his horror that several of the large purple demons were making their way into the combat is well. He had fought them before. He was not excited about doing so again.

Holve came up next to him.

"We're gonna have a hard time fighting them," he said. "Especially without my spear and Gorplin's ax. Those things only go down to rimstone and magic."

"Did somebody say something about a spear?" Ealrin spun around at the sound of the familiar voice. He knew his eyes lit up at the sight of them. He couldn't believe it. Out of the shadow of a few trees and a rock came Silverwolf and Serinde. Silverwolf, the assassin threw Holve's spear to him. He caught it deftly in the air. It was glowing white. Serinde handed Gorplin his ax with it's glowing red stone embedded into it.

With a somber expression, she handed Ealrin his sword.

"Barton didn't make it," she said.

Holve nodded, but said nothing else to her. Serinde then made her way right to Olma.

Turning around, Holve gave them all a grim battle plan.

"Everyone pair up with someone who can do magic or is carrying a rimstone weapon. Fight along the edges and make your way east. We want to avoid as much of this as we can."

Ealrin nodded at Silverwolf.

She winked at him.

"Maybe we could find a better place to rendezvous next time?" she asked.

Ealrin shook his head. Even in the midst of immediate death and danger, she was still the same Silverwolf. Ealrin stood next to Blume.

"Ready?" he asked her.

"Never," she replied.

45: Fresh Blood

"Try not to get separated!" Holve shouted at the group as the battle began to draw closer to them. Running to the east, they made their way alongside the base of the mountain and the plains on which the battle was ferociously intensifying. Ealrin saw a burst of blue and heard a scream. The wailing screech rose above the tumult of the battle.

Another blast of magical cannon fire rained down close to where they were and shook the earth. Ealrin felt himself being thrown into the air ever so slightly and losing his footing. Holding tightly onto the sword Serinde had returned to him, he felt it grow icy cold in his hands.

He wondered if that was the thrill of battle, or something else. Returning to his feet as quickly as he could, he stood and saw that the only people next to him were Blume and Holve.

"Where are the others?" he asked frantically. There was no time to discover the answer to that question. The battle was around them.

Blume threw up her hands to create a wall of magical protection as several bolts of energy flew at them. Her red shield absorbed them but Blume withdrew her hands as if burned as soon as the magical energy had hit the wall.

Holve jumped out in front and let his spear sing through the air. Ealrin saw one speaker fall to Holve's thrusts and another back away, surprised at the magical weapon that was sending out sparks with every stab.

Trusting that Blume would be able to take care of herself for the time being, Ealrin jumped down and charged the other speaker. He knew words of magic were coming from his mouth and could feel the hair on his arms rise up with the thrill of energy. Ealrin brought his blade down as hard as he could, silencing the speaker before he could finish the spell. The air around him burst with unfinished magic and Ealrin crouched down, hoping to avoid the worst of the blast.

He felt the back of his neck singe with a burning pain. Letting out a yell of fury, he rose to his feet and charged forward again. Thankfully, he saw Blume and Holve were next to him as they continued to run east.

Blume threw two more shots of magical energy in the direction of a group of speakers. One of them hit the mark and sent several of the troops from Isol flying. The other shot too close and only sent dirt flying everywhere. The explosion at least was enough to screen them for a moment as they continued to flee.

Ealrin found himself filling with dread.

Where were the others? How could they have gotten separated so quickly?

He knew he had to trust the plan. Looking over the battlefield, he saw several flaming beasts of purple holding their giant weapons in the air and bringing them down in devastating arcs that caused death and explosions whenever they touched the ground.

He knew a moment of panic as he remembered the terrible war in Beaton. How could they all survive this?

Ealrin felt a firm grip on his arm that pulled him forward.

"Don't stop!" Holve shouted in his ear.

It took everything Ealrin had to obey. He rushed forward, making sure that he could see Blume right beside them. Another blast of magical energy shot over their heads and sent rocks and debris flying everywhere.

Ealrin heard Blume shout out in pain.

"Blume!" Ealrin called, running to her as quickly as he could.

He fell down beside her and did his best to get her to her feet. She wasn't bleeding, a fact he was grateful for. But he could tell she was shaking.

Between him and Holve, they lifted her up and kept her feet moving. Without her medic, they were going to be in dire straits.

Ealrin had just completed this thought when he saw something that made him freeze in his tracks, even though everything around him was screaming at him to run forward and escape.

It was children. Boys and girls younger than Blume. Their faces were gaunt and their eyes were blank stares of terror. But what made him most terrified were the bloody weapons they all carried. Each of them were covered with fresh blood. It consumed every part of their bodies.

"What type of devilry is this?" he asked.

"Demons," Holve replied with a grim expression, pushing them out of the way. "Something we'll have to deal with if they come for us."

Ealrin kept stumbling forward with Blume at his side.

"They're just kids!" he said, seeing that one of them could be no older than ten.

A group of soldiers had seen the three of them and began to rush toward them. Before the soldiers could make it to them however, the bloodsoaked children engaged. Ealrin screamed as he watched them. There could be no other response.

The teenagers moved with uncanny speed and what looked like superhuman strength. They leapt upon the soldiers with a bloodlust Ealrin had never seen before. Men screamed in pain and agony as the young ones killed with farming equipment and rusted, broken swords.

Holve got them moving forward again.

"There's nothing worse than someone who's been possessed by a demon," he said.

Ealrin remembered his instructions to Blume. Hit them both. Kill the demon. Kill Olma.

There was no time to think anymore about it. They had to keep moving. The battle was growing more intense and the last soldier was falling to the seemingly demon possessed band of kids.

Ealrin had seen war before.

But this was a new kind of terror.

46: Racing For It

"Curse you flaming horses into the depths!" Gorplin shouted as he rose to his feet after being blasted off them. He didn't know if the blast had come from the giant demon who was approaching them, but he felt justified in blaming him anyways.

He had fought them once before and thought that he might never fight them again. Gorplin wouldn't admit he was wrong to anyone. Not out loud at least.

"On your feet stumpy!" Silverwolf shouted at him.

"And curse you, you white-haired harlot!" Gorplin added as he got to his feet. "Couldn't you fight alongside somebody else?"

Gorplin was not excited about having to face what could be his last moments next to the smart-mouthed assassin.

At least she was good at her job.

"Coming right for us, ya know!" Tratta shouted.

Gorplin looked up and saw that she was right. A demon holding a giant ax over his head was bearing down on them. Standing to his feet, Gorplin raised up his own ax. He was glad to see it glowing with a red light. His magical weapon was back and thirsting for demons.

"Come and get it, four hooves!!" Gorplin shouted as he charged the demon. Silverwolf and Tratta were right beside him.

Tratta let several arrows fly up towards the demon's helmet. The first two bounced harmlessly off of his protected head. The third, however, drove itself deep into its slit and the demon roared with pain.

Bringing down his ax wildly, Gorplin dodged out of the way with Silverwolf right beside him.

"Get up there, short stock!" she shouted as she grabbed onto the demon's arm and shoved a dagger deep within its purple flesh.

The demon swung his arm furiously, and Silverwolf hung on as she was thrashed about.

Gorplin ran under the demon's leg and swiped at it with his rimstone ax. With an arc of red energy, the blade sliced right through the armor the demon was wearing. It reared back up on its hind legs as Gorplin ran underneath it and sliced again at its rear right roof. This time his ax did not go all the way through. He found his glorious weapon stuck in the demon's armor.

"Blasted underworld!" Gorplin shouted.

Tratta came up beside him and shoved him. He had only just gotten the ax free as the demon crashed down to the ground. He and Tratta rolled out from underneath it just in time.

The pair scrambled away as the demon thrashed wildly at the ground, its wails and shouts of pain sending tremors through Gorplin's head.

"Finish him already!" shouted Silverwolf.

Gorplin couldn't help but agree.

He righted himself and then leaped onto the demon, throwing his ax down as hard as he could into what he guessed should be where the heart of the thing was. Giving out one final wail of pain, the demon began to glow as it split into a thousand pieces of fire and red hot metal.

"Get outta there!" Tratta yelled. Gorplin could feel her hands pulling him away as he held desperately onto his ax. He had only just gotten back this blade and he was not going to lose it now.

The next explosion was worse than Gorplin remembered as the demon's energy released itself onto the battlefield. Tratta and Gorplin both went flying forward as they ran from the chaos. A hot ringing filled his ears even as he heard the words come into his head.

"That still only counts as one!" the assassin was saying to him. "There are two more coming and I'm going to claim at least one of them."

"Like the devil you are!" Gorplin shouted.

He looked up and saw that she was fiddling with a dagger that held a green rimstone in its hilt.

"Hey," he protested. "Where did you get that?"

Silverwolf's only smirked as she replied.

"Race you for it."

As a demon begin to charge at them, it swung a giant mace wreathed in purple flames over its head.

"You won't get there first just because you've got longer legs!" Gorplin shouted.

He did not enjoy spending time around the assassin.

But he certainly loved fighting next to her.

47: The Bravest

"Miss Rivius!" Jurrin called out as loud as he could. "This way! Run this way!"

The halfling was doing his best to get Miss Rivius moving to the east. For a moment she seemed to have misunderstood Holve's instructions and ran south towards the battle instead of east alongside it. Master Ferrin was running beside her and doing everything he could to pull her in the correct direction.

"I don't believe the woman has ever seen battle before," Galp was chattering away. "Most unfortunate for the circumstances, although it may be rather fortunate if one really considers the ramifications."

Jurin shook his head.

He was still getting used to the skrilx who spent most of his time talking instead of being silent.

"Miss Rivius!" he shouted again. Master Ferrin appeared to have a good hold of her now and was directing her away from the soldiers who had taken an interest in them.

Galp held a short sword in his hands. Jurrin had his slingshot and had found a dagger on the battlefield. Master Ferrin had a shield and a sword as well.

Jurrin wasn't sure that Miss Rivius had any type of weapon on her.

Although he knew he was capable of fighting, Jurrin still did not enjoy it. He would much rather try to get back with the rest of the group. He scanned the battlefield and couldn't see any of their friends. Mister Holve and Mister Ealrin had run off with Miss Blume. A demon had separated them from Gorplin and the others.

Jurrin realized with a start that no one in their group had any magical weapon or abilities to fight off the demons or the Speakers.

They were on their own.

Master Ferrin came running back with Miss Rivius on his arm. She looked pale and white.

"We've got to go this way Mister Ferrin!" Jurrin said, pointing the way Holve had directed them to go. "That's where everyone else was heading. Let's try to make our way around those demons, though."

Jurrin definitely did not want to face those monstrosities without any magical weapon. He had been close enough to one before to know what kind of folly that would be.

The four of them begin to move slowly east, skirting around any soldiers that they could. Jurrin managed to take down one soldier who wandered too close to them with his slingshot. Master Ferrin had taken care of the other four.

Jurrin was still feeling rather small, even though Szabo had told him he was one of the most well-traveled halflings he'd ever met.

It was hard to feel large and important next to such chaos and death.

"This way!" he shouted, pointing the group towards a hill that looked like, if they could get behind it, would shield them from most of the fighting.

The group managed to follow his directions easily. They made their way around the sandy dirt hill and saw that they had come upon the cave like formation in the side of the mountain.

"I didn't know this was here!" Jurrin said as he walked past the mouth opening.

The suns were beginning to set as the day wore on. It cast just enough light into the mouth of the cave for Jurrin to see something that caught his eye.

"Do you see that, Master Ferrin?" he asked as he peered deeper into the mouth of the cave.

At first he only saw a pair of red dots. Then several more appeared next to it. Then a large pair of yellow orbs blinked into existence. There was no time to do anything but push Master Ferrin along and shout.

"Run!" Jurrin commanded, shoving the much larger man as hard as he could. "Run now!"

The lizards burst out of the cave as if commanded by during his words. The four of them ran as quickly as they could away from the cavern as an army of the lizardmen poured out of it.

Jurrin was not ready to fight these things again.

His feet carried him as fast as they could with Master Ferrin and Mis Rivius up ahead and Galp right by his side.

A lizard ran up next to him and thrust a spear in his direction. Jurrin managed to dodge it and swipe at the lizard with his slingshot. He actually hit the thing in the nose, but at this range and with his short arms, he doubted he did any real damage other than to make it more mad.

Just as they ran alongside the other side of the hill, Jurrin saw a contingent of speakers who had been focusing their attention on the magical cannon at their side. Turning to look at the commotion, Jurrin saw one of them raise his hand to cast a spell. He raised his hand in order to loose a stone, but found that he did not need to let the projectile fly. A spear of one of the lizards had pierce the man's chest before he could let it go.

"Up this way!" Jurrin said. The four of them ran up the hill they had been skirting around as the lizards and speakers below began to engage in a battle.

Looking over his shoulder, Jurrin saw that only a handful of the scaled beasts had decided to follow them.

Galp swung his sword weakly at one that had come up on their heels and missed. Jurrin stabbed his dagger at the hand that stretched out for him and saw that he pulled back a blade covered in the cold blood of the lizard.

At least he had managed to do one of them harm.

Master Ferrin was looking over his shoulder at them, and waved them on towards a spot that he was running towards. The redheaded man still steered Miss Rivius along.

They ran until they found themselves on top of a steep incline of rock at the base of a the hill.

"Let's get everyone up here!" Master Ferrin suggested.

Jurrin certainly thought that it would be better than running wildly around the plains. They could wait for the skirmish between the speakers and the lizards to die down before heading past the battle. He helped Master Ferrin get Miss Rivius climbing upwards. Galp was next.

Master Ferrin looked down at Jurrin with a wide smile on his face.

"You're certainly one of bravest creatures I've ever seen!" he said.

Jurrin's chest swelled with pride.

"Thank you, Master Ferrin!"

It was at that exact moment that a spear hurled through the air and lodged itself firmly into Ferrin's chest. With a great gasp he reached a hand out to Jurrin and flung the halfling up onto the hill. Jurrin hardly had time to look down after he landed in a heap on the top.

Ferrin fell with a crash as the lizards began to scramble towards them and the speakers of Isol closed in around them.

48: Possessed that Fight

As soon as she had seen the little girl, Serinde had rushed to her and given her a warm embrace. Holding her back to see her more clearly she grabbed some of the locks of her hair and asked the obvious question.

"What happened to you?" she said with a grin.

All this time she had been traveling with Barton and Silverwolf, she had only thought of Olma. She wanted to return and see the girl safe and unharmed.

It was beyond her wildest hopes and dreams that she sat here right now safe.

She did look different, however.

Serinde felt her skin where the strange markings moved and twisted. They seem to respond her touch with degrees of fleeing from it and moving towards it.

"They say I'm possessed," Olma said quietly. "And I suppose I am. I've done extraordinary things even though I don't know how I'm doing them or even why. But there's something in my head. A small voice. It's quiet now, but it was loud at first."

Serenity tried her best to not look concerned at this news. She saw that her face betrayed her, however, by the look Olma gave her. The young girl faltered.

"Am I going to be OK?" she asked quietly.

Serinde nodded and tried to fix her face with what she hoped was a reassuring mask.

"Of course you will be!" she said

Holve finished giving the instructions that Serinde heard snippets of. Head east and take someone magical.

The choice was made clear for Serinde. She stood up and took Olma by the hand.

"I'm going to get you out of here safely," she said. "I'll help you find your uncle after this is over. We'll find him together."

Olma looked like she was on the verge of a smile. That alone gave Serinde hope. Then the world fell apart around them as a blast of magic ripped through the sky and landed just in front of their group. Serinde leaped forward, hugging Olma with all of her might, hoping to protect the girl from the worst of the blast.

When she shook her head and came to her senses, she saw that a red orb had encased the pair of them. Dirt slid off the top of it as Serinde looked around. Olma had her hands outstretched, like Serinde had seen Speakers do when they summoned up magic.

"Olma?" she said quietly.

The girl blinked and the orb disappeared. She shuddered as she lay on the ground. Serinde helped her get up.

"See?" Olma said. "I don't even know I'm doing it. I don't know *how* I do it. It just happens. I..."

She paused.

"I'm scared."

Serinde heard the sound of the battle growing closer to them. She grabbed Olma's hand and looked around. Most of their party had already fled east. At least she hoped they had. There weren't any of them in sight.

"We'll figure it out together," Serinde said. "But for now, we have to run!"

They began to trot away from the blast. The elf couldn't see any of their companions lying down on the ground, injured or worse. She prayed they had all made it. That they were way ahead of them.

A demon had come crashing forward, its purple flaming body swinging a massive ax. Serinde saw Gorplin, Silverwolf and Tratta running after it.

"We need to help!" she shouted.

Olma resisted her pulling when she tried to take her in that direction. Serinde looked back, and gasped. Olma had turned a shade darker. Her skin was moving as one fluid pattern. A red glow began to emanate from around her.

"We need to fight," said a voice that was Olma's, and yet not hers.

"What's wrong?" Serinde asked.

Olma had turned her attention toward another demon that was charging forward. Serind turned to shield the girl from it, wielding her sword but knowing it would do little good against a demon of unnatural flame.

Then a blur of red sped past her.

"Olma no!" Serinde began to say, reaching out a hand to grab the girl and stop her. But she was too quick. She was running full speed, faster than even Serinde could, towards the demon as it bellowed its terrible roar. Seride ran after her, still. She would not allow the girl to go off against such a monster alone.

Arcs of red energy shot out of Olma's hands as what looked like large red blades replaced her forearms. The demon held up its giant sword and shield as it charged forward. Olma jumped into the air and swiped at the demon. With one fluid motion, she rent the shield into four parts and the demon shrieked a horrible noise that assaulted Serinde's ears.

Still, she ran forward just as Olma hit the ground from her impossibly high jump. Serinde took a swing at the demon's leg. Her arm jerked violently as her sword bounced off the unnatural armor. The demon turned to her with its helmeted head and giant breastplate. It began to swing its sword at her when a terrible wail escaped its mouth. At the same moment, a red blade shot through its armor and deep into its flesh.

Olma flitted gracefully out of the way as the demon fell to the ground.

"Run!" she shouted, as tiny lines appeared in the demon's flesh and Serinde felt the air fill with energy. Following the order without second guessing turned out to be the right choice. The demon's form exploded and they were propelled forward, running as fast as the pair of them could.

Serinde grabbed Olma's arm, no longer glowing red or in the shape of a blade, and ran with her east. The demon the others had been fighting was gone as well. To her horror, however, she saw that the Isolian army had caught up to their position.

"Woah!" she said, pulling Olma back. "Not that way!"

She was pulling Olma back just in time to see a rush of lizards pouring out of the base of the mountain. The foul beasts had somehow found their way here. One the size of a house came running out towards them and Serinde shrieked, even as she pulled Olma back.

The girl wouldn't budge again. Something was wrong.

"What is it!?" Serinde yelled. They were hemmed in on all sides. It was important they move. Or do something other than just stand here.

Serinde looked down at Olma and saw her glowing again.

"He's here," she said, pointing out at the battle.

Serinde turned to look.

All she saw was a blaze of red falling to the ground, away from a pillar of blue light.

A cry of rage echoed over the battlefield as the shape of a man soared over the fight in a blaze of purple flames.

49: Sacrifices

Blume sat up on the hill Ealrin and Holve had fought to get her to. Jurrin was consoling a shaken Rivius as Silverwolf, Gorplin, and Tratta climbed up the steep incline as well.

All around them was death and destruction. Demons were raining down on the battlefield from all directions. The three magical cannons had been decimated by a host of demons that had pummeled down on it.

Apparently they had some type of grudge against the Speakers of Isol who wielded them. Blume remembered being forced to use one of those abominations and hated that she felt a slight sense of pleasure at seeing them torn apart.

Ealrin had not made it up the hill yet. He said something about Serinde and Olma and ran down again into the fray. They were protected up here for the time being, but for how long? What would happen to them if they stayed on the the hill? Would they ride out the battle here? Or would it overtake them?

Serinde climbed up onto the hill and Gorplin rushed over to her.

"Where's the lass?" he said, helping the elf up onto the small patch they had claimed for their own. Tratta ran over to bat down a lizard who had attempted to follow Serinde up and over.

Serinde just pointed.

There was an explosion of blue and purple over towards the rear of the Isolian line. Blume could feel the brute force of the magic emanating from the two bursts of color. Feeling the rimstone in the bangle the Potion Master had given her, she knew it wouldn't take long.

The battle was growing more intense, with all sides taking heavy losses and the demons raining down death wherever they came.

She also remembered the last time she had gotten involved in such a battle, what it had cost her and those who cared for her.

So many people had sacrificed for her. Her friends had laid down their lives for her. Ealrin and Holve had protected her from so many dangers, many of which she got herself into. So many had fought for her.

Perhaps it was time she return the favor.

Blume saw Holve pulling Ealrin up over the hill and the two exchanged a conversation. She didn't hear much of it. She had made up her mind. Standing up, she walked towards the edge of the hill, her bangle glowing as she began to feel its power grow within her.

Words were said that had little meaning to her. There was only one thing that kept her going forward. One thought that resonated in her mind other than her need to keep her friends from death.

"I'm not weak," she said again to Ealrin.

She meant it. She knew it. She had a power within her that was untied to the ancient artifact Silverwolf was supposed to have gotten her.

That Yada still had.

Blume was a powerful speaker. She had called down magic others could not and stopped magic far greater than most saw hers as. She was not weak.

"I've stopped this before," Blume said. "I'll do it again."

"Blume!" Ealrin said, a pleading tone in his voice. "You've done so much today! If you go up against them now..."

It pained her to hear it. Before she gave any of them time to consider, or talk her out of it, or try to hold her back, she ran toward the edge of the hill and jumped.

Using her magic to slow her fall, she blasted a path of destruction from the hill to the place where the three magic users were dueling. Dirt solidified into a solid wall on either side of the blast, preventing the soldiers of Isol and Theocracy from attacking each other. The channel she had dug with the blast served as a small buffer. The battle continued, albeit fractured, on either side of the divide she had made. The war in front of her, however, continued. She would stop it.

No matter the sacrifice.

50: Split

Octus was still fighting, despite the fact that some magical confrontation was happening just above him. He didn't care. This was his chance to do something. To overcome.

Fortunately for him, the battlefield had been littered with the spears and swords of the deceased. He now had a sword on his belt and a spear in his hands. He was Octus, hero of the south.

And he was fighting for his freedom.

Captain Oberon had taken Yada's personal guard away from the place where she had erupted in magic. After the cannons were destroyed, Yada had burst into a sphere of blue magic, just as a demon flew in and attacked.

The fight was terrible and sent wild bolts of magical energy flying all over the place. In order to protect against damage to their own troops, the companies of Isol had fled from the palanquin they had protected all this way from their homeland.

It was now just a matter of time.

Octus had managed to break free of his captors by fighting alongside the battle lines. No one concerned themselves much with the fighting of a slave. Moving from company to company, Octus gradually worked his way to the front lines. If he could just manage to get there, he could make his plan a reality.

All he needed to do was to get to the Theocracy troops.

"You there! Slave!"

Such words were not uncommon to Octus. He pretended not to hear whoever it was that was calling to him. Unfortunately for him, the man was far too close for him to disappear into a crowd. He felt a rough hand on his shoulder as he was forced around by a man who was at least a head taller than he was.

Captain Oberon's rival.

"You don't belong in this company!" Captain Fortan shouted as men ran forward from all sides. He was so close to the front. Just a stone's throw away from Ladis' troops.

"Captain Oberon sent me to deliver a message," he invented wildly.

It could be true. Oberon had often told her company to tell Captain Fortan she thought he was a bumbling idiot.

"Well let's have it!" Captain Fortan said, crossing his arms over his chest. "The battle's going so poorly not much can possibly make it worse!"

He was wrong.

At that moment a line of magical energy shot through the spot they were standing. Octus felt himself lifted into the air and thrown away from Captain Fortan and his company. The blast had split the battlefield into two parts. Octus got to his feet, feeling that his sword was still in his belt and his spear was just in reach. A six foot wall of dirt now rose up in front of him.

"What in the name of the gods..." he began to say.

Then he realized that he had accomplished his goal. Looking around, he saw no Isolian troops. It was only the green of Ladis that was nearby. They too looked like they were recovering from the explosion.

A second explosion followed the first, this time closer to where Yada was, towards the back of the line.

Octus didn't care. He didn't even look back to see what had happened, though a part of him wished the worst of fates on the old hag.

Now he was with Ladis.

It was time to find a captain of the Theocracy.

51: Keep the Men Alive

The mass of the armies pressed in around them. General Brand's last orders echoed in Pul's head.

"Keep your men alive and fighting the heretics!"

Pul was certain he could push his men forward to fight. Last night, Brand had given his commanders orders concerning how they were to proceed against the second wave of Isolian fighters.

He was no longer certain he could keep them alive. The beach cut them off to the south. There was no way he could lead his men towards the sand. They'd lose their footing and their heads in the process. He had to get them to better ground or they'd all be crushed to death by the throes of the battle or the demons that kept appearing and stomping over the battle, causing devastation at every turn.

There was no use ordering his men with words. His voice had gone hoarse before the dawn had broken on this new day. Noticing the other sides lining up to prepare for another round of battle, Pul nudged his company's standard bearer. Then he raised his hand. The flag of the company he had inherited rose up and behind him soldiers put their spears into position. They were preparing for the battle ahead.

A combination of magical blasts has separated the battlefield into two, with Juttis fighting the Theocracy on one side and Isol fighting the rest of the Theocracy on the other. Split into two in such a way, the largest empire on Ladis had been cut down to size.

Would they really be able to fight two armies in such a fragmented battlefield? They would soon find out.

Tars managed to use what was left of his own voice to cough and offer some encouragement of a sort.

"We may not all be dead by tomorrow, eh Pul?"

Commander Pul, he thought. But he was too worn to offer any correction. Not that Tars would ever listen anyways. *And he has a point. Not all of us may die.*

"Keep your men alive..."

Those had been the last words of Brand before he dismissed what was left of his commanders to command what was left of the Theocracy reserves from the south.

Juttis was above them. Isol was ahead. The Theocracy's reinforcements were most of what was left of their army.

How many would live to see the next sunrise?

Pul didn't know. But he would keep every man he could alive.

He lifted his sword high, and the banner went up alongside it. His men rushed forward with him. The battle lines had shifted so much throughout the day. Now with Juttis to the north and their own lines to the west, the battle was quickly becoming a group of smaller skirmishes between each company and whatever enemy they could find.

Pul charged his men right into a block of Isolian Speakers. They raised their hands to cast their spells in response and Pul braced himself for whatever death may come.

Before the heretics could cast their magic and destroy his company, however, the ground between them rose up in a blast of dirt and magic.

His men pulled up short as they collided with the wall of earth. That had not been something Pul had expected the Speakers to do. Looking left and right, he couldn't see any Isolian troops who were trying to block them in. Instead, he saw lizards to the north, pouring out over a hill and into the battle as well.

He took a deep breath before rallying his men.

"Over there!" he shouted through the hoarseness of his voice.

This battle continued to bring the unexpected.

52: Screams

The battlefield was a blur of blood and death. David no longer cared who came near to him. All he needed was to kill for the goddess of blood. It was his job to cause as much carnage as he could. He and the others who had shambled to the war had seen only red this day.

Blood smeared his body from his neck to his battered feet. He wasn't sure whose sword he had now. He only knew it was not the one he had begun his journey with.

The only thing that was different now was the screaming. It was no longer in his head. It was outside on the field of battle.

Men screamed and died at his hands. With the superhuman strength he had been given, David continued to spill the blood of any man or soldier who came near to him. Over and over again he killed.

But the screaming in his head was now quiet.

Graxxin had not commanded him for some time now. The flow of moments was lost on David. Whether he had been at war for a day or a week, he couldn't remember. The suns rose and fell at their own desire.

He only killed.

Taking his sword from the belly of his last victim, David turned to strike at whoever was closest. Then a blast of magic came hurtling down towards him and landed next to him, causing the earth to shake and David to lose his balance. He feel to a knee into the soft, sandy dirt. One hand kept him from falling down entirely, while the other grasped tightly onto his sword.

Looking up, David saw that a crater had formed right beside him from the blast that had wrecked the nearby battlefield. In the middle of that crater was a winged creature,

One David recognized, even though he had never seen her before.

The battered and ragged looking demon clawed at the ground as she attempted to get to her cloven hooves.

David slid down the side of the crater, coming to rest right beside the creature he knew and feared.

And hated.

"Why does she scream?" he asked, holding his sword tightly in his hand. Blood caked every part of his body. Dirt and mud mixed with his own sweat. His breathing was heavy and ragged.

"Filth," Graxxin said. "You serve me. I am your mistress!"

"Why does she scream!?" David called out louder. He knew the screams in his head were someone he knew. Someone he may have cared for. But there was no one he felt such emotion for like this demon at his feet.

He raised his sword. He feared this thing. He would end it.

Others came down into the crater with him. Those same ones who had marched from the west to the battle. Others who hated Graxxin as much as he did.

"Why does he scream?" a girl asked.

"Why do they scream?"

"Why does she scream?"

David did not give the first blow, but he added his to the flurry of stabs and cuts. They launched into Graxxin with reckless abandon.

"Stop!" she yelled. "I command you! Stop filth and waste!"

There was no way to stop them. The demon struggled to her hooved feet, but the children were on top of her, cutting and biting and clawing at every inch of her demonic flesh they could reach. Pain meant nothing to them, even as she tore them away. More and more piled onto her. Their lust for battle had been stoked by the demon. Now she was the one who would receive their wrath.

She had been their mistress.

They would be her undoing.

53: Proven

There was a pull in her that Olma couldn't explain. Something was forcing her forward. Not from behind, as if someone was pushing her, but like she was being thrown off a cliff and propelled towards the ground.

She ran.

She ran as fast as she could, which, for her small size, was surprisingly quick. The power that had indwelled her was something beyond her reckoning. Something otherworldly.

It made her fast. Made her strong. The feeling of it filled her being.

And pulled her forward.

The blue and purple lights ahead of her called her forward. It was important, vital, that she intersect those two lights. That she be between them and feel their power within her. She was greater than they were. Stronger than they were.

And she had to prove it to them.

Leaping into the air, Olma found herself jumping impossibly high, her arms outstretched and, as they had done twice before this same day, long blades of magical energy came out of her forearms.

She wielded these as if she had always had swords for arms. They were a natural extension of her. And she sliced the air viciously as she collided with the orbs of purple and blue.

The two who battled here were both foreign and familiar. She knew them by their magic. The old woman who wielded the blue magic at her looked livid at the intrusion. She threw her hands out in order to repel Olma's blades. But Olma sliced through boths blasts of magic with ease.

The white haired man looked more perplexed than angered. With a shove of his hands he sent hundreds of smaller, more concentrated blasts at Olma. She dodged the ones she could, the others she deflected with her blades.

Instinctively, Olma knew that the bigger threat lay with the purple-wreathed man. She threw herself at him with all of her energy, sending out powerful arcs of energy in his direction. For each one she loosed on him, he raised his hands to absorb it. Not deflect or dodge. He took her magic within himself.

Olma sent more and more arcs of energy at him, becoming more and more frustrated with each blast he absorbed.

Then something hit her from the side. A blast of blue magic from the woman who had taken advantage of Olma's distraction. That would prove to be her undoing.

Olma stabbed her blades in the direction of the woman in blue. She sent arcs of energy soaring towards her. The woman kept deflecting the blasts, sending them crashing into the hills behind them or the plains below. Olma was barely aware of the destruction that her power was causing. She needed to end this woman. She raised her blades as powerful red bolts of energy cascaded from her.

Then a blast of purple hit the woman in blue from the side, alongside Olma's blasts. The combined attack sent the woman soaring to the ground, sprawling in a heap and causing an eruption of blue magic.

Olma turned her attention back to the white haired man in purple. She knew he would be more difficult to defeat. That his magic was superior to the woman's. But she didn't care. She had to prove herself to the power that coursed within her.

Instead of sending blasts of red arcs, Olma went straight for the man with her blades. She sliced the air, coming down hard on a shield of purple magic the man put up in front of him. Olma shoved her blades down, forcing them harder and harder into the shield he had put up.

Then he began to laugh.

Olma continued to force her blades on him. She put all of her power into those swords of light. All that was coursing through her went into the blades. They sparked and burst with power. One she kept on the shield. The other she pounded again and again against the man's powerful magic.

And still he laughed.

"I don't know what power you've discovered little demon," he said. "But do not fool yourself! I am power and death incarnate! I am Farnus! I have the power of the destroyer of worlds and god among demons! There is none who have bested the power of me! For I am Rayg! There are none who have defeated me!"

"I have!"

Both Olma and Farnus looked down at the ground. Standing over the crumpled form of Yada, was a girl Olma knew. Her name was Blume. A green amulet a blazed around her neck.

"You!" the man with the white hair shouted.

Olma felt a huge burst of energy and was blown backwards until her feet touched the ground and her arms became hands again. She felt herself slam against the force of the blast.

Looking up to see the man who had called himself Farnus, Olma saw that he had been enveloped in an even darker shade of purple that shone brilliantly against the night sky. The effect of it hurt her eyes, but she continued to look up at the man who was transforming.

Where white hair had been, black hair begin to sprout. Plates of metal began to encase him as his face changed. Olma heard a scream and cry from the man, as if the transformation caused him great pain.

Looking over at Blume, she saw that the girl was wrapped in a sphere of green light. There was a look of ferocity on her face.

"You may think you had bested me once," the transformed man said, his voice now deep and threatening. "But I am Rayg. I know no limit to my power. I feel no end to my might. I underestimated you once. You will receive no such luxury from me ever again."

The man raised his arms above his head and a giant sphere of purple light appeared within his grasp. He threw it down to the earth in the direction of Blume.

And the world exploded.

54: Defiance

She had prepared herself for this frontal assault. The demon who called himself Rayg was back. Blume had felt his presence on the battlefield. She had felt him back in the cave. His power had emanated out from the host body he had borrowed. From the body he had now destroyed to claim his return fully to this world.

Now it took all of her skill and might just to deflect this first burst that came down on her.

She was tired. She could not remember the last meal she had had, or the last time she had slept a good night's rest.

Several spells had been wasted on lesser speakers and smaller demons.

Now, she was facing a trial that could not be easily won.

This was a demon of great power. If he was to be believed, he was the god of demons.

But she had her necklace back. The family heirloom from which she had done great works of magic and produced powerful spells. The thing that a dragon once called powerful and ancient. A first rimstone. She was the master of it again.

"I put you back in your cage once," Blume said, mustering up all the strength and courage she could find within herself. "And I will do whatever it takes to put you back!"

The earth and rocks that had burst into the air with Rayg's first assault flew to her side and floated at her command. With one hand she held back the magic of the demon, with the other she forced the rocks to encase him.

The stones began to enclose around him. While continuing to throw his assault at her, Rayg expanded the purple orb around himself to keep the rocks away.

"Insignificant girl!" he shouted. "I could do away with you with the snap of my fingers."

"I have more power than you realize!" Blume shouted back at him. She had no idea if it was true or not, but, she would show him she was not insignificant.

Even from this distance, Blume could sense a change in the demon. A shift in his assault and a change over his face.

"True," he said.

Throwing his arms wide, the rocks exploded with great force. He scooped his hands in the air, and the earth that had been Blume's to stand on now rose up with her on it. She fell to one knee near as he lifted her up to his level.

The earth held together, giving her a platform just as he held her within his gaze.

"You have power," Rayg said as he looked her in the eye.

His stare was going past her eyes, into her very being. Blume found herself unable to look away. Her fists balled as she drew in power from the amulet. She wanted to look away. She tried to turn her face. But she could not. All she could do was stare into the eyes of the demon. And she waited.

"I am not a patient being," he said. "But I may find a place for such a human as you who can defy my power."

A wicked grin showed on his face. He looked like he had just found a treasure of great value.

"If you join us, I can increase your power a hundred times. I can show you the secrets of the stone you wield. I can unlock the mysteries of why that one in particular calls to you."

He breathed and raised a hand high into the air. Stones from below rose in pillars of purple light.

"I can give you purpose, Blume Dearcrest! I can show you a world of power and infinite possibilities beyond this one. I can tell you the mysteries of the stars!"

Blume felt a hesitation in her spirit.

Could he really show her the answers to her powers? Why could she wield such power out of one stone, when others were just able to use it to do normal magic? Could she find a sense of purpose? Would she be able to find it, with him? A demon?

An allure rose up inside of her. A feeling that she was missing something. That there was something more powerful within reach but just beyond her grasp.

She closed her eyes.

When she opened them, she saw that Rayg was just a hand's breadth from her face. She gasped, but could not pull away. He was no longer the terrifying demon who had haunted her dreams. His face was kind. Enticing.

"Join me," he whispered. "And all will be made clear."

Blume breathed out. Looking into the deep purple of Rayg's eyes, she could see her future. One where she was powerful. One where she was in control and never faltered in her magic or failed to save her friends.

Her friends.

What would she need with insignificant beings who could do no magic? Why should she need others when she had power?

The longing in her heart grew more burdensome as if a weight had been placed inside her chest. Pulling up on an energy-filled hand, she began to move it towards the demon Rayg.

"Get away from her!" came a shout from the side.

Everything about Rayg's face changed in an instant.

Blume saw Olma jump up from the edge of the earth Rayg had suspended in space. She sliced through the air with her giant red blades. Rayg turned to engage her.

At that same moment, Blume snapped out of her trance. Join Rayg? The demons? Impossible!

She let a devastating blast of energy fly from her fists, still balled in a fury, at Rayg.

The one who had taken so much from her.

A blinding light overcame her just as Rayg and Olma collided in midair.

And her blast of magic consumed them both.

55: Deeper Caverns

Snart felt his right arm hanging down limply at his side. He knew he was lucky. The thing should have fallen off. If he had a few days, his bones would heal and he would grow back whatever skin he needed before he would need to use it.

He looked around him and saw dust and fire.

The magic had been strong and potent. Snart could feel that he had been exposed to the power of rimstone beyond his reckoning. It didn't matter. Whatever forces those had been were gone now. Perhaps they had been blasted into the sky above. Or maybe one of the fires that burned around him belonged to one of the magic users.

Making the decision not to stop and check, Snart continued on.

The skin on his feet burned him. The very ground felt hot. He didn't like it, but going next to the water at this point would bring him close to the armies that were left still on the shore. The island nation was getting back on their boats. Snart didn't want to fight anyone. Not right now without the use of his arm.

He would heal first. Then he would find a place that was just the right warmth and rest his bones.

He had earned such a rest.

"Going going?" came a loud booming voice from behind him.

Snart froze as he heard it. Surely the enormous beast hadn't followed him all the way here?

The rimstone around his waist began to glow and crackle. He had damaged at least one of the stones in the fight. Hopefully, they would serve him well.

"No glowing, glowing," the voice said, much closer than Snart was comfortable with.

He spun around, grabbing for his spear with his left claw, fumbling with the shaft even as the massive bulk of Vallin came rushing at him. The first thing that hit Snart was a tooth of the monstrous cave dweller. Its teeth were so large that Snart's own head would have been impaled clean through if Vallin had gotten his mouth around him.

For the time being, that wasn't the case. Fumbling as he was, Snart was able to dodge the first bite of the beast and use his spear to stab the soft part of Vallin's under jaw. His opponent let out a gurgling howl of pain and flung his head wildly. Still holding onto the spear, knowing it was one of his only two weapons, Snart went flying into a rock.

He was just grateful it wasn't the fire that burned next to it.

"You lying, lying, nasty cheating, cheating lizard!" Vallin yelled. "Taking, taking all our troops and wasting, wasting them! We are dying, dying! All running, running!"

Snart took full advantage of Vallin's bad mood and ranting. Focusing every fiber of his being into his claws, he created a fire of blue flame and hurled it at Vallin. It seared the skin of the giant beast, but it didn't put it down. Snart let out a long hiss. A blast of fire that large would have ended the lives of at least four Veiled Ones.

It didn't even appear to have slowed Vallin down.

He let out another great roar of pain and hatred. Snart put his good claw down on the ground, ready to leap out of the way if Vallin charged. It certainly looked like the beast was ready to.

But then, jumping from all sides of him were Veiled Ones. Blues and purples and greens were falling on Vallin, stabbing him with spears, mercilessly poking holes in the thick hide of the cave lord.

Vallin screamed and threw his arms wildly, taking off one or two of the lizards. But it wasn't enough. Soon the sheer amount of wounds and blood loss was too much, and Vallin fell to the ground.

He heaved one last great sigh, reaching out a massive claw, and then fell still and silent.

Snart was breathing heavily as he picked himself up out of the sandy ground. His arm was pulsing with pain as it had been jolted around when he had been thrown. If any other part of his body hurt, he was unaware of it at the moment. He needed to get somewhere he could rest and recover.

The battle with Vallin taxed him more than he would like to admit. It was alright now, however. He looked up to see his fellow Veiled Ones who had come to his aid. He would continue to lead them, and they would continue to follow He was boss, boss, after all.

"Sssnart, boss, boss," he said as he righted himself fully. "Re-wardsssss faithful Veiled Onessss."

He looked at their faces, expecting to see elation or relief or pride. None of those emotions were in front of him. Instead, anger, resentment, and disgust registered on the lizards who had taken down Vallin.

"Sssssssnart failed ussssss," a blue one said.

Snart was suddenly very aware that his spear was lodged under-neath the bulk of Vallin's dead body. There wasn't a way for him to get it. So that meant he only had one option of fighting back.

His claws exploded with blue light.

"Sssssstupid lizardssssss," he spat. "Dare defy Ssssnart!? I'm bossss bossss!"

"Not our bosssss," said a green, with a flick of its tongue. His claws clicked against his metal spear.

Snart acted first. He shot a ball of magical energy out at the blue lizard to his right. A cry of pain told him he had aimed true. But now the other two were charging forward, spears raised and eyes filled with their own kind of fire.

Another blast ended the second Veiled One with a snarl and a sizzle of flesh. As Snart pointed his next blast at the third, a spear tip jutted out from his chest. The blue fire faded from his hand as he let out his own, strangled cry.

Snart glance behind him. A man stood there, looking down at him with hard, determined eyes. Another blur rushed by him and the other lizard fell to another man with a spear.

"Good one, Captain Pul," said the first man. "With Isol pulling away we can finish up these last few lizards. There's a few more over there."

"Good eyes! Rallet! This way!" the man whose spear had impaled his chest. "Gods save us, what's that thing?"

The captain moved on quickly, not paying Snart a second glance. Snart looked up and saw the darkening sky as he slid off the spear and onto the ground. His vision blurred as he coughed. It looked like a cavern with a light towards the end of it. The glow called to him, and he followed after it.

It was like the darkest cavern he had ever traveled. New and uncharted lands.

He was Snart.

He was boss, boss.

No more.

56: The Shores of the Saved

Ealrin was calling as loud as his voice could carry.

Where was she?

"Blume!" he shouted again and again. "Blume, where are you!?"

He knew the rest of their party trudged behind him, almost unwillingly. It had been such a battle of magic. So many lives lost in one final sacrifice. Isol had been devastated by the blast that had encompassed the sky.

The Theocracy was nearly done tearing itself apart with Juttis still vying for control of what was left of the empire. And Ealrin cared for none of it. All he wanted to do was to see Blume safe. And Olma in one piece. They had both left in such a rush. They had tried to run out after them, but they couldn't run nearly as fast.

And then the armies had swept up over them again. It had been a miracle that they had made it out alive. After the explosion, the battlefield went eerily quiet.

The suns had just barely risen, showing the catastrophe below. So many were dead. Many more were dying. Ealrin prayed the ones they sought weren't among them. He wouldn't search the piles of the dead. He refused to.

The sands of the beach crunched under his boots as he walked. The skin by his sword was the only part of him that felt warm. All the rest of his body was cold with fear and the winds from the sea. Sprays of mist lashed out at him as he called over and over again the name of the one he wanted to ensure was safe.

She had to be safe.

Blume was so powerful, so very gifted with magic. Surely she had survived again. That's what she had done over and over against all manner of demons and magical opponents. She had survived. And he was going to find her. She was going to be alright.

She just had to be.

"Blume!" he called again.

He refused to believe she was defeated. She was too powerful. Too strong. She was Blume. What world could exist without her?

"Blume!"

"Ealrin," came a voice from behind him.

He didn't want to listen. He didn't want to hear anything he had to say. Whatever Holve was thinking was wrong. Blume had to have survived. That's what she did. Even Holve had survived magical trials before.

Ealrin spun on the spot.

"When the demons took you to the comet," he said rapidly, grabbing Holve by the arms. "When they imprisoned you. How did you know you were there? Did they take Blume? Could she be up there as well?"

Ealrin looked up at where the comet floated in the sky. He refused to acknowledge the look on Holve's face. It was not one that said he believed what Ealrin was saying.

"They wouldn't have taken her there," he said quietly. "They certainly want her gone. She may be..."

"Don't!" Ealrin roared, throwing his hands up in the air. "She's out here somewhere! Blume!"

"Mister Ealrin," Jurrin's calm voice came from behind Holve. Ealrin didn't like the tone of his little friend. He refused to believe that he had seen the impossible. He turned around to search the beach more. Blume was fine. She was just...

"Blume!" Ealrin shouted and began to sprint at the same time. She was there. Right there. Sitting on a rock.

"Blume!" he said again, coming to a skid next to her, landing in a pile of sand and grabbing her hands. They were warm.

He thanked whoever was listening and began to say over and over again.

"You're alright. You're alright. You're alright."

He looked her in the eyes, trying to see what was going on inside her mind. She just sat there, blankly staring ahead. Her mouth was moving slightly as if trying to form words. Ealrin didn't care. She was alive. She would be alright. She was just tired from the battle. There had been so much magic coursing through the land in those moments.

Perhaps she was exhausted and drained?

Of course, she was, Ealrin thought.

He took off his jacket and threw it over her. She didn't react to the gesture. She just continued to stare ahead.

Serinde came running up behind them. Ealrin knew it was her by the sound of her shaky voice.

"Where's Olma?" she asked. Ealrin could hear the pain in the elf's voice. She had taken a liking to Olma. Ealrin guessed she was as concerned for her as he had been for Blume.

At the sound of Olma's name, Blume jerked and began to seize up. Almost at once she started to claw at Ealrin as if trying to escape from him, though he wasn't holding her.

"No! NO!" she said over and over again, with increasing volume and terror. He didn't know if he needed to grab her, to hold her still.

She seemed to recoil at his touch. He tried harder to grab her, but she scrambled away and clawed away from him on the beach, looking back at him as if he were a pursuer. Like he was a demon.

"Get away from me!" she shouted. "Don't come any closer! He nearly got me! If she hadn't... I would have... But she..."

"Blume..." Ealrin said, knowing the pain that was in his voice was coming straight from his heart.

What had happened during the battle?

How had Blume been affected?

"Don't come near me!" she shouted.

"Blume," Serinde said from a ways off. "Where's Olma?"

Her words sounded desperate and frantic, nearly like Blume's own.

At this second mention of Olma's name, Blume stopped short. She froze in place and looked from side to side as if she were searching for something. Then, slowly, with what seemed to Ealrin like a considerable amount of effort, she looked up at his face.

He could see the tears freely flowing there.

"Olma..." she said quietly. "She's.... Rayg... He..."

Ealrin closed his own eyes. Blume didn't need to finish. He knew what she meant. Olma was dead by Rayg's hand. He heard a gasp and a wail from Serinde's direction and he knew the elf was tortured by the thought of Olma's death.

More death.

There was always death.

It followed them everywhere they went. No matter what continent they were own, no matter where they went, death was always close by. He hated it. Ealrin wanted it all to stop.

But it wouldn't.

There were still demons around. There were always men who hated each other for the gods that they worshipped. There were elves who detested the dwarves, who sought to kill off those who threatened their mountains.

There was always death.

A cry of rage came out of Ealrin's mouth. He hated death. He hated pain. Why couldn't it all just go away? Why was there such hardship in a land filled with enough trails as it was?

He opened his eyes to see Blume still in front of him, looking tortured.

What could he do to console her? How could he make it better? She had faced demons and pain herself. She was in a state of shock. What could he possibly do to help?

"Miss Blume?" came a voice from Ealrin's side. He looked over and saw Jurrin standing there, now at eye level with him on his eyes. "Remember that song you sang, Miss Blume? The one on the ship when we were headed to the island?"

Ealrin didn't know what Jurrin was referring to. It had been so long since he had heard Blume sing, he had nearly forgotten what the sound of her song was like.

Jurrin cleared his throat and coughed. Then he sang a tune, slightly off-key and with a wavering voice.

"How far does the bird fly?
How low does the valley go?
How far do the suns glide?
How vast do the seas flow?
How tall do the mountains climb?
How high do the blizzards snow?
I don't know how far the birds fly.
I don't know how high the mountains go.
But I'll love you until I can find them.
And I'll love despite all I don't know."

The last note of the song hung in the air. Far off there was the sound of men marching away from the destruction that had been left in the wake of the battle. Isolian ships sailed south to their own lands. Juttis and Prommus both headed west. The Veiled Ones had fled underground as soon as the fire had rained down on them from the demons above. The demons, for their part, were dispelled for now. But Ealrin knew how this worked. As long as that comet remained in the sky, they would return.

"Do you remember that song, Miss Blume?" Jurrin asked. "You sang it to me when I was sacred in that terrible storm. You told me it was going to be alright. It will be alright Miss Blume. Just give it some time. It'll all be alright."

Ealrin took a deep, ragged breath. He looked around at their party. Bruised, battered, beaten, and tired.

They had endured so much.

Yet here they were.

Being sung to by a halfling who had not lost hope.

57: Hope

The suns were nearly halfway finished with their journey across the sky, yet their light gave off no warmth to Octus. This was the part of any battle that he hated.

The aftermath.

It was always a slow, painful gathering of the living. The long, dreary process of sorting out the dead. Both armies had left in full now. Isol had sailed back to their islands on boats that looked terrible and hardly seaworthy. Demons, or so the rumor had been.

Juttis had overtaken what was left of the Theocracy's army. The devastating explosion that rocked half the battlefield had wiped out nearly all of the military that had marched from Prommus and some of the reserves as well.

Only a quarter of those who came to war now took the weary road home.

Ladis would recover, but it would take years. Decades, perhaps.

The only good Octus could see out of this was the slow, peaceful years they might endure while the rebuilding took place.

It was a dream if it was anything.

He meandered slowly west. There would be no welcome party for him. No hero's welcome. Octus hated being a hero. The only thing that had given him such a title was his ability to survive another battle. That was all.

The wars that had consumed Ladis, Isol and the Disputed Lands had consumed him as well. There was hardly anything left to live for.

Crows and birds of prey circled above, waiting to feast on the dead below. Octus watched one swoop down and begin to pick at a body, only to be shooed away by two people kneeling on the ground. Octus kicked aside an old, torn and tattered book as he walked towards them.

One wore the brown robes of a temple guard. The other was...different. Not just someone, Octus realized.

An elf.

He walked closer to the elf realizing that the long ears that poked out from its head were hidden by long locks of hair. A female?

Elves had not walked the lands of Ladis for generations. He had only heard tales of them from long ago on other continents.

What was one doing here?

Without even realizing it, Octus was walking up to the elf. His hand was on the sword he had scavenged, something made in the land of Isol and possessing a rimstone in its hilt. They were valuable and usually well maintained. And he would use it if he needed.

Turning to face him, he saw the elf had tear tracks running down her face. The temple guard appeared to be unsure of what to do. She held a small flask of water and was wetting the wounded person's mouth.

"Please spare us," she said. "She's wounded and needs help."

Octus raised an eyebrow as he looked down and saw a girl who had the strangest color hair he had ever seen. It was brilliantly red, the same red as a flame. But her face was...

"Olma?" Octus said, not believing his own voice had spoken her name. He bent down beside the elf and looked over the girl she cradled in her lap. Her skin was covered in strange markings. Her hair was a different color. But her face. It was the face of his brother and his wife. There could be no doubt.

"What..." Octus began to say. "What happened? Why is she here? How did she?"

"Shh," the elf said calmly. "In time. Right now she needs to rest. Luca here is being helpful to us, right Luca?"

The woman nodded, though she cast a wary glance up at Octus.

Octus could see that the elf was caring for Olma as tenderly as if she was her own. That gave him some comfort, but also made a dozen more questions fly through his mind all at once.

"Who are you?" the elf asked. "And how do you know her?"

Octus stared into the elven eyes that looked deeply into his own.

He let out a soft, slow breath, realizing that even in the midst of death and destruction and chaos, there was something worth fighting another day for.

"I'm her uncle," he said.

58: Eastward

Holve guided them east when the armies had cleared. He told them that he had written a letter a month ago that he hoped had gotten out past the war on Ladis and made it to its recipient. If it had, they should go to Tremus and wait there.

Now that they had his spear, Blume's amulet, Jargon's spells books, Gorplin's ax, and Ealrin's sword, there was no reason to stay on Ladis. They were the most precious items they possessed.

Save for Ealrin's journal.

He wrote in it often. Some days it was only a few lines by the firelight of their camp. Other days, like when they stopped at a village who had offered them a barn to sleep in for the night, he wrote considerably more.

It was surprising how Ladis continued on even after the collapse of the war and the heads of the Theocracy. The wars of the high and mighty seemed to matter little to the farmer and his family who were just trying to make the land grow.

Ealrin watched them eat a meal around a fire by their house. The father lifted up the bread he had gotten from inside their modest hut and kept it there for a moment. Then he brought it down and tore off a piece for his wife, then his daughter, then his son.

Ealrin raised an eyebrow at this, unsure what was going on.

Serinde sighed next to him.

"He's being thankful for what he has," she said. "Thanking the old god Decolos for blessing their farm and praying that they would have a good spring and that none of their family would be ushered to death's door before their time."

Ealrin turned to look at her.

"Olma told me," she said simply. She didn't take her eyes off the family but instead stared intently at them. The daughter turned to

267

see them sitting just outside the barn and waved at Serinde. The elf nodded in return but did not wave.

"You really were close to her," Ealrin said. He didn't mean it as a question for Serinde to answer. More of a statement that he had just realized was true. The two had shared many conversations together late into the night. Serinde seemed fascinated by the girl. Like she was learning from her. It was odd that an elf who was so much older and had lived through so much could glean anything from one so young.

But Serinde had. And she was recalling it now for Ealrin's benefit.

They had sent Olma on with her uncle and Miss Rivius. A small village one day behind had agreed to help them and care for Olma. She was in no shape to travel. But she was alive. It was more than he could have hoped for. Serinde had promised them she would return and visit again with her. Olma had smiled weakly at that prospect. Serinde had cried silently most of the day after they had left. She really did care for the little girl.

It was like him and Blume. Well, when she was in the right state of mind.

He turned to look over at her in the barn. She wore his coat, as she had done since the battle. A constant state of cold followed her wherever she went and no matter how close she got to the fire. At least she wasn't unconscious, and beyond reach, Ealrin reminded himself. She was in shock. Still fighting the demons, but only those in her mind.

She would come out of it in time.

That's Ealrin told himself over and over again. That Blume would get better.

They traveled the week it took them to walk from the shores of the battle to Tremus, never going more than a day would allow and ensuring they had enough food to travel between villages. Szabo was extremely helpful in this. He knew the land so well that most of the time, Holve allowed the halfling to tell them the path they should take.

It was a day before they would reach their destination that Ealrin began to feel the winds coming from a different direction. Instead of up from the south, he felt a calm west wind. One that carried with it the smell of the sea.

They had not been far from the southern shores, so when the smell found him, he was surprised. Had he not been paying attention to it before this? Or was this a different body of water he could smell?

Holve looked at the countryside around them. Ealrin wondered if he could sense the change as well.

"We'll be there tomorrow," he said.

That was it.

Ealrin let his shoulders slump. There were many questions he had yet to find answers to. And, for some reason that he could not yet understand or determine, he left them unasked.

He hadn't thought of what would happen once they reached East Town. Perhaps they would find Holve's contact and then they would get off of Ladis.

Where they would go from there, Ealrin didn't know. He wasn't quite sure he cared. The desire to flee this continent was burning him from the inside. He needed to get away from the land that had brought him here against his will. For once, he even considered returning to Ruyn. Maybe even Good Harbor. There was a feeling of home that the place gave him when he remembered it. Home. The thought struck him as they crested a hill and looked down on East Town.

Good Harbor wasn't his home.

There was another place that had to be.

He surveyed the port that was laid out before him. There were three ships docked there. At the sight of one, however, his spirits lifted considerably.

Because it had red sails.

59: Towards Unfamiliar Homelands

Blume sat uneasily on the railing of the *Skydart*. It had been a year since she had last sat on the vessel, and it had not been under the greatest of circumstances that she had left it. Their last adventure into Ladis had revealed much about the companions she sailed with.

She took a deep breath. The sea air was both refreshing and disheartening. Both times she and these friends had sailed away from a continent, it had been with plans of adventure ahead of them and sorrows behind them.

Would they see even more sorrows unfold in their new quest?

"I know that look," came a familiar and comforting voice. Blume didn't even have to turn around. She let Ealrin put a hand on her shoulder as she leaned back against him. They had almost lost each other so many times during their travels.

This last time had been the closest one yet.

She had really felt the pull of that demon. That Rayg. He had nearly convinced her in her state of magic to tap into the power he had offered her. To see Olma nearly torn apart in her wake was what had woken her up.

Had she not attempted to sacrifice herself to save Blume, would she really have gone over? Could she be so persuaded by power to give in to a demon's call?

She shuddered. Ealrin gripped her shoulder more tightly. She knew it was to comfort her. But was she someone who ought to be comforted? Or should she be feared?

"We're going to find out what my story is," Ealrin said. "We're going to find my family. If they're out there."

Blume closed her eyes tightly before opening them again, hoping to regain a bit of herself.

"They are," she said. He was doing so much to comfort her. She should at least return the favor. "I'm sure they are."

Ealrin didn't say anything. He just put his other hand on the railing and looked out over the sea in front of them. Blume turned her head so she could look up at him. His eyes seemed unfocused, almost as if they weren't looking at the sky or the water, but at something Blume couldn't see.

"What is it?" she asked.

Turning herself to get a good look at him, Blume saw that Ealrin had an expression painted on his face that she could tell did not communicate what was going on in his heart. There was something darker behind his eyes.

The other members of their party went about their normal activity. Felecia and Urt stood at the wheel, steering the ship onwards. Galp was close to them, eyeing the larger Skrilx with an appraising eye. Gorplin and Jurrin sat over a stack of blades, sharpening and inspecting them as they came to them. Holve was nearby, huddled over a railing himself.

Blume remembered that the older man didn't care much for the sea.

Ealrin's attention was drawn up to where Silverwolf sat in the crow's nest with Wisym. From the looks of it, the pair kept a silent vigil over the horizon. The assassin hadn't said much since they had made their way eastward. That didn't bother Blume too badly. She had proven to be a useful ally at times. She was also a pain in the neck.

A growl from below reminded her that Panto and Amrolan were also along for the ride. They were whole again.

As much as they could be at least. Teresa moved from the front of the ship and nodded at the pair of them. Ealrin took his gaze back to the horizon, not meeting Blume's eyes.

Was it something he felt about her?

He had seen her power. Her full power. Had it scared him? He had been the one who had nursed her back to health. She had returned the favor when the wars of Irradan had nearly done him in.

Had he experienced something this time that he couldn't reconcile? Was he going to distance himself from her, even as he kept a hand on her?

Maybe it wasn't to comfort her, but to make sure she was watched over? To keep the rest of them safe?

"You fear what you do not yet understand," came a voice from Ealrin's side.

Blume nearly fell off the railing of the ship. The only thing that stopped her was Ealrin's firm grip on her arm. Pulling her back onto the deck, Ealrin looked behind him.

"Did you hear that?" he asked.

"What was that?" Blume asked, just as confused as Ealrin seemed.

"The correct question," the voice said again from Ealrin's hip. "Is who is that? And I am more than willing to speak."

"I know that voice," Holve said as he took several steps up the deck to the pair of them. "Is that really you?"

Ealrin looked to his left and right, a puzzled expression on his face.

Holve shook his head, pointing to the sword at Ealrin's side.

"Draw your blade," Holve said shortly.

Slowly, Ealrin stood up straight and did as he was told, eyeing Holve cautiously.

The sword slid out of its sheath and shone in the twin suns. Other members of the crew had directed their attention at them now. Blume looked up to see that even Silverwolf was looking down at them.

"Ah!" Ealrin said. "It's hot!"

"Sorry," the voice said again. "I've been having difficulty changing since I found my voice again."

Holve shook his head. Blume even saw a small smile on the old man's face.

"Edgar it is good to hear you once again!"

"Mister Ealrin," Jurrin said quietly. "I believe your sword is talking to us."

"Well, I'll be a princess," Felicia said, putting her hands on her hips. "Edgar!"

"Who is Edgar?" Blume asked, not understanding why Holve had named the voice coming out of the blade, or why there was a voice coming out of it at all.

"The spirit in the enchanted armor?" Ealrin asked. "From the White Wind? It's... You're in my sword?"

These last words he spoke to the blade in his hand.

"And have been for some time," Edgar, the voice of the blade said. "My voice has been silent for so long because I could not yet find a way to speak. The last duel between the forces of magic seemed to have unlocked that for me. I wish I could be more excited about the prospects of speech. For I have news that may not be so well received as I am."

Blume looked up at Ealrin. He looked down at her with confusion on his face, but not in fear. That alone gave her hope.

"Hey!" came Felicia's call from the wheel. "Do you call yourself a captain or do you reckon I should learn how to fly this thing? We'll take three times as long on water!"

Ealrin looked down at Blume with a smirk before running back to take the helm from Felecia. Blume felt the ship lurch and bump as it began to slowly rise out of the water, its sails jutting out to the side, and soar into the sky.

"Easy, flyboy!" Silverwolf called down from the crow's nest.

It seemed that even as they flew towards the west, there were new adventures in store for them and the odd family that they had turned into.

Blume leaned herself against the rails of the *Skydart* and shook her head.

No matter where they went, magic and mystery followed them. She leaned her head to the side and observed the oddly shaped blade Ealrin had carried for the last two years that had, inexplicably, learned to talk.

A smile found its way to her lips.

They were off on an adventure again.

Author Notes

This particular title deserves a small note from me.

It's my ninth book and the third trilogy in my "Legends of Gilia" series.

When I first started writing these books back in November of 2013, I had this massive and wild idea that I should write five trilogies for the five continents of the world I had created in my head.

We've now explored more than half of them!

But there is more to come and I'm so excited about the next trilogy! I've been dangling the carrot out in front of you for a long time, and you have been so patient in waiting. That's why I'm so excited for this next trilogy story arc.

Because we're finally going to get an answer to the question I've put to you since the second chapter of Sword of Ruyn:

Who is Ealrin?

Well, now we're flying off to Redact.

It's time we found out who our hero is and where he came from.

The wonderful thing for an author, I've discovered as I've been writing, is to find that his or her readers are excited for what's to come. There is a bit of mystery still to be had. I've known since I wrote the first book who Ealrin was and what he would find when he arrived in Redact.

I'm so excited to share it with you!

But, even more exciting to me, is that there is a second and much more burning question that I hope you've been asking yourselves this whole time. It's not a thing that I've alluded to directly. I've actually intentionally kept it secret. But it's there. And it's something more pressing for the world of Gilia than the history and backstory of our protagonist.

Fate brought Ealrin his companions.

And fate will determine that it is those very same one who has been under our noses this whole time with secrets far greater than Ealrin's.

Thanks for coming along with me!

Enjoy the journey,

RG

The Story Continues

The next exciting adventure is "Crystals of Redact", book ten in the Legends of Gilia series. It will be released January 8th, 2019.

Want to be the first to know when the next exciting adventure in Gilia is ready?

Sign-up to my email list by visiting this website: www.rglongauthor.weebly.com/subscribe[1]

Also, if you want to connect with me, I'd love to hear from you! Find me here:

Facebook: www.facebook.com/rglongauthor[2]

Twitter: www.twitter.com/rglongauthor[3]

Instagram: www.instagram.com/rglongauthor[4]

Website: www.rglongauthor.weebly.com[5]

Thanks for reading.

Enjoy the journey,

RG Long

---

1.   http://www.rglongauthor.weebly.com/subscribe

2.   http://www.facebook.com/rglongauthor

3.   http://www.twitter.com/rglongauthor

4.   http://www.instagram.com/rglongauthor

5.   http://www.rglongauthor.weebly.com

Made in the USA
Coppell, TX
26 July 2022

80488795R00166